SIX-GUN FROM TEXAS

G. WAYNE TILMAN

WOLFPACK
PUBLISHING
— EST 2013 —

**WOLFPACK
PUBLISHING**
— EST 2013 —

Six-Gun From Texas

Paperback Edition
Copyright © 2020 G. Wayne Timan

Wolfpack Publishing
6032 Wheat Penny Avenue
Las Vegas, NV 89122

wolfpackpublishing.com

Paperback ISBN 978-1-64734-129-9
eBook ISBN 978-1-64734-128-2

SIX-GUN FROM TEXAS

ACKNOWLEDGEMENTS

My sincerest appreciation goes to Denise Kearns, Rebecca Thomas Payne and Susan Stecker for their careful scrutiny of the manuscript as the Beta readers.

DEDICATION

This book is dedicated to my beautiful wife, Georgia, my toughest reviewer and best fan.

FOREWORD

Six-Gun from Texas is a classically good Western novel with action, twists and surprises, and a lot of real history woven in. In the story, a Frontier Battalion Texas Ranger moves north to Colorado and ultimately becomes a county sheriff. He's a fast gun and honest lawman.

As a Texan descended from a Frontier Battalion Texas Ranger and having served as a three-term County Sheriff, this is right up my alley!

G. Wayne Tilman writes Westerns, mysteries and thrillers with the real-life experience to back them up. I know what he's done, and it shows in all of his books. Turn the page and hang on for a great ride!

Bob White, Sheriff (Retired)
Pasco County, Florida

CHAPTER 1

The rider was heading out of Texas, leaving disappointment behind.

Disappointment because his boss and mentor, Captain Leander McNelly died. His men believed McNelly to be indestructible, though he was a slight man wracked with a constant cough. His integrity and bravery were far above most men's. But, in the end, he died from consumption, not a bullet.

The rider turned in his warrant and rode away from politics. Texas Rangers did not have badges to return in 1878. A few Rangers were commissioning "cinco peso" star and circle badges to be made by jewelers at their own expense. The rider reckoned he could save the considerable sum for land or cattle and relied on his warrant of authority and his black book of suspects to prove his authority. But, nobody had ever asked for proof he was a Ranger. His look and his Colt were proof enough.

Texas had made it through the War of Succession without a Union invasion. A lot more Texans served the Union than many would admit. After, it was not scalawags or carpetbaggers who caused dissention. It was the alternating administrations of liberal pro-Union Republicans and conservative pro-Confederacy Democrats. Virtually all were native Texans trying to do what they thought best for the Lone Star state, but from different perspectives. So, a state employee like a Ranger never knew what new silliness was coming down the pike. Without McNelly to ride interference, it ceased to be fun.

He figured he would ride until finding a place he liked and pin on a deputy badge. Loose and free, he had only the black gelding, the set of clothes he was wearing and Model 1873 Colt and Winchester in matching .44-40 caliber. The interchangeability of cartridges had been convenient in his many firefights with hostile Indians, Mexicans and Anglo rustlers and other criminals. Sometimes, he felt however, having a longer range rifle would be nice in instances where he wanted to reach out further to touch someone.

His route was northwest and had taken him into New Mexico. He would know his bearing had been true when he hit Raton.

He planned to check out Raton and see if any lawman jobs were there. If not, he would move on across the border to Trinidad, Colorado and check. If not, maybe Denver. He wanted some green trees in his future and a bit less desert and prairie.

The sky was dark and he was not sure about the time. He seldom had a need for a watch, but reckoned he might get one sometime.

He noticed Cisco seemed to be slowing down a little.

"What's wrong, boy? You think we've come far enough today? My butt's in full agreement. Let's call it a day and get you some water and feed."

The horse whinnied and shook his head. The rider was convinced the horse spoke English better than some folks he had met.

He found a stand of pinon pines along a creek he had been following for several miles. They would provide some shelter, fuel and water. There was not much for Cisco to graze on, so he would finish the feed in a saddlebag and replenish it in Raton.

He pulled the saddle and placed it near where he planned to sleep. He stuck his number one canteen in the creek and filled it with cold, pure water. He put about half in his Stetson and gave it to the horse before refilling the canteen. A couple handfuls of feed would supplement any grass Cisco sampled for grazing. He put a hobble on the powerful horse.

He used a small trowel to dig out a fire pit and his Bowie knife to secure adequate wood to build a medium fire.

Dinner was bacon, Indian fry bread and coffee. It

was his pretty usual dinner….breakfast….everything on the trail. On special occasions, he might add pinto beans and finish off with a can of peaches for dessert.

It was getting cold and damp, It felt like rain. He slid into his bedroll, propped against the saddle and covered himself, his saddlebags and guns with the small waxed tarp and went to sleep. He expected to arrive in Raton, New Mexico tomorrow.

******

The rider was up and on the trail early, man and horse refreshed. Both were glad it had not rained after all.

They rode along the old Oregon Trail. Nearing Raton, the telegraph lines and railroad tracks he saw signaled how advanced the town was for the times.

As he approached the town, the sun was getting high, but not in his eyes. He shed the long duster and lashed it behind him, over the top his bedroll.

The rider was dressed in black pants, dark gray shirt and a black vest. His hat and horse were black.

His gun-belt held a Colt, a Bowie knife standard to all Rangers, and cartridges. It and his boots were dark brown.

The rider walked his horse slowly into town as he was wont to do when a Ranger. He scanned side to side and people stopped to look at him. Was he a killer? A lawman? He looked like he was somebody all right. Somebody looking for somebody.

The town marshal was watching, too. He was relieved when the young man dismounted and tied to the hitching post in front of the Marshal's Office.

"Howdy," he greeted the marshal with a pleasant grin. The marshal did not hide the fact he was putting a ten-gauge away in the corner as the rider came in.

"Wonder if you might have need for a deputy. I have some good experience," the rider offered.

"What kinda experience, son?" the older man queried.

"My name's Tate. I rode for five years with the rangers. Most of the last was under Captain Leander McNelly."

"A Ranger, huh? It would count for a lot if I had a job for you. But, the new marshal up the road in Trinidad is looking for someone to tote a badge with him. You mighta heard of him, lawman name of Masterson," the town marshal said.

"The one out of Dodge City? Sheriff of Ford County?" the Tate asked.

"The very same," the marshal said.

In the midst of their conversation, they heard a woman scream and then several shots.

The marshal, a man named Hawkins, grabbed the ten-gauge and headed for the door.

"Call me a special deputy and I'll back you up," Tate said.

"My deputy has the stomach gripe. You are officially a deputy - for now. C'mon!

Tate loosened his Colt in his holster and walked purposely from the office onto the main drag of Raton.

The two lawmen saw a farm wagon. The farmer, a man beyond middle age, was leaning against it holding a bleeding shoulder and seemed to be in shock. His rifle lay on the ground.

Several men were dragging a screaming young woman towards horses tied to a hitching rail across the dirt street.

The marshal called out.

"Y'all unhand the woman!" and one fired a shot at him and the former ranger.

The two lawmen separated. The marshal had the big-bore shotgun to his shoulder, but could not fire at the man with the woman without killing her also.

"I got this," Tate said.

He walked towards the group, gun still in holster and an unreadable look in his eyes. It was not threatening, however.

"Why don't we talk this out, 'fore somebody else gets hurt," he suggested.

The three men already had revolvers in hand. One was still holding the young woman who was terrified. Her captor looked at Tate like he was crazy.

"Who in hell are you? This ain't none of your affair," the man with the girl said as he held a Smith & Wesson Schofield revolver pointed at her.

"I'm nobody. But, why don't you point the revolver

at me? I'm the threat here. The young lady has no way to hurt you."

The man obliged and pointed it towards Tate.

"You ain't answered my question. I like to know the names of folks I kill."

"Name is Tate. Former Texas Ranger. But, right now, I'm just helping the marshal over behind me there. I'd appreciate it if you dropped the Smith and let me take you into custody," Tate said.

The man looked at the woman and cocked his revolver. The young woman, unbeknownst to Tate, had experienced a lot of hardship and trauma in her life. Her dress was threadbare and her pretty face drawn. Dying in the street would more than she could add to her burdens. She lost color and her breathing became labored. Then, her eyes rolled up and she became dead weight on the kidnaper's arm as she passed out.

The second she was clear and Tate had a good target, He drew and shot the man between the eyes. The gunman died instantly where he stood.

But, Tate did not see his bullet strike. He was already swinging his gun toward the other two.

Both raised their guns and Tate heard the marshal's shotgun and simultaneously saw one man's vest get shredded.

Tate redirected his Colt to the other man, aimed his front sight blade above the man's belt buckle and fired twice, as fast as a Colt Frontier model could be fired.

The two shots sounded like one. The man sucked in his gut and folded. He stood for a second as Tate aimed for another shot, but then the man collapsed on the street. Tate un-cocked the Colt, looked around, replaced the spent shells and slid it into the holster.

Tate and the marshal covered the twenty feet between them and the bodies in the street. They kicked the guns away from the fallen men. But, there was no need. All were dead.

Tate knelt at the prone woman. No sign of an injury was visible. He lifted her shoulders up and supported her with an arm and knee as she regained consciousness.

She recognized him and asked "Did you get them, stranger?" she whispered.

He nodded. Looking past the stark fear still on her face, Tate thought, "Lord, she's beautiful," he thought.

"We did. They won't bother you anymore."

"My uncle?" she asked.

"I don't know. The marshal's checking him now. He was standing, last I saw. Tate took a quick glance over his shoulder. The uncle was hit, but still leaning against a buckboard wagon, the horse skittish from all the gunfire.

"He's still up. I'm no sawbones, but he doesn't look hit too bad," he told the woman.

Now he could focus on her instead of the threats, he saw she had auburn hair, green eyes and a pretty face and a shape he knew would make any man who saw her keep looking and accidentally walk into a post or trip over a watering trough.

"What's your name, Miss?" he asked.

"Evelyn Hudson. Everybody calls me Eve."

"My name's Tate. I'm proud to make your acquaintance," he said, wanting to stretch the conversation as long as he could.

"I passed out like a little girl when the man cocked his gun. I thought I was gonna die," she whispered.

"It was a bad situation. But, the important thing is none of those men will bother you — or anyone else — ever again."

"Did you shoot them dead?" she asked.

"I shot the one threatening you as soon as you dropped and I had a clear shot. The marshal shot one and I turned and got the other. It all happened pretty fast."

"How long was I out?" she asked.

"Just long enough to miss the shooting part. Seconds," he told her softly.

Several women from town came up, helped Eve to her feet and began to lead her off to tend to her. Eve turned and mouthed "Thank you" to Tate. He nodded, a half smile on his face.

He rose and walked over to the buckboard. A doctor had arrived and was checking on the uncle.

"You gonna be okay, Hiram. It's a pass-through. It will hurt like hell for a while, but you won't die and you won't lose use of anything. We need to get you over to my office and sew up the holes. Maybe cauterize them."

Several townsmen helped support the man and he was walked to the office several buildings down the street.

The marshal was questioning a group who had materialized from the saloon at the first shots.

He ascertained the names of the men and their ranch affiliation. The undertaker and his assistant had already arrived with a two-wheeled hand cart to put the bodies in for transport.

Tate turned to the marshal.

"Well, I guess unless you need me for something else, I'll head the twenty or so miles up to Trinidad and call on Bat Masterson," he said.

"Tell me your full name, ranger, in case Bat wants to contact me for a reference. I'll give him a good one after this."

"It's Morgan Tate, Marshal Hawkins. I'd be most grateful for a reference if it comes to it. Will the girl be okay on her own for a while?" he asked.

"I'll try to see to her," Hawkins responded. "Her uncle's ranch is in the direction you are heading. It's over the line just a few miles from Trinidad. Her uncle Hiram Stone has friends here, so he drives a few miles further to shop. You might mention to Masterson about her. He might know something."

"I think he might have a deputy commission for the county, too, but I'm not sure. Anyways, thank you for your actions. It could have ended up bad for the girl.

She came here a year or so ago real sick. She's a pretty thing, but has a sad look about her.

Good luck in Trinidad," said the marshal as he proffered his hand. Tate shook it and said "I'll get a hotel here and ride over in the morning, I think, Marshal. Thanks for the good words. Maybe I'll see you in the morning before I leave."

CHAPTER 2

Tate picked a likely hotel and checked for a single room. They had one and he paid for it for a day. Most hotels in towns like this rented a bed not a room. Tate did not like to be too close with strangers, especially when he was asleep. He would sleep under the stars first and had chosen camping as an option over a room full of smelly drunks many times.

Room secured, he found a livery and boarded Cisco with instructions for feed, water and a rubdown. He asked the liveryman to check the right hind shoe. It seemed loose to him.

He slung his bedroll, saddlebags, canteens and carbine scabbard over his shoulder and walked back to the hotel. The room had a lock. Weak, but a lock. So, he chanced leaving his rifle while he went to dinner.

There were a number of likely restaurants in town and he picked one at random.

He ordered a steak with potatoes, green beans and sweet tea. The tea was actually cold. On the trail for days, he rewarded himself with pie. It was some sort of berry and was good. He did not know what kind, but could care less.

He finished with strong coffee, knowing nothing would interrupt his sleep this evening.

Tate went back to the hotel. He inquired about baths and found there was a bath room with several tubs in a shed out back. A hot bath could be reserved and the price was two-bits for a half hour, soap included. He reckoned it to be a bargain and scheduled one for just after sunrise.

By dark, Morgan Wood Tate, former Texas Ranger, was sound asleep. Music from the rinky-dink piano in the bar next door came in the open window, but it did not hamper his slumber a whit.

The next morning, he took advantage of a big tub and several buckets of steaming water to clean a week's trail dust off. He shook his clothes and brushed them with his hands.

He went out for a real breakfast and spotted the marshal finishing his cup of coffee. The marshal motioned him over.

"You look rested, Tate. It's a good thing. Sit down and order while I finish my coffee."

"Thanks, marshal. I sure will. How are you this morning?"

"As well as can be, I reckon. Checked on the fella got shot by those boys we settled with yesterday. He is in more pain from the cauterizing than the bullet. But, he's a tough old buzzard and he'll survive."

"I'm glad to hear it. How about his niece? She still in town?" Tate asked.

"Yes, one of the ladies put her up last night, but she had to ride out by wagon to feed her chickens and milk the cow. I showed her how to reload his old Mexican War musket. She's a fine figure of a woman and probably needs some protection," Marshal Hawkins said.

"You think she'll come back and forth between here and the ranch for a while?" Tate asked.

"Probably. It's only fifteen or sixteen miles. Her uncle comes here 'cause he's got friends. She might go up to Trinidad to shop. It's a lot closer to where she lives. She can't let the ranch go to pot because her uncle is all she's got left on this earth. He's put everything into it.

She has a story. I don't rightly know what it is, but there's a story there for sure."

"Well, I hope she does okay. She was in a bit of a pickle yesterday. I'm glad you and I were able to get her out of it," Tate said.

"Me, too. You riding up to see Marshal Masterson today?" the marshal asked.

"I am."

"He sure has become a dandy for a Canadian turned

buffalo hunter turned US lawman," Hawkins observed.

"I did not know he was a Canadian," Tate admitted. "A dandy how?"

"He wears a derby hat, a gun to his specifications ordered directly from Colt and a dark color suit and vest every day," the marshal commented.

"Hmm....you reckon I should get a suit for when I talk to him?" Tate asked.

"If you can afford it, might be a good idea. You may be expected to wear one anyway. Who knows?"

"I have a little grubstake so I can rent a house wherever I land. Mebbe a suit would be in order."

"I don't mind sending him a telegram saying I sent you up there with my recommendations after your actions yesterday, if you want," the marshal offered.

"I'd sure appreciate it, Marshal. He doesn't know me from anybody. I could give him Capt. Lee Hall's name. He's the fella who took over after Capt. Mc-Nelly died. I worked for him a little while."

"I'll go ahead and send a telegram to Bat. It might help and sure won't hurt."

"Thank you, sir. I really appreciate it."

"Do you know, marshal, why a man who was a famous sheriff of a big county with Dodge City in it would give it all up to move to Trinidad with probably only a couple deputies?" Tate asked.

"I have my suspicions. I'll share them with you, but keep 'em to yourself, 'cause they are just guesses."

"I will. What's your suspicion?" Tate asked.

"There was a pretty and famous singer name of Dora Hand. She studied in New York and I heard, even in Germany. She weren't no barroom soiled dove with a voice. She was a trained lady and did lots of good in the community. Well, the story goes, she was staying at Dodge Mayor Dog Kelly's house. He wasn't there. Dog was in the hospital over at the fort with some ailment.

A fella who had a beef with the mayor rode past his house and shot it up with his revolver early one day. Killed Miss Hand dead layin' in the bed asleep. Was a mistake, but a murder any way you look at it.

He rode out and a helluva posse rode after him. Was Charlie Bassett, Bat Masterson, Wyatt Earp and Bill Tilghman. Now, the first three are already pretty well known. But watch for Bill. He has a gun hand about as fast as yours. He will be the comer.

But, back to the Dora Hand matter. The killer was a fella named Kenedy. His pa had been co-owner of the King Ranch in Texas." Tate nodded in recognition of the massive spread.

"The posse chased him down and Bat shot him in the shoulder with a buffalo gun. He was hurt something fierce. They brought him in. His pa hired a big city lawyer and he walked. Bat was so peeved, he resigned not long after. He just got here a month or so ago, hired in to replace a marshal who left before end of his term."

"Thanks for the background, marshal," Tate said, "if he says anything, I'll be surprised."

"Changing the subject, old Hiram's ranch is just about three miles south of Trinidad. You could check in on them periodically, I suspect," the marshal said.

"I don't know what the girl's prospects are, but she is fine looking and seems, with my limited contact, to be a good person," he added.

"I will. I feel responsible for her. I know it doesn't make any sense, but I do."

"Sounds to me you ought to follow up on her. I suspect it means something. Beats me as to what, but let it play out. Unless Bat hired somebody yesterday, I think you will get the deputy marshal job with no problem. It may lead to bigger things. Bat Masterson fancies himself a gambling man. This lawman stuff is just for a regular income to pay living expenses. He'll be moving on sooner than later, leaving the marshal job open. Earp and his brothers gamble, but mainly invest in whore houses. The brothels are where they got their common law wives, word has it. Next silver or gold strike and they are gone, too," said the normally quiet lawman, trying to help this young protégé understand the type men he might be dealing with. He went on to explain how difficult it was for towns to find lawmen and some straddled the line they enforced. Some were worse than the people they served or even arrested. It was the way it was in a violent land.

Tate appreciated and took the candor seriously. He had seen lots of violence and bad men, but virtually none had been wearing badges. This was a different side of things. He wanted to pattern himself more like Hawkins and maybe this Tilghman fellow. The latter was about his age from some further conversation, but sounded like he was dedicated to the job, not just wearing a badge passing by. Or, so Hawkins felt.

He thanked the marshal for his tutelage and headed for a general store to see if they had suits. They did and he got a dark gray one with a vest and a white shirt and tie. He checked the jacket for how it draped over his Colt. It was okay. He just had to get used sweeping it aside to draw. With a little brushing, he thought his Stetson was acceptable with the suit.

His trail clothes rolled up in his bedroll, Tate set off to meet Marshal Bat Masterson.

He rode the twenty miles in two hours, with Cisco at a trot. Tate rode down the street as he had entered Raton and any other town, slowly and scanning for threats. He found the Marshal's Office before any threats and tied Cisco to the hitching rail and went in.

There was an older deputy working the desk. Tate figured he was a jailer, not a deputy who would patrol and collar drunks and other miscreants. He had a bit of a pot belly, but still looked like a tough customer. And, who knows, Tate thought. He might also be the world's best shot.

"Howdy deputy. Is Marshal Masterson in?" he asked.

"Naw, he's out walking around enforcing. He walks around every hour or two and covers most of the town."

"Showing the badge, huh?" Tate prompted.

"Yeah, I guess it's what you could call it. What can I do for you?"

"I need to talk with the Marshal."

"'Bout a job?" the deputy asked.

"Could be," Tate replied.

"Got any experience?

"Passable." Tate said.

"Where 'bouts?" Tate did not want to talk so much, but also knew men like this sometimes ran offices, were knowledgeable about everything going on and useful to have on one's side.

"Texas Ranger for ten years."

The man perked up.

"Under who?"

"Capt. Leander McNelly. Capt. Lee Hall for a little while after McNelly died."

"McNelly was right up there with Hays, Walker and Jones among the greats," he said.

"You know your rangers, deputy."

"Ought to. Served in the rangers just after the war. The Sharps and cap 'n ball rangers," he said, identifying the period by the guns they carried.

"I'd sure like to hear some of your stories about those days," Tate said, meaning every word.

"Wal, let's get you on board and we'll talk over coffee during quiet times," he said.

"What's your name, sir?" Tate asked.

"Hulon Parker. From El Paso," he said.

"Glad to make your acquaintance. I'm Morgan Tate, from over by the Concho River," Tate said.

They shook and Tate sat at his desk as bidden.

"Marshal ought to be back shortly. Usually takes him a half hour or so to make his rounds. You ever met him?" Parker asked.

"No, sir. I have not."

"Medium height, strong stocky build. Limps and uses a cane, though the cane is kind of a handy accessory to him. Dresses like a dude. Don't let it fool you. He's tough as nails and fast on the draw."

"He was a buffalo hunter wasn't he?"

"Yep. He and his brothers all were. All the Dodge City lawmen except, I believe, Charlie Bassett were buffalo hunters. The Earp brothers, Pat Garrett, Bill Tilghman. Hunters, scouts and Indian fighters. Their grit and gun skills turned them to the law jobs, a pressing need to tame towns. Sometimes there's a fine line between good and bad," he hinted to Tate without further elaboration. Marshal Hawkins had given Tate the same impression. This was something he had not seen much of in the rangers, operating mainly in the wilds in a military format.

The door opened and a man with a black suit and

derby hat walked in. He was carrying a black cane with a silver head. If it was not Bat Masterson, it was someone doing a good job of impersonating him.

"Bat, come over here and say howdy to Morgan Tate, late of the Texas Rangers. I been getting' to know him. He's got something he wants to talk to you about," Parker said.

"I already know a bit about Mr. Tate," Masterson began, flashing a telegraph form.

"Marshal Hawkins sent me a little *billet-doux* about him wanting a deputy job," the marshal said.

"There you go, speaking Canuck again," Parker said.

"It means 'love letter,' Hulon."

Continuing, he aimed his comments at Tate.

"He said you were fast as hell and cool under fire in the one incident he saw and he would hire you himself if he had an opening. I'll pay you twenty-five dollars a week and a split on arrests and on the fees and taxes we collect. Since there's only Hulon and two other deputies and me, the extras should exceed the salary by a good margin."

"Sounds good to me, Marshal. I'll hold up my hand anytime you want," Tate said.

"Hulon, grab the Bible and the extra badge."

Hulon Parker did and Tate placed his hand on the Bible.

"Do you," he started, nodding for Tate to say his full name, "swear to uphold the Constitutions of the United

States and State of Colorado, the laws of Colorado and the ordinances of the Town of Trinidad and Las Animas County, so help you God?" Bat Masterson asked.

"I do," Tate answered.

"Well, then. I guess you are a Deputy Marshal and by agreement with the Sheriff, have full deputy powers for the whole county. Makes things easier for posse's and such. We had the same arrangement in Ford County when I was sheriff there."

Hulon gave him a silver star, which he pinned on the left side of his vest, just visible under his jacket lapel.

"I like my deputies to look official and presentable. You don't have to wear a suit every time you walk out the door. But, a vest and nice shirt and a tie are appropriate all the time, depending on weather. Right now, you can wear a coat over your vest if you want instead of the suit jacket. Your choice. But, some drunk is gonna puke on you and once I teach you how to buffalo somebody instead of shooting them, you might get a few specks of blood on yourself," Bat said.

"Buffalo, sir?" Tate asked.

"I know you are a Southerner and all, but, you don't have to say 'sir' all the time. Not like I could be your father. Now, Hulon, could be your great grand pappy," Bat said grinning at his older deputy, who might be fifty at the most. "Just call me Bat, okay?"

"Okay, Bat."

"Where are you living, Tate?"

"Out of my saddlebag. This was my first stop when I rode into town," Tate replied. "If there was a cottage for rent in town or not too far out, I'd call it lucky. Otherwise, I'll put up at a hotel for now."

"Go over to the town office. Tell 'em I sent you. Ask if they know of any houses for rent. If anybody would know, it would be them. Out the door, take a right and walk half way down the street. For now, Town Hall just looks like any other house. I'm sure one day we'll have a brick edifice so some puffed up blow toad politician can think he's a big deal."

"Okay. I'll get settled and come back."

"Naw. I won't start paying you until tomorrow, unless you have to shoot somebody today. Take the rest of the day and get settled. There's a livery down the street, too. I'm assuming the fine looking black tied out front is yours?"

"The black is my pard, Cisco. He's a fine horse, Bat." Bat nodded.

"Tomorrow, we'll start off with the fine art of buffaloing an uncooperative cuss. Have a good rest of the day and see you around seven in the morning, okay?" Bat said.

"Sounds good. See y'all then," and Tate headed to the town hall, such as it was.

The clerk (of the court, he presumed) said there was a small cottage one street over from Main, near its intersection with Commercial Street. Having left Cisco at the hitching rail by the Marshal's Office, Tate walked over.

The place was clean. It had one bedroom, a fireplace for cooking and heating, one combination living room and kitchen and a stable out back with a small corral. At the far end of the yard was a privy. He read the price and how to get in touch with the owners from a sign in a front window. Two hours later, he had rented it for two months with an option for more. He needed to buy some basics to make it livable. He decided to leave his bedroll and trail gear intact and store it in the stable, ready to use at a moment's notice.

His last bit of shopping was for canned goods, bacon and dried food, especially pinto beans. His first meal was his normal trail fare, with bacon, fry bread and a fair amount of the bacon going into a pot to simmer overnight with the beans. Ham and bean soup would be good, he reckoned. There was a bit of split oak beside the rear of the house. He needed to find out where to replace it when it ran out.

As a ranger, he had lived in a wall tent with a wooden floor with several other rangers for ten years — when he was not on the trail and sleeping on the ground. Tate was enthusiastic. This was his own home for the first time ever. Even if temporary.

CHAPTER 3

Tate showed up at an estimated seven o'clock the next morning. He decided it was time to get a watch. Hulon was there fixing coffee, but Bat had not yet put in an appearance. Hulon said he probably dealt faro most of the night. Tate could tell Hulon felt this would ultimately be the marshal's downfall.

The marshal came in later. His eyes were bloodshot and he was moving slowly.

"You look like a man who was up dealing last night, Bat. Were the cards good to you?" Hulon asked.

"Not particularly. You got coffee?" he mumbled as he sat at his desk. The deputy brought him a steaming mug of the life-saving brew.

"You know what my old Pa would say don't you, Bat?"

"No, but I suspect I'm getting ready to find out."

"He'd say your eyes look like two pee holes in a snowbank."

"Wal, thank you, Hulon. Makes me feel better all ready," Bat said.

"What's on for today?" the marshal asked.

"You were going to teach Tate how to buffalo somebody."

"Couple cups more and we'll get to it. Tate? You want to take the first patrol? The saloons have not opened yet, nor the sporting houses. Should be pretty quiet."

Tate stood up and put his waxed cotton coat with the tartan wool lining over his shirt and vest. He donned the Stetson, saluted both lawmen and headed out the door.

As he walked down the street, he checked the locks on doors of businesses not yet open for business. Some deliveries were being made, but the streets were not busy. He kept his coat open so the badge would show.

The few people he saw were mostly men and looked suspiciously at the stranger walking and trying doors so early, until they saw the silver star on his chest.

Some grunted "howdy," others nodded and just went about their business. Colorado was not the South, Tate noted, as far as politeness went.

He heard snoring in the shadows of an alley near a saloon and investigated. It was a drunk sleeping it off. It was not cold enough for a man with a coat to die of exposure, so Tate left him alone.

It took him about forty minutes to cover town and get back to the office.

Bat Masterson seemed to have found his second wind and showed Tate how to draw and use his revolver as a bludgeon instead of shooting iron. Done quickly, it was surprising and efficient.

Thinking about how close he had come to running out of ammo in the gunfight in Raton, he asked the marshal a question.

"Bat, what do you think about carrying a second gun? We did on our saddles sometime afield in the rangers. I got real low on cartridges the other day in the street at Raton."

"Tell me what happened at Raton. Hawkins didn't go into details," Bat said.

"We were talking and shots rang out. He grabbed his big ten-gauge and we went into the street. An old man was shot and leaning against a wagon. His musket was on the ground and three men were dragging off his niece. Marshal Hawkins called for them to stop. He could not take a shot at the one holding the girl because of the scattergun.

"I approached them. The captor cocked his Schofield and the girl fainted. She gave me a clear shot and I drew and dropped him and the guy next to him. Hawkins cut the other one down with the shotgun," Tate said.

"You had your gun holstered?" Masterson asked.

"Yes. I wanted to try to calm things down. Drawing slowly as I walked over to them might have gotten the girl killed. I knew I could get my Colt into action quickly if I needed to. And, I did."

Masterson considered this and did not comment further, nor answer the earlier question about a backup gun.

"Why don't you spend time before the next patrol familiarizing yourself with the Colorado law book and our wanted posters. Oh! You got a long gun?" he asked.

"I have a '73 Winchester in .44-40 to match my revolver."

"Why not leave it in the rack here, loaded, so it will be handy and not stolen from your house while you are on duty. My Sharps Big-Fifty is in the rack, along with Hulon's rifle and several shotguns, all loaded."

"I'll pick it up on next patrol," Tate said as he thumbed open the law book Hulon just handed him.

He read the laws for an hour and asked periodic questions of Hulon, the professional peace officer with years behind the badge. Particular emphasis was placed on murder, rape, kidnapping, robbery and assault and battery. Tate broke the head off a match and dropped it in the spittoon. He used the stick to mark his last page read and got up to commence his next tour.

"Enjoy the sun in your eyes, Tate. Next week, you are going to be patrolling nights, when the bars and whore houses are rolling and the drunks are trying to kill each other for some reason they won't remember," Bat told him. He just nodded with a half-smile in return as he stood and headed for the door.

This tour, the stores were open. He went into each and introduced himself to the shop keeps as he toured. Several asked "You a gambler, too?"

He replied with the truth. "Nope, I don't play. I also don't drink anything stronger than beer either." One man asked "What kinda man don't have no vices?"

Tate laughed.

"Oh, I'm sure I have plenty of vices. I just don't gamble or drink." His response seemed to satisfy the questioner.

But, it did get Tate thinking. What were his vices? He knew he was not perfect. He cussed on occasion. He smoked a pipe in camp sometime. He looked lasciviously upon pretty ladies, the rare instance when he saw one he thought was actually pretty. Like Eve Hudson.

Eve. Her name led him to a whole new line of thought. What *was* her story? Marshal Hawkins alluded to her having one. A woman ought to have a bit of mystery, he thought. What if he did not like the story?

He would sure like to know. Maybe he would see her again and get to know her well enough she would volunteer it. Or, maybe frogs wouldn't bump their butts on the ground if they had wings. He walked on, frustrated.

During his next office time, he finished his initial scan of the Colorado laws. Most were the same as Texas. His time in the rangers had been one of transition. He and Hulon talked about it.

"Hulon, I 'spect you mainly fought Indians and Mexican raiders and rustlers?" he prompted.

"Just like you probably did during your first few years," Hulon said.

"True. It was only towards the last when we started being lawmen instead of a border paramilitary, as Capt. McNelly called it, protecting Texas' outlying ranches and trading posts against raids," Tate answered.

"We had some pretty nasty pitched battles against hostile raiding parties. Unlike the damn army, we didn't ride into villages and slaughter everybody," Hulon said.

"One thing I never figured. We were issued Sharps rifles. Now, a Sharps is a fine long distance rifle with a lot of power. But, it's a single shot. We fought Indians who had repeaters. Henry's and Spencer's. They had us outgunned. Sometimes, the bows and arrows had us outgunned. Purely a matter of bureaucrats selecting guns, not the men who were on the line using them. Was it so in your time, Tate?"

"Maybe a little less. McNelly was a Confederate officer during the war. He led a group of guerilla raiders and scouts. Like Mosby and others, we often had repeating rifles and two Colts on our saddle horns during field maneuvers. Of course, we wore at least one on our belts when in town or purely law enforcement missions," Tate said.

"I guess Bat forgot to answer your question about a backup firearm," Hulon began.

"He carries one. A Marlin .38 with a spur trigger. Small, but fairly powerful. Hides it in his vest pocket."

"Interesting. One of the rangers carried a new Colt 1878 in .44-40 as backup. It was bigger than the 1977 Lightning model, but a lot more dependable. I was thinking about one of those in an inside holster, covered by my vest. What do you think?"

"It would work, but heavy and hard to hide. The gun cabinet down at the general mercantile stays pretty well stocked. I'd take a look down there before deciding," Hulon recommended. Tate nodded appreciatively.

On his next patrol, he stopped and checked the gun cabinet.

He asked to see a new Colt New Line spur trigger in .41 caliber. It was small, had an easy to hide bird's head grip and two and a half inch barrel. He bought it for ten dollars and added a box of cartridges. He planned to test it soon, but knew despite the big bullet, it was woefully weak. Power and size were almost always a trade-off in handguns.

The left pocket of his vest was pretty deep, so he loaded it and tucked it in there.

Not great, he thought, but better than a sharp stick in the eye.

Back at the office later, he asked Hulon a question.

"You seem pretty fit. Don't you get bored sitting here most of the day? Of course, walking patrol in a small town is boring enough by itself," Tate said.

"I guess I'm fit for a short fight. I took a ball in the leg a few years ago. It's still in there and impedes my running after somebody. So, I'd rather stay here and run things. Marshals come and go. Most are happy for me to run the administrative stuff. We, as you see, just have a small two-cell lockup. The county jail is outside of town and run by the Las Animas County sheriff. Not trying to get rid of you, son, but you'd be better suited as a county deputy. Patrol a big area on horseback. Exercise your great-looking black."

"I appreciate your thoughts, Hulon. I figured I'd be a tumblin' weed until I found the place and job really appealing to me. Growing up where you and I both did, I'd kinda like to live where there are real woods. Green. Tall trees. Maybe I'd find it a bit farther north and west. Maybe Manitou Springs."

"Bat's reputation has kept violent crime down ever since he's been marshal. But, some powerful do-gooders let their Bible stuff get in the way of reality. They don't like him dealing faro all night. Doesn't look seemly for town marshal, they think. I personally only look at what's *not* happening on his watch. Little things like murder, major robbery, rape, kidnapping. A Wild West town is always gonna have fights and drunks. And, gunshots. The good thing is most cowmen and even most lawmen, can't shoot worth a damn. But, Bat can. And, everybody knows it."

"How long you think he'll be marshal?" Tate asked.

"Hard to tell. He's popular with most folks. It's the powerful, monied do-gooders who will support somebody else soon. He's up for reelection this coming month. It could go either way. But, what I hear is it is likely to go against Bat. The other side's candidate is a church-going businessman. We may have to teach him how to carry a revolver. Hell, we may have to furnish him one!" Hulon said.

"If Bat keeps the peace and has you run an efficient office, who cares whether he deals cards at night? He's awake, dressed and armed for any criminal event."

"I agree. But, we don't run the town. The banker, big shop owners, coal mine operators. Those are the folks who determine elections in a place like Trinidad…and, much of the West," he added.

This did not convince Tate he had come to the right place to stay very long. He would make some money and learn some more under a famous lawman and maybe move on.

His soliloquy was interrupted by the sound of several shots. He and Hulon went to the door and carefully looked out. A man in a suit was firing a revolver at three men fleeing the bank on horseback.

The man saw them and pointed to the riders, yelling "bank robbery!"

Tate grabbed his Winchester off the rack and Hulon got a sawed-off shotgun. They went across to the bank.

"Anybody hurt?" Hulon asked.

The banker shook his head.

"How many men?" Tate asked.

"Three men," he said.

How 'bout a facial description of each?" Tate asked.

"One with dark beard, one with a brush mustache, light colored. Other one had blonde hair, clean shaven. All carried rifles."

"Did you hit anybody?" Hulon asked.

"Maybe. I don't know for sure whether the shot was close and the man jerked from fear, or I actually hit him," the banker said.

Tate turned to Hulon.

"I will get Cisco and go after them. If you or the marshal can put together a posse, it would be good."

The older deputy nodded and Tate sprinted for his house and saddled Cisco in the stable out back. His trail gear was already lashed to the saddle, his canteens full.

Less than ten minutes after the shots were fired, Tate was heading out of town at full gallop. On the way out, he met a buckboard in-bound. Eve Hudson was driving and looked him in the eye.

He rode with his rifle out and across the saddle behind the horn. It was something rangers did a lot in hostile country.

The road was part of the Santa Fe Trail and cutting sign was virtually impossible. Knowing the only person he had passed was Eve and nobody but the robbers were in front, he safely assumed the dust was his only sign from the robbers.

They apparently had fresh horses, because he surely was not catching up with them very fast.

He knew Cisco's endurance and let him run. After about eight miles, he met another wagon and stopped.

"You see three men riding this way?" he asked the driver, an old farmer with a load of vegetables.

"Yep. Riding hell for leather. 'Bout ten minutes ago. Had some fine horseflesh. They was pushing them ponies hard, I'll tell ya."

"Thanks," Tate said as he galloped off.

He let Cisco drop down to a canter for a while. The way they were headed would take them into the mountains eventually. He doubted the three would stay on the main road much longer. It would leave too many witnesses like the old farmer.

Now he slowed down. He leaned as far off the horse as a good rider could and searched the road below.

Finally, he saw it. A large drop of blood. The banker *had* winged one of the robbers. It just got a little easier. He was not bleeding badly, but he was bleeding enough to leave a trail and slow them down.

Over the next half hour, he saw larger droplets of blood. By best reckoning, he thought maybe it had finally soaked through a couple layers of clothes and was dripping off the man's vest or something.

The dust seemed to be growing, indicating he was catching up with the three horsemen. There was a stand of woods paralleling the road. It was about a hundred yards off to the left. Tate moved Cisco over near the woods so he could duck out of sight if he came up on them too quickly. He knew it was too early for them to expect a posse, so the outlaws probably would not be too wary yet.

In another hour, he smelled cigarette smoke in the distance. Tate learned in the rangers by blowing air from one's nose and sniffing in the open, it was possible to smell man, animals and other odors with an efficiency unimaginable to most town dwellers.

Tate dismounted and led Cisco into the edge of the woods. They moved furtively for about half a mile until he saw the men. They were dismounted and counting cash. Dividing the money was a sure precursor to separating, so he had to act quickly to apprehend all of them.

One of them had poured canteen water into a tin mug, probably for the wounded man. The mug was sitting on a log and Tate had a clear rifle shot at it from fifty yards.

He steadied the Winchester against a tree and pressed the trigger. The mug went flying, splashing water on several of the robbers.

"You fellas, drop your guns and throw up your hands. Or, the next one will ventilate somebody."

Shocking Tate, the men did as ordered. He stood and walked towards them, rifle at his shoulder and finger on the trigger.

"Unbuckle your gun belts. Do it slow and easy. No-body wants to be the first to die." All dropped their belts.

"Now, move several feet back from them and sit on your asses. Do it now!" Tate ordered.

He whistled and Cisco came trotting up. Drawing his Colt, he held it unwaveringly as he sheathed the carbine in its scabbard.

Tate had no nippers in his saddle bags to hand-cuff the men, so he ordered one to retrieve a lariat from a saddle and use a pocket knife to cut three one yard long sections from it. He had one man tie the wounded man with a piece of rope. Then, he had the same man tie the second man. Both were tied in front so they could ride and relieve themselves. Now, he wondered how to get the third man tied. Clearly, the man could not tie himself. Tying a conscous man would guarantee endangering himself in a scuffle. So, he made all of the men squat down and walked behind the third, untied man. He swung the Colt hard against the back of this head and he went down.

"Hey! That warn't nice!!" one of the men said.

"You rather I'd shoot him? I could have killed all of you and brought you back over your saddles instead of on them. I could still do it, if you'd prefer," Tate said.

He knelt and tied the unconscious man tightly himself, his Colt ready to hand.

Tate picked up the three piles of money and put them back in the white cotton money bag from the bank.

"Okay, Mr. Wounded Bank Robber. Can you ride back, or should I shoot you now? Of course if I shoot you all tied up, I'll have to kill your pards. They'd be witnesses then."

"I'm a little dizzy from where the damn banker shot me, but I can make it back," the wounded man said.

"We are going to ride straight through. No way I'm gonna camp with you girls," Tate said. What he was really hoping was meeting a posse led by Bat Masterson on the way back to Trinidad.

"Here's the way it's gonna be: I will ride in back with my rifle out. You will ride at a fast walk three across. Nobody in front. Anybody takes off, I shoot his horse. If you are not killed by the horse falling on you, you will walk all the way back to Trinidad while we smart ones ride. Got it?" Tate asked.

All nodded and they started to backtrack to Trinidad.

Mid-afternoon, Tate spotted a big dust cloud ahead. He reckoned, correctly, it was Bat and the posse.

They pulled up and stopped fifty feet in front of the three prisoners. The banker, who had proven to be a good, or lucky, shot, rode next to Bat.

"Well, I'll be damned!" Masterson said. "What you got there, Tate?"

"Just three fellas I have arrested for bank robbery and some money from said robbery. Nuthin' else."

Bat Masterson shook his head, remembering the long, cold trail four of the best lawmen in history had ridden to bring back one murderer.

Tate nodded to the banker and tossed him the tied bag of cash.

"I have not had a chance to count it. Been kinda busy. But, I would like a receipt. And, if it doesn't tally with your robbery amount, then somebody at the bank counted wrong. This is everything they had. They were just beginning to divide it when I sent a bullet their way and brought them to the Lord. The fella in the fancy vest is the one you shot. I knew I had the right ones once I was able to cut sign on his blood drops along the way."

The banker was happy enough with the way the day ended up, he did not even get peeved at the part about someone counting wrong. He was not a fan of the gambling marshal and would not have put it past one of his deputies to kill all three and disappear with the whole proceeds of the robbery. But, maybe he misread. Here was the deputy leading three tied men back to Trinidad at gunpoint and tossing him the bag of cash.

The triumphant combined posse of one deputy and of a marshal and ten men rode into Trinidad before dark. The town turned out and the men were cheered. The prisoners were temporarily lodged in the two-cell Marshal's Office. A doctor was called in to treat the wounded man.

The next day, they were transported several hundred yards to the court and formally charged and turned over to the sheriff for custody until the trial date.

The sheriff caught Tate on the way out.

"I'll be needing another deputy in the next month or so. You might stay in touch. There's a marshal election coming up and it could go either way. I will be here another three years before election. The salary is the same and the share of taxes and all is higher since it's for a whole county, instead of a piss ant town."

"Thanks, Sheriff. I'll sure keep your words quietly in mind."

The sheriff doffed his Stetson and walked off, leaving the town deputy deep in thought.

A week later, the bank robbers' trial was the big thing everybody was talking about in Trinidad.

It was like a circus coming to town. A hanging was about the only thing better for most folks, but the bank robbery did not rise to capital punishment.

The bank's cashier and president and Tate were the only people testifying for the prosecution. A local attorney handled the defense, but no witnesses were called, since the three were seen running out of the bank being shot at by half the town and then were caught red-handed by Tate.

The bankers elaborated about the robbery and fearing for their lives.

Tate, though serious, caused a round of laughter prompting the judge to slam his gavel down, when he mentioned shooting the mug off the stump. A *soto voce* comment by a viewer prompted it when he said, "Gol, dang! I bet them boys 'bout whizzed themselves when the mug went flying!"

Tate saw Eve in the gallery smiling as he testified. At the recess for the jury to deliberate, he made a point of catching up with her.

"I saw you high-tailing after those three the other day when I was coming into town," she told him.

"I know, Miss Eve. I saw you too. Excuse me, please. Seeing you called for me being more polite, but I was in a powerful hurry to catch them.

"I figured it out pretty quick, Deputy."

"You can call me Morgan, if you want," he ventured.

"Alright, Morgan, I will. And, I'm just plain Eve. No need for' Miss Eve'."

"Eve, you are anything but plain. Any man who sees you wants to turn and enjoy another look," he said.

"Thank you, Morgan. I am afraid I am not the type woman a good man would want to be seen with. But, it's nice to hear your words."

"Why on earth, Eve?"

"Maybe one day, I'll share it with you. Now, I'll keep my shame to myself."

He chose not to press her, though his curiosity was aroused.

"Might I ask your uncle if I could come around and call on you?" he asked.

"I am fully emancipated, so I can answer for myself.

Regretfully, the answer is 'no.'"

"Is there someone else?" he asked.

"No, I don't have anybody else. It's…complex."

"I would like to pursue the matter again soon. But, in a less public place," he said.

"The answer is unlikely to change."

He walked away wondering what was wrong with a tall fellow with white teeth, a paying job and a nice suit. In school before the rangers, girls had chased after him. How had he changed so much for the worse in less than twelve years? He had added a pretty nice mustache and all, too.

The three bank robbers were found guilty and sentenced to five years each in the state penitentiary in Canon City. Tate and one of the county deputies were tasked to take them to the prison in a wagon. This time, the men were properly shackled with nippers and a logging chain. Along the way, Tate investigated what it would be like to be a Las Animas County deputy sheriff.

Bat Masterson was a natural teacher and Tate availed himself of the learning opportunities. He learned tricks about how to read people, how to interrogate them, hints about how to detect the options a fugitive was mulling over as he stood in front of a lawman. He learned when to not arrest someone in order to catch a bigger fish, something generally irrelevant in the rangers.

Night patrols were less boring than day patrols in Trinidad. Any night worth remembering always included arresting four or five drunks.

Tate got pretty good at buffaloing. He thought about a black jack, but sometimes it was better, Bat said, to have your six gun already in hand.

Tate was on patrol and went into the Lazy Deuce Saloon. A poker player was getting loud. Very loud. It was the whiskey more than the cards, Tate thought.

He stood close to the man, his right hand away from his gun and propping him against the wall. It was something he had practiced at home a lot.

The drunk had a bureau drawer special junker revolver tucked in his waistband. He eyed Tate's gun and his gun hand, mentally wondering if he could outdraw the deputy marshal.

Tate could see him arriving at a conclusion, probably a stupid one.

In a flash, Tate drew the .41 from his left vest pocket and had it cocked under the drunk's nose before the fool knew what was happening.

The drunk stared at it with crossed eyes, it was so close. He missed the blur as Tate drew his big .44 and slammed it into the side of his head. He was out before the stars began to sparkle in his addled brain. Tate took the junker gun and left him lying in the corner. He dropped the gun in the privy before somebody lost a hand shooting it and continued his patrol.

At Miss Epperson's Social Parlor, he stopped and accepted a cup of coffee. It was welcome to get out of the rain and get a hot cup. Miss Epperson and a couple of the girls sat with him and chatted.

Tate didn't have much experience with soiled doves. Actually, none at all.

But, these women talked just like any other folks.

One seemed open to conversation, so he asked her a question.

"Miss Alice, what brought you to this line of business?"

"Deputy, I am just like the vast majority of other women in this work. I was a widow with no prospect of a job. There was nothing available in house cleaning, sewing, or serving food in a café. This was the only choice. It is the last thing in the world I wanted to do, but I had to. At least at Miss Epperson's you deputies or the marshal are patrolling and she has Rufus to remove anybody who gets abusive. About all I have to worry about is pregnancy and disease. We have ways to try to avoid both, but they are primitive at best. So, I pray a lot."

Tate listened, nodding. He had never given the subject much thought, but it made sense. Despite what the church ladies thought, but for luck of the draw, it may be them working here. These were just regular women without better choices.

Tate thanked the ladies and told them to call out if they needed a deputy to help and then he left, wiser than when he entered.

The rest of the patrol was more like work, since he was walking in pouring rain after stepping in at the several saloons and sporting houses still open.

CHAPTER 4

City politicking season had gotten well underway. Tate heard both Bat's and his opponent's speeches.

Bat Masterson was by far the more eloquent speaker and the more competent person to serve as town marshal.

Wyatt Earp and several of his brothers rode in to support Bat.

Tate thought they were all handsome and well-dressed, but he plain just didn't like them. Apparently, the voters felt the same about the Earp's support of Masterson either.

Money talked and Bat walked, losing in a landslide vote.

One month into his two-month house lease, Tate decided to resign and ride north. He did not worry about Hulon. The professional lawman had weathered a series of marshals and would likely have more during the next twenty years or so of his career.

Tate told both the marshal and Hulon he was going to just ride north and look around and would return before resettling anywhere. Both shook with him and he rode Cisco out of town. He planned two more stops.

On the way out of town, he stopped at the sheriff's office. The sheriff was at his desk.

"Howdy, Sheriff. Just wanted to tell you I have been giving a lot of thought to our conversation. I have resigned from the Marshal's Office and have to ride north for a little while. I will check and see if you need some help once I get back."

"Know when you will return?" the sheriff asked.

"I don't for sure. Shouldn't be much more than a week or two. I have to go up to Manitou Springs on some personal business. After, I plan to ride back down to Trinidad," Tate said.

When they parted, he turned south towards Raton instead of north. He wanted to speak with Eve before he disappeared with no notice.

The ride was an easy three miles, but two miles into it, he saw her driving the buckboard towards him and Trinidad. He waved her over.

"Hello, Eve. I was coming to see you."

"I thought I was clear, Morgan, there was no bene-fit to you calling on me," she responded, her tone not as sharp as her words.

He smiled. "I'd rather be the judge, if you don't mind."

"Do you mind pulling off the side of the road so

we can chat for a few minutes? I am heading out of town for a little while and didn't want you to think I was gone forever without saying anything to you."

She pulled the buckboard over and set the brake. The horse, more a towing creature than one for long rides, immediately began to munch on a clump of grass.

Tate rode Cisco around to the side away from the road, dismounted and dropped the reins, knowing the black would stay close. He climbed aboard and sat on the hard wooden board seat beside her.

"So, how are you today?" he asked.

"Fine. And, you?" She replied in kind.

"Look, Eve. I think you are a kind, lovely person. I'd like to get to know you well enough to see if we might have something worth chasing after. Is there something about me you find offensive?" he asked, jumping straight to the point.

"No! Of course not! You are nice looking, seem honorable. You even have a job. You have a lot more than any prospects I see drifting by," she said.

"Then, what's the problem? Why don't you want me to call on you?"

"The problem is *me*, not you!" she exclaimed.

"Will you share this secret and let me decide for myself?" he asked.

"Can I trust you?"

"You trusted me with your life not so long ago. I think I earned your trust."

"But, you will think awful about me."

"Please, just spit it out, Eve."

"I am a widow. No kids. My husband was killed in an Indian raid over in Kansas a couple of years ago. I did not have any prospects. No sign of an available job. So, I went to work at a brothel. I'm a whore," she said, tears welling up in her pretty face.

"How long were you employed in a sporting house?" he asked gently, pulling off his kerchief and blotting the tears from her cheeks.

"Not long. I immediately got pregnant. The madam got rid of the pregnancy almost instantly. But, the process tore me up inside. I almost bled to death. While I was healing, I came here. My uncle is the only one I have left. I'm physically okay now, but I seriously fear I won't ever be able to bear children again. So, now you know. I am a scarlet woman. A woman no honest man would want to be seen with."

Tate paused, knowing what he said next had to be absolutely the right words.

"Eve. I have learned a lot since I have been in Trinidad. One thing is about the limited choices woman have when widowed or orphaned."

"In patrolling, I have had coffee with the ladies at several of the sporting houses. They opened my eyes with their stories. They were not any different from any churchgoing wife in town. Just unluckier. Fewer choices. You did not willingly choose your profession.

It was all you had left other than starving."

"I would be proud to call on you. I *will* call on you if you will let me. I think we have something together already. Let's explore it to see if we can go further."

"One thing you said was not quite right. I am not employed. I resigned from the Marshal's Office yesterday. I have a job with the sheriff if I want it. But, first, I am going to ride up towards Manitou Springs. I would like to look it over. After spending my life in deserts and prairies, I'd like to live where there's trees. Real trees," he said.

"I know what you mean. I grew up on the prairie. I hate those winds and the grass forever without a tree in sight."

"Morgan, do you really, really mean what you say about not being put off by what I did before coming here?" she asked.

"I really, really mean it, Eve. On my word as a Texan."

"I hate the prospect of leaving my uncle. He will need help soon. The bullet slowed him down a lot."

"I would never ask you to neglect your responsibility to your uncle. Let's deal with those things when we come to them. In the meantime, can we consider we are in a relationship? Undefined for now, but a relationship anyway." Eve nodded and smiled.

She leaned over and kissed him on his cheek. His mustache tickled her nose and she giggled. Tate considered the kiss her bond and gave her a big Texas grin.

He reached in his left vest pocket and removed the small .41 caliber revolver.

"Here. Keep this hidden about you in case some toughs bother you and I am not there."

She had a pocket in her skirt, under the apron. She placed the Colt there and smiled again. This time her kiss was a little better aimed. Actually, a lot better.

Tate climbed down, very satisfied with how the talk had gone. He told her so and promised to call on her as soon as he returned. She gave him a smile he would take on the trail with him, all the time wishing for a daguerreotype or ambrotype of her to carry with him. It gave him an idea.

"Would you pick up something in Trinidad for me?" he asked.

"Of course."

"Go by the photographers on Commercial Street and have a small likeness taken. Have him put it in a locket so I can carry it with me all the time. Here is some money to cover the costs. I will return with a gift to you very soon. I promise."

He folded her hand over a ten dollar gold piece and held her closed hand for a long time before mounting Cisco and riding north along side of her.

"Oh, you already gave me a romantic gift!" She patted the revolver in her skirt pocket.

"Flowers will die. This might keep me from dying," she said. "I would take a practical gift over a silly one any day. This proves you care about me a lot more than a box of candy or French perfume."

They parted at the photographer's shop and he rode on towards Colorado City, soon to be merged with Fountain Colony into Colorado Springs. The use of the name preceded the legal change. There, he would turn west seventeen or eighteen miles to Manitou Springs.

Eve tied the horse to the hitching rail, with the buckboard pulled in diagonally to block as little of the street as possible. She went in and spoke with the photographer about what she wanted and what her budget was. He offered her an ambrotype miniature in a case appropriate for a man's watch chain for the gold coin. Eve had on a clean white, sun dried and bleached blouse she had donned in the morning. She combed her hair and sat as he took several shots. She picked one to pick up in several days. For the first time in several years, she smiled prettily without having to force herself to do it. And, she changed her purchase before leaving the shop.

******

Tate rode into Colorado City about lunch time. He stopped at a café and ate. He added a half dozen biscuits to go. He had beans and bacon and some canned peaches in his trail larder and cook kit.

He left Cisco tied outside the café and walked around town.

At a general store, he found beef jerky and a duplicate of the revolver he had given Eve. He bought both as well as a box of cartridges. There was plenty of space where he would be exploring to test fire the Colt .41.

Then, he remounted and rode west to Manitou Springs and the Rocky Mountains.

Tate immediately liked Manitou Springs. He considered it the ideal Western small town. It even had carbonated springs from which folks could drink the bubbly water or bathe for the claimed relief of a multitude of ailments. Pike's Peak, named for Zebulon Pike, was near the town. There were streams and trees of all sizes and type. He did not see the area as being ideal for ranching. To stay there, he might have to resume the badge. He sure as shootin' was not going to be a shopkeeper or laborer.

Tate found several plots within a few miles of town meeting his mental vision of ideal. Each had nice cabin sites on a stream or pond and wooded surroundings. He inquired about the prices and made notes. He found a builder outside of town and received bids on several sizes of log cabins.

Just after nightfall, he found some remote woodland and pitched camp. There was plenty of browse for Cisco. After dinner of bacon, biscuits, and canned peaches, he set the peach can on a log and backed off fifteen feet. From fifteen feet, he was able to drill every shot into the can. Certainly good enough for a backup gun, he thought. He shaved a stick to fit the barrel and chamber holes of the small Colt and got out a small brass bottle of light oil he carried. He thoroughly cleaned the New Line Colt revolver by pushing an oily, then clean, patch through the barrel and chambers with the stick.

He banked his campfire and pulled up the bedroll. He stared at the stars for a long time, then closed his eyes and thought of Eve before drifting off to sleep to the scent of evergreens.

The next day, he rode into Colorado Springs to meet the Sheriff of El Paso County. The sheriff was out, but his chief deputy was in and indicated a deputy job was generally available and preference would be to experienced lawmen. When Tate listed his experiences, the chief seemed impressed and said someone like him could be hired by the large county about any time such a person might apply.

Tate spent several more days camping and riding around the area, especially looking at federal land available for homestead. He could claim one hundred sixty acres and build a house on it, then farm or ranch it for five years and it would be his. Alternatively, he could do those things and buy the land after six months for one dollar twenty five an acre and have the hundred sixty acres paid for and title transferred within half a year. The eligible land he found in the area was five to ten miles out from Manitou Springs. He thought it might be possible for her uncle to homestead an adjoining parcel to double the ranch size, but needed to verify whether it could be done.

It was too far to leave Eve alone on and ride to and from a deputy job. Particularly worrisome at night. He would have to do some deep thinking and talk with her further before deciding on anything.

******

Tate had seen everything he needed to and pointed Cisco back to Manitou Springs. He stopped by a store and picked up a gift for Eve and headed south towards her uncle's ranch.

He rode up the short lane to the ranch in mid-afternoon. The buckboard was sitting out front, unharnessed. She should be there.

"Hello, the house!" he yelled out. The uncle came to the door, holding the musket loosely. He immediately recognized the rider as the one who had saved Eve along with Marshal Hawkins.

"Git on down, Ranger. There's cold spring water if you are parched."

Tate swung a long leg over Cisco's back and lightly stepped down.

"I expect you want to see my niece."

"Yessir, I do," Tate replied.

"Eve, it's the lawman from town. C'mon out and say hi," Hiram Stone called.

She came out a few minutes later, having done a bit of emergency grooming. Eve Hudson was even prettier than the images of her floating through Tate's mind for the past few days and nights.

"Howdy, Eve. You sure look nice," was the best he could come up with. She smiled at him.

"Morgan, why don't you sit on the porch here and talk with Uncle Hiram. I will get the two of you some cold water and be right back," she said.

Tate and the older man sat on ladder-back chairs.

"How's ranching, Mr. Stone?"

"It's not worth the trouble. My riding and lassoing days are over. I'm afraid the place is going downhill fast. I am about ready to sell out," he said.

"Given good land, would you be better doing a little farming?" Tate asked.

"Mebbe. I grew up farming. Grew hay and corn and such. Didn't get rich, but I got by. I spent more time fighting Indians than tilling the earth, seemed like."

"Bloody Kansas. It must have been a rough place to live," Tate commented.

"Still is. There are about five tribes still raiding outlying farms and ranches. The army does more harm than good. They wait for some family to get burned out and scalped, then ride in with a bunch of cavalry and burn a village down and kill every living soul. Us acting like them don't stop the Indians. It just makes them madder. And, I don't blame them. Sometimes, I think we are savages, as much as them. I'd kill any attacking brave I got my sights on. But, no way in hell I'd ride to his village and kill his babies and his grandma. It ain't right."

"No. It's not right at all. We live in a violent place out here in the West. I hope it gets more peaceable, but it won"t happen real fast. And, if anybody would be in a position to see it, it would be a lawman," Tate said.

"I was really more worried about the raiders from both the anti-slavery and pro-slavery. More often than not, the Indians would steal your horses and ride off. The whites would burn you out and shoot with wild abandon. It didn't seem to matter which side you were on. They rode and killed with a frenzy."

Tate nodded, knowing the man was dead right. Though something seemed a bit off in his history. Tate couldn't quite put a finger on it.

Eve interrupted with cold water in tin mugs. Tate stood as she walked out and she gently touched his shoulder to sit back down.

"I brought some .41 cartridges for your revolver. Do you want to try shooting it? I replaced it with another, so we match! I shot mine and it surprised me with its accuracy. It is a Colt, after all," he said.

"It probably would be a good idea for me to fire it without it being an emergency," she said.

The men finished their water. Hiram suggested they shoot in the field behind the barn.

Tate got a second box of cartridges from his saddle-bags and they walked to the barn. He picked up some big clods of hard earth and set them on a clear spot. Again, he paced off fifteen yards with his long stride.

Eve stood sideways to the targets, put one hand on her left hip and extended the gun hand out as she cocked the hammer. She fired and knocked up dirt beside a chunk. She fired again and it exploded. She gave a giggle and fired at another chunk and hit it, also. By the time the cylinder was empty, there were no more targets.

"I guess I won't have to be teaching you how to shoot, will I?" Tate asked, with more than a modicum of pride in both voice and expression. She just smiled.

"Okay, Mr. Lawman. I'll pick some targets and you shoot now."

She walked the fifteen yards and found five smaller clods of dirt and lined them up.

After she returned and stepped behind him, he stood there and stared at the five small targets.

"You gonna will them to disappear?" she asked.

He drew in a flash and fired five times so fast it sounded like perhaps two shots. Within two seconds, there were no clods of dirt downrange.

Eve and her uncle just stood looking in shock. The clods were there, then they were gone almost immediately.

Eve turned to her uncle.

"Now you see how Morgan to saved me, Uncle Hiram. He killed two men in about a second. Nobody alive but him could have done it. I'm sure of it!"

"Thanks, Eve. I just did what I was trained to do," he said with genuine modesty.

"I have some gun oil in a small bottle in my saddlebags. Let's clean these guns up and put 'em away," Tate said, changing the subject.

Hiram went off to do some ranch chores. Tate noted he moved stiffly, maybe from his wound, maybe from age. Or, most likely from both.

Tate showed Eve how to clean the two revolvers and reloaded both. She tucked hers back in the pocket under her apron as he holstered his.

"Why don't you wash the oil off your fingers before looking at what I've got for you?" Eve suggested.

He went to the well, dropped the bucket in and raised it to scoop a dipperful of water on his hands.

She handed him a bar of homemade soap and he lathered the grease off and dried on a cloth.

Eve took him by the hand and led him back to the porch. She took a small bag out of her pocket and presented it to him.

Inside was a nickel pocket watch. He opened it and the lid held a photo of a beautiful smiling Eve. He could literally see her eyes sparkling in the ambrotype.

"Nobody ever gave me such a fine present," he exclaimed. But, I did not give you enough for a watch, too," he said.

"I had a little egg money to add to it. I have been doing a lot of thinking. I am convinced we do belong together, Morgan. You are kind, polite and protective. You are understanding about my past. I have smiled more since I met you than I have in the last five years all together."

"I have been thinking and smiling, too. And, wondering how some old boy like me could possibly deserve an angel like you. But, stick with me and I'll promise to make you keep smiling."

She took his hand and they just sat there for a long time enjoying each other's presence and not talking. Tate looked at the watch. It was not expensive, but it did not matter. It was his first one. And, the fob with his beautiful Eve's picture made it special. *His* beautiful Eve. He liked the way it sounded in his mind, so he said it aloud.

"My beautiful Eve." He pressed her hand and saw a tear start down her cheek. But, he knew this one was happiness, not sadness.

CHAPTER 5

They sat for a long time, enjoying being together and enjoying the silence.

"I found some real pretty land up west of Manitou Springs. If we homesteaded it and built a house and planted something or raised a few horses or cattle, we could buy it for a buck twenty-five an acre after six months and own it free and clear. It's only two hundred dollars. I have it and enough to build a house already saved. Otherwise, it's free after five years. But, why wait?"

"My dilemma is it's almost eighteen miles from the county seat at Colorado Springs. I'd have to be a deputy. The sheriff all but said he'd hire me any time. But, I am leery to leave you out in the wilderness all alone while I am on patrol for the sheriff's office all over a big county."

"What if my uncle came with us? He loves farming, especially since he can't wrangle cattle any more.

Maybe we could build him a separate cabin a hundred yards from ours," Eve thought aloud.

"Would he give up on this ranch?" Tate asked.

"I think he hates it. The soil isn't right for what he wants to grow. How is it up there?"

"It looks pretty black. A lot better than what we had in my part of Texas, and we grew crops there."

"Morgan, why don't you let me ask him alone. Then, you would have an excuse to come back to dinner tomorrow night."

"Good idea. Especially since I can test your cooking before committing the rest of my life to you," he said, earning an elbow in the ribs.

"What time, Eve? Now I have a watch and can be precise."

"Then, be here at six twenty-seven on the dot!"

He leaned over and kissed her.

"See you exactly then," and picked up Cisco's reins and mounted the black.

He rode back to town and went to his rental house. Things were falling in place, he thought.

He brushed Cisco and let him loose in the small corral by the one-horse covered stall.

There being nothing else pressing, Tate did something he had never done before. He allowed himself the luxury of a mid-day nap.

******

The next day, Eve and Uncle Hiram got up at their usual daylight. She fed the chickens and milked the cow while the old man walked out to the pasture and checked the small herd of cattle there. It bothered the Kansan he could no longer get onto his horse unassisted. He had never come back to his original level of fitness after being shot at Eve's kidnapping. He knew why she was kidnapped. He knew also they would be back. And, he knew why. What he did not know was today was the day they would return.

By mid-morning, Eve was busy in the house baking bread and preparing a stew for the first-ever dinner with Tate.

Hiram Stone was pleased for his niece. They were all each had left. He hardly knew her growing up and really only got to know her a year ago when she wrote him asking if she could come to live with him.

She came a broken, sad woman and it saddened him to see his sister's girl in such dire straits. It was rough, he knew, to be a woman on the frontier. He knew first hand as his wife had died of pneumonia a year after he enlisted in the army. He had been unable to get leave and tend to her. It was something he always held a great personal sadness and guilt about. And, it had been the beginning of a story which still had not played out.

Hiram kept his .58 Springfield rifle handy. He called it a musket, but only because it had the stock and appearance of an old musket. The army adopted a rear-loading cartridge version in .45-70 caliber only a year ago, so it was not an antique.

He knew his niece wore a .41 Colt revolver in her pocket every day.

Hiram was repairing the latch on the corral when he heard the horses. He knew in his heart it was them and started for the house to get the rifle.

"Eve! Raiders coming! Take cover and stay out of sight!" he yelled as he shuffled as fast as he could move towards the rifle.

Before he got to the house, they were on him. There were five of them. Warden McGillivray, Lt. Langston, Sgt., Kelly and two others he did not know.

1865 was the last time he had seen the three ex-military men. It seemed like yesterday and the nightmare returned.

They came in fast and had their revolvers out like Confederate raiders. The first shot hit him in the leg. The second in his arm and the third passed through the loose skin of his side. Luckily for Hiram Stone, the last shot looked like a solid torso hit by the shooter.

He fell to the ground.

A loud boom sounded from the house. It was Eve with the .58 Springfield. But, Hiram was already unconscious. She missed her main target, Warden McGillivray, but killed his horse. The horse went down hard and he was pinned, injuring his leg.

The other four sent a flurry of revolver rounds

towards the door of the house. Eve was already re-loading, using a paper cartridge and a percussion cap. Lt. Langston helped his former commander extricate from under the dead horse. As the former sergeant and two others approached, she fired again, winging Kelly. They knew it was a single shot, so the other two rushed the house thinking it was safe.

They met three rapid .41 Colt rounds headed their way and turned and ran for their horses in fear. Before turning, one had lost his hat, and the other had a bullet go through his coat, although missing his body.

The raid had not gone as the three army men had planned it. But, it had been a long time since they were in the army and even then, they had run a small prison, and not been battle hardened troops. The additional two proved their mettle to be virtually worthless.

They rode off as fast as they could with the leader seriously injured from over a thousand pounds of dead weight horseflesh landing on him and having to be dragged out from under the animal.

Eve reloaded the Springfield and the small Colt revolver and eased out of the house.

She scanned from side to side and listened as the sound of the hoof beats, one horse with double riders, disappeared in the distance.

She knew it would be several hours until Tate arrived. Kneeling at her uncle's side, she found the three wounds. None were fatal, or even very serious. However, his condition before being shot and not having fully recovered from the previous shoulder wound increased the new wounds' danger to his well-being.

Hiram Stone was still unconscious. She knew shock may be the greatest danger to him. None of the wounds were bleeding badly. Nonetheless, she went into the house and got some white linen she used for personal times and cut it into handkerchief-sized squares to fold for compresses.

The shot in his arm was a through-and-through as was the one in his side. She put compresses on both sides of each and tied them tightly. The bullet was still in the leg wound. She held the compress on it for a while, then tied it tightly, too. It would require surgery, she knew.

Eve was strong, but her uncle was a large man and now dead weight. She would have to wait for Tate to get him into the back of the buckboard.

She led the horse over to the buckboard and hooked him up. Eve left him tied to a tree near where her uncle laid. She propped the Springfield up against a wheel and put the bag with paper cartridges and percussion caps on the seat. She wished several times during the incident for a repeating rifle, or at least a double-bar-reled shotgun instead of the single shot Springfield. Still, the 575 grain Minié ball behind sixty grains of double-F powder had proven pretty powerful in sound and effect. Thank God Tate had given her the small

.41 revolver. But, like most folks who have been in a gunfight, she wished she'd had a bigger gun.

Eve got a mug from the house and put water in it. She sat in the dirt and put her uncle's head in her lap. She poured small sips between his lips. He came to and she was able to get him to take larger sips.

"Eve, I know who these people are. Am I at risk of dying right now? Tell me true, girl."

"No, Uncle Hiram. You have a bullet in the big muscle in your leg. It will have to come out, but it's not bleeding enough to worry about. You have a pass-through in your arm and side. Neither are bleeding much and I have both bound tightly. You will live unless you fall off the buckboard on the way to town to the doctor," she said. She mentioned she had winged the sergeant.

He smiled at his niece and continued.

"When is your lawman gentleman friend coming?" he asked.

"Probably about an hour from now."

"Since you say I won't expire first, I'd like to wait until he gets here and tell both of you my secret and why those men tried to kidnap you and these old enemies from my past tried to kill me today. When they find out I'm alive, they will be back. Both of you need to know about this matter I've hidden since 1865."

"Okay, you rest and you can tell Tate and me once he gets here and we get you up on the buckboard to go to the doctor's," she said, wondering what the secret could possibly be. And, how it was connected to the three men Tate and the Raton marshal had killed while trying to drag her off.

******

Tate rode in at the appointed time. Once he got there, he wished he had come a couple hours early and burned some powder.

Eve told him what had happened and he expressed his pride in how she thwarted the attack. She shared the fact her uncle knew who and why her attempted kidnapping and today's attack had occurred.

They got the man into the bed of the buckboard and the effort and pain caused him to pass out again.

He came to shortly and motioned both close to him.

"Tate, I lied to you and my niece about who I am. I have been living in the shadows for thirteen years. I hope you both will forgive me when you find out why.

There was a secret Union prison near Baxter Springs, Kansas during the last part of the war. Its existence and what happened there was a secret. I am going to divulge the secret to you. Do with it what you wish."

"Go ahead, Mr. Stone," Tate urged.

"Along with Wilkes Booth, Belle Boyd, Rose Greenhow, John Surratt and many others, I was a Confederate spy. We reported to Confederate Secretary of State, Judah P. Benjamin. He was a Jewish man from Louisiana. The most honest and smartest man I could ever hope to know.

All my 'history' living in Kansas was a cover story based on a man I had to kill.

Other than some of the famous women spies, like Rose who Allan Pinkerton tracked down and arrested, about twenty-five of us were so deep nobody other than Benjamin knew about us. Most were captured during the last year of the war and put in the secret prison in Baxter Springs. It was hidden inside a Union fort which was supposedly had been shut down before the end of the war. We were regularly tortured, starved and denied even water while they questioned us.

By April, 1865, Lee surrendered. The war was shortly to be over and the warden —who was here today and Eve shot his horse from under him — and his top two men were in a panic.

They had run a secret and illegal prison and were facing courts martial. They knew the few senior officers who had approved the prison would not back them up. It was every criminal for himself.

So, they locked everybody in a wooden barn and set it afire. I had been in the privy and stayed there as I heard what was happening. I will never forget the screams of men burning to death or the laughter of Warden McGillivray, Lt. Langston or Sgt. Kelly. They were all here shooting today and they paid those three in Raton to kidnap Eve to exchange for me.

They were too busy trying to gather anything of value from the prison before it burned to the ground to account for all prisoners. I hid behind the privies and by dark, disappeared into the woods. One of the other guards was riding away separately. I jumped him, pulled him of his horse and strangled him. His body was weighted down and dumped into a deep creek. I took his uniform, horse, gun and identity papers and rode into Kansas instead of away. As a spy, I knew to hide in plain sight. I wrote my sister and told her my new name and never to divulge who I was. She didn't, even to Eve here.

Using Corporal Hiram Stone's identity, I claimed veteran's rights, got some land in Kansas, then here in Colorado. I shaved my beard and became a new man."

"But," Tate began, "how did the warden and his cronies find about you. They should have thought you were dead."

"Well, Tate, I wasn't as careful as I thought. The real Hiram Stone was not dead and made it out of the creek. He knew what he had done was as wrong as McGillivray and the others, so he kept quiet. Apparently, he accidentally met his old warden and the lieutenant and the sergeant five years ago and told them one of their prisoners was still alive and using his name. The quest to locate and kill me began. There is no statute of limitations for murder, either in the civilian or military courts. The three men here today could all hang. I don't know who the other two idiots were. I'm thinking go-fers MacGillivray hired along the way.

Anyway, we need to get on the trail of these five and finish the job Eve started today. She caused a dead horse to crush McGillivray and winged Kelly. They need to die, Tate. It's a stretch to think the Judge Advocate General would believe the testimony of a Confederate spy against the word of two Union of-ficers. The Warden was a major. Them against me. They'd win in court. If it ever came to court, the army would cover it up.

So, we have to kill them or they will keep coming back until Eve and I are dead."

"Well, we just aren't going to let them get their way. But, realistically, by the time you heal from four different bullet wounds, they will be long gone. I need to get on the trail," Tate said.

"I recommend getting you to the doctor's. Eve, tell the chief deputy at the marshal's office this story. He is a Texan and would listen sympathetically. Tell him I am trying to trail these attempted murderers. Then talk to your uncle about our conversation and maybe selling this place and homesteading further up the road and living with us like we talked about.

Now, I have to refresh water in my canteens, load some chow from your larder and ride," Tate said.

"I have a Mason jar. I will put some stew from to-night's planned dinner in it and bread, coffee beans, cornmeal and some jerky Uncle made. I will include salt and flour. Enough you think?" she asked. He kissed her in response and stayed with the wounded man until she returned and slung a burlap bag on Cisco's saddle horn.

Tate had gotten a detailed description of the raiders from Stone and got Eve to corroborate it. He kissed her again. Tate lightly touched the old spy on the shoulder and rode off on what he knew could be a long bloody trail.

CHAPTER 6

It was a late start at six in the evening. Tate picked up sign almost immediately. He was helped by having one of the four horses carrying double. Its tracks were readily discernible from the others. He knew from Eve he was about an hour behind. The four horses were galloping, then trotting away on a heavily travelled road south. They would have already hit Raton. From there, they had several options. He would stop at Marshal Hawkins's and see if anybody stopped at the doctor's within the past hour.

The marshal was outside with the deputy who had been sick the day of the gunfight and several other men, all armed. It sure looked to Tate like a posse in formation.

"Howdy, Marshal. I'm on the trail of five men on four horses. One was crushed some when his horse was shot out from under him and fell on him. Another has a possibly minor gunshot wound. Anybody ride in for the doctor? Or, to buy another horse?" Tate asked his friend.

"How 'bout *steal* another horse? Or, two?" the marshal asked, emphasizing the operative word.

"Could be," Tate responded.

"Five men rode into town about half hour ago on four horses. They stole two fresh horses from the livery and shot the liveryman. I suspect you might want to join our posse?" Hawkins asked.

"I sure do! They shot Hiram Stone three times. Eve fired a bunch of shots and scared them off. One killed the boss man's horse and it fell on him. He and his number two rode the same horse here. Explains why they stole two. Which way did they go?" Tate asked.

"You operating for Colorado?"

"Nope. I'm riding for me."

"I'll deputize you this time with a badge. We might hit a state line or go too many counties for my posse, but a deputy in hot pursuit could continue on legally," Hawkins said.

"Might be real handy Marshal."

The marshal walked into his office and came out with his ten gauge and a spare deputy badge. He handed the latter to Tate, who pinned it on.

"To answer your question, we don't know other than south outa here. None of us are much trackers. You might earn the dollar a day a posse man gets."

"Forget blowing your town budget on me. I'm in for the whole dance on this one, with or without a posse."

"Okay, men! Let's ride!" and the six men took off at a gallop southbound out of Raton.

The posse rode for an hour and the sun was dropping fast. Tate looked at the men's' saddles. They did not appear to have food. They definitely did not have sleeping or storm gear.

Marshal Hawkins noted Tate's glances.

"This kind of posse is based on the prospects the hurt man would cause them to stop before dark. Does not look like it's going to be the case here. I suspect you know who these people are and what's going on. You want to share?" the marshal asked.

"The injured man is a former Union officer. A Maj. McGillivray. His number two is his former lieutenant, a fella named Langston. Their sergeant is called Kelly. I don't know first names. Hiram Stone can possibly tell you. They hired the men who we killed a while back. Today, they shot up the Stone spread, trying to kill Stone. He knows something incriminating on them going back to the war. Something, if prosecuted might cause their necks to be stretched," Tate said.

"You know what the information he has is?"

"It has to do with a bunch of prisoners in a secret prison. Anything else, I think you should get from Stone. He related to me in confidence," Tate answered.

As they were talking, the marshal noticed Tate was leaning left on Cisco. He finally held up his hand to stop the posse. He dismounted and studied the dirt road, part of the Santa Fe Trail.

"One of the two stolen horses threw a shoe during their fast getaway. Here's his tracks here. They show the five turned left off the road we've been on. They are heading due east. I can't begin to think when they will stop. They did not have what appeared to be lots of trail gear on their horses. I doubt the two from the livery did. So, they will have a dry hungry camp.

Are there any towns due west?" he asked.

"No. Not really. Some little clusters of houses every now and then. Nothing you'd call a town. What's your best bet for where they are heading?"

"Well, as I remember, you could vary only a few miles either way from here and end up in Indian Territory going a bit north, or Texas a bit south. Since they were Union officers, I'd think Texas might not be their first choice. But, who knows? Ticked off Texans or ticked off Indians? Not a good choice to have to make."

"No, Tate. A lousy choice," the marshal said.

"This is where we have to stop and think about heading back to Raton. This is just a town posse, so we are out of jurisdiction. If you go on, keep the badge for a while and say you have been chasing them the whole time. Ought to work with any lawman you bump into. I'll wire the US Marshal for Northwest Texas and the one at Ft. Smith, Arkansas for Oklahoma and Indian Territory. I'll let them know a deputy is trailing five men wanted for murder, assault and horse stealing," Marshal Hawkins said.

"Sure would be help. I'll get the badge back as soon as I can. Will you get murder warrants on the three whose names we have? For killing the livery man?" Tate asked. The marshal nodded as the posse turned back and Tate rode on into the darkness.

Most lawmen would ride with apprehension. But, Tate was happy to be on his own.

He reckoned the odds were pretty good. Two injured men, two idiots who ran with a woman shooting an underpowered revolver at them, missing. And, the ex-army men who were not combat experienced according to Hiram Stone.

The likelihood of a successful trial based on the testimony of a former Confederate spy was low.

Therefore, to stop the threat, Tate determined he would not seek to take prisoners. And, he would just as soon not have a posse of witnesses with him.

He rode on into the dark for a while and then decided there was just too much chance of riding up on them unexpectedly. So, he picked a good spot off the road and pitched camp.

Since he had no idea how close his quarry was, he considered a cold camp, but chanced a fire and trying Eve's stew and bread. Both were excellent.

Luckily, it was not terribly cold and his bedroll and the tarp sufficed.

In the morning, the wind was hard in his face, blowing away from the fugitives.

He put some fuel in the fire pit and built enough fire to brew coffee to go with a breakfast just like his dinner.

"Wal, Cisco. You 'bout ready to trail these fellas? Like always, it's you and me."

The horse shook his head up and down and whinnied. Tate unhobbled him and saddled him.

The two rode on, slowly until he could see the signs and determine the men were likely still half an hour ahead.

He rode up on their abandoned camp. No fire. They must be pretty hungry. They would rob the first traveler they saw for food and maybe more water, though the Cimarron, Corrumpa Creek, and other streams flowed nearby.

Mid-morning, he heard distant shots and spurred Cisco on faster. He figured they were getting food by hunting or thievery.

Shortly, he saw an oxen-drawn freight wagon coming towards him.

He made sure his badge was showing and removed his Winchester from the scabbard.

It was entirely possible some of the fugitives were hiding in the back of the wagon, so he had to be ready for anything.

"Deputy marshal! Halt there!" he cried out.

The wagon came to a slow halt and the driver held up his hands.

"Anybody in the back of the wagon hiding? They pop

up on me and you will be first to go down," Tate promised.

"Nope. I already been robbed by five men. Stole my canteen and my food."

Tate rode around the wagon, rifle at the ready and saw nothing but freight of various categories.

"Did anyone appear to be injured?" he asked.

"The older one was in pain. You could tell. He sat real uncomfortable on his horse. Two of the others did the talking. They came up and fired some shots to get me to stop. One of them had a bloody shirtsleeve. They stole my shotgun, my food and water. Good thing there's plenty of water between here and Raton, where I'm going."

"You will be there today. Tell the marshal what happened and you met Tate on the trail. He may or may not meet you with a posse on the way in. I don't know. These men are wanted for murder and other crimes," Tate said.

"You going after them by yourself?" the freighter asked.

"I am. Not my first time doing something like this."

"Wal, good luck, deputy. One against five don't seem too healthy to me."

"I'll be fine. Surprised these fools didn't shoot you. You ought to stop off at the church in Raton and give some thanks."

"I might just do it, deputy. Be careful. These fellas seemed panicky."

"Thanks. Good luck to you," and Tate spurred Cisco down the trail.

He suspected the five would stop and fix coffee or make some food instead of eating in the saddle. He had to ride carefully. The time they took to rob the freighter reduced the distance he was behind them.

He was close. Really close.

He found out how close when he felt a burn in his left arm and heard a shot following. He rolled off Cisco and moved behind a rock, rifle in hand.

Tate saw a bit of smoke down the trail and fired at it. He saw a man get up and started running from about a hundred yards, maybe a bit more.

He looked through the buckhorn sights on the Winchester '73 and fired. The man stumbled and fell.

He heard horses gallop off, leaving the man laying by the edge of some woods. "Real heroes, these people," he thought.

The bullet had creased his left bicep. It hurt like hell. He splashed water on it from his canteen and tied his bandanna tightly around it. He would get or make some black walnut salve or put some wild honey on it later to hold down infection. Now, he had business to do.

Tate walked towards the downed man. He held the Winchester ready.

The man was dead. He was one of the non-army ones Eve had scared off, by his description.

Tate took the man's shortened barrel Colt Open Top 1871, the transition gun between cap n' ball and Tate's Frontier Model 1873. It was in .44 Henry rimfire like the 1866 carbine he recovered. He thought both would be better choices for Eve than the weaker .41 and put the revolver in his saddlebag along with a box of cartridges he found. The man had ten dollars, so Tate confiscated it. He strapped the 1866 Winchester onto Cisco's saddle.

Tate's last action was to unsaddle and free the man's horse. He left the body and the saddle where they laid and rode on. Very carefully. The fugitives would know their "throw-away" sniper was down when he didn't return. And, know someone serious was on their trail.

"Well, so what do you think, Cisco?" Tate said to the black gelding. "Terrified people get real stupid. And, real stupid is good for us, buddy." The horse did not respond, but Tate felt he agreed.

The remaining four must have sped up, because Tate could tell he was not closing in on them. In the morning, he had been within ten or fifteen minutes. Now, he reckoned thirty to forty-five minutes.

It was fine with him. He could easily outlast them and pick his battlefield.

He rode on.

By dusk, Tate thought he must be in the area known as Oklahoma and Indian Territory. There were no signs, but he was confident he was in the panhandle of the territory. There was no sign of the four men by dark, so he and Cisco climbed a small hill looking for a place to camp. He found a likely spot and hobbled the black and unrolled his bedroll for the night. There was a black walnut tree on the hill and Tate picked up a passel of newly-fallen nuts.

After a long and eventful day, he dug another fire pit for some much-needed coffee and to make a decoction of black walnut. By having an air hole and short tunnel to the main pit, he eliminated much of a campfire's telltale smoke and intensified the burning, taking less fuel and heating the coffee faster. While the wood was burning to usable coals, Tate walked a several hundred yard circle around his camping spot. There were no hostiles lying in wait, so he came back and prepared his repast and medicine. He used his pocket knife to cut the green outer layer off the black walnuts he found lying on the ground. He boiled these outer layers several times. Tate then chopped them up on a flat stone. He mixed them in some of his petroleum jelly in its almost empty jar. He now had black walnut salve and immediately put it on his gunshot wound and would twice daily until it healed or the salve was gone. He would have to replace the jar of Vaseline at the next town to keep his guns lubricated. He had an almost empty small can of gun oil, but it depleted as quickly as his coffee beans. Somehow, the jelly lasted longer.

Tate propped up against a tree, sipping coffee and munching on some of Eve's very good bread. The stew had been good too. Stress might have made her faint when the hired thug cocked the revolver pointed at her head, but she'd returned shots in kind and given her uncle medical attention with coolness and efficiency. And, it looked like she was not only real pretty, but a damn good cook. He took a look at her likeness on the watch fob. Yep, he was making the right decision with her.

He fell asleep, the Winchester under the blankets and tarp and Cisco patrolling close on hobble. He knew Cisco would whistle if anyone or anything came around.

His school marm in Texas had been from South Carolina originally. She had many attributes, including being the prettiest woman he as a boy had ever seen until a month ago. One of her intellectual attributes was a love of history and the willingness to teach more history than mathematics.

She taught the children about Roger's Rangers in the French and Indian War, Francis Marion, the Swamp Fox in her native Palmetto State, and Mosby, the Gray Ghost of the Confederacy. Young Tate learned they survived by picking off troops one at a time. Hitting and running. Not out of fear, but good tactics.

He already had one of the five dead. Today or tomorrow, he'd try to take out another. It didn't matter who, but maybe he'd try for one of the prison men.

His chance came earlier than expected. About noon, he spotted their dust cloud and sped Cisco up to a fast canter.

Tate closed on them fast. They were coming up on a cut between two large hills. The right side of the road was wooded. Tate moved Cisco over to the right and rode at the same fast canter through the woods to the other side of the right-hand hill.

He had cut them off and beaten them! Tate slipped off Cisco and lightly tied him to a branch. If he called, the horse could easily break free and come to him.

Tate took his rifle and slipped through the woods and found a good sniper's nest. A downed tree was at a perfect angle to provide a rest for his Winchester.

The four men came into sight, walking their horses.

They were single file, though the road was wide.

Tate drew a bead on the third man in line. From the description, he must be Kelly, the sergeant. He wanted to have a face-to-face with the two officers before killing them.

Tate aimed at the man's ear as he rode by fifty yards away in profile. He took in a breath and let half of it out. Good sight picture. No breathing to move the sight picture. Tate pressed the trigger slowly backwards, holding the picture until the rifle bucked against his shoulder. He saw pink spray come out the other side of the ex-sergeant's head. Kill shot!

Tate watched at the two leaders spurred their

horses into a full gallop to escape. The last man absolutely panicked. He turned and rode in the direction from which they had come. The warden yelled for him to turn around. He did. Tate shot at his head. He knocked his hat off instead. He levered the Winchester, but the man had ridden out of sight. Tate was pretty sure the man soiled his pants.

As always, Tate rolled to a new location as soon as touching off his shot. But, there were no responding shots this time. Just escaping riders. Down to three from five. The odds were just getting better and better.

Once the three were out of sight and he could still see their dust getting smaller, he rode to the fallen man and his horse. Kelly had Eve's wound festering in his arm. He sure would not die from it now.

The man had a decent Colt like Tate's. Luckily, he was left-handed, so Tate strapped on his gun belt and checked the Colt. Loaded with five and the hammer on an empty chamber like most folks with any sense carried to prevent a negligent discharge from the gun falling on its hammer spur.

The man's rifle was a .45-70 Springfield carbine. A single shot. Tate left it on the saddle he had stripped off and checked the man's pouch. He retrieved twenty-three dollars. There was nothing else of value in his saddlebags, so he slapped the dead man's mount and made him run off.

He left the body and the saddle in the middle of

the road and continued on at a comfortable pace, knowing the other three were probably wearing their horses down with a mad dash away from him.

Tate grinned, congratulated himself and Cisco verbally and rode on.

CHAPTER 7

The trail continued to lead eastwards into Indian Territory. The country was desolate and generally unoccupied.

Late the following day, Tate rode up on an odd wagon and an encampment.

The wagon was something he had heard of but never seen. It was a Black Maria prison wagon. Five men were sitting around a campfire, though it was not yet dark. A sixth man, probably the driver, was cooking beans in a black pot over a roaring fire.

It was the seventh man who captured Tate's attention.

He was preaching to the captive men. Preaching hellfire and brimstone. And, he was black and wearing a half-moon over star Deputy US Marshal's badge.

A handsome man with a thick mustache curving down below his bottom lip, he had to be the famous Bass Reeves. Deputy for Judge Isaac Parker out of Ft. Smith, Arkansas. The judge ruled Indian Territory with an iron gavel and a piece of rope. He earned the name "Hanging Judge."

Tate rode in, badge very obvious and slipped off Cisco.

Reeves stopped preaching, but Tate smiled at him and waved for him to continue. He sat on a log and listened. Though real strict Baptist, Tate felt Reeves was a good preacher. Tate had not been to a church service for ten years and enjoyed this one.

The two men introduced each other. In response to Tate's question about whether they had seen the fugitives, Reeves said he had been south, arresting one of the men chained with the logging chain. His driver spoke up and said he had seen three men riding fast about lunchtime. They had waved and just seemed like normal riders, just in a hurry.

Tate explained they were more than normal and Reeves frowned.

"I've filled all the warrants in my bag. Judge Parker will have his docket filled with these guys and Deputy Maledon will be tying a lot of thirteen loop knots," the deputy said referring to the infamous hangman.

"We were going to turn around anyway. You want me to ride with you to catch these fellas?" the respected lawman asked.

"I'd be honored to ride with you, but I have them whittled down to a workable number. It's probably not worth your time. These men are in a panic and will make mistakes. Should be an easy capture," he said, though capture was not the word he was planning.

"I have a suspicion they are using the Cherokee Strip here to hide because it's not very populated. I believe, based on what I know about them, they will turn north and head up into Kansas very soon. They left from near the southern boundary of Colorado. Almost New Mexico. Had they gone north, they would have been on a main road and passed through Colorado Springs, Denver and other populated places. A wire from the marshals of Trinidad or nearby Raton, New Mexico would have had posses' waiting. This way, they rode through barren country. Now, they can ride north through similar country into their home turf of Kansas," Tate explained.

"Hmm….makes sense and it sounds like they'll soon leave my jurisdiction. I have an obligation to get these prisoners back to Judge Parker. I could have ridden towards Ft. Smith with you, but can't ride up into Kansas. I will pray for you though, Deputy."

"And, I for you, Deputy," Tate responded, struck by this deadly, yet Godly man.

"But, let the good judge provide you with some beans for dinner before you ride on," Reeves offered.

"I'll take you up on those beans, then hit the trail," Tate said.

They ate together, after Bass Reeves offered the blessing over the beans. The two lawmen chatted. Reeves lived up to what Tate had heard about him.

He was the consummate lawman. Dedicated and with nerves of steel. A man who would compassionately serve a murder warrant on his own son because it was his duty. And, did.

Something about spending time with the tall, powerful ex-slave made Tate feel good. The world seemed like a better place because of men like Bass Reeves.

Tate rode on in the dark for another hour.

He was starting to worry about riding up on McGillivray in a dark camp. He stopped for the night and made his usual camp, albeit without a fire. He thought about his meeting with the famous manhunter. He'd had plenty of coffee and beans cooked with ham hocks and cornbread at the Reeves camp. It was much more than he usually ate for dinner.

Tate was a tall, lean man, built like a rider. Reeves, on the other hand, was the same height as him, but built like the professional boxer John L. Sullivan.

As he fell asleep, he wondered how the former Confederate spy was recovering. And, how his Eve was doing. Did she miss him and think of him as much as he did her?

***** *

Eve missed Tate and thought of him much of her day and all of her nights. But, she stayed busy with a project.

She was concerned about the unknown chapter of history where a prison of non-criminal military prisoners had been murdered by burning to death by the order of one man. A man who had tried to have her kidnapped and who knows what else? A man who had caused her kind uncle to be shot. Shot four times, because he knew the truth about the man's criminal acts.

So, while Hiram Stone, though she now knew it was not his real name, was recovering, she wrote down his exploits as a spy in detail. None of these things were secret anymore. And, the last chapter was about the prison and what happened.

Her epilogue told about how her uncle escaped and lived a hidden life for a decade before the prison's senior staff tried to kill him.

Eve was careful to use a different name for her uncle, since he had killed one of the guards and stolen his identity. She further distanced her uncle from the story by saying the person telling the story had heard it from someone on his deathbed.

But, she didn't bother to hide the names of McGillivray, Langston, and Kelly. She figured her Tate would bring them in for their punishment or see they received it on the trail.

Her uncle read the story and made a few additions and declared it historically correct. She wanted to keep it as family history, maybe for release after everyone in it was dead.

Hiram Stone disagreed. He wanted her to send it to a New York publisher and have it published as a novel.

If a New York publisher was not interested in a rebel spy's story, there were publishers in Dallas, Houston, Atlanta and other places more sympathetic to a Southern perspective.

Stone also saw the justice in his family making a return on the hell he had experienced. And, the evil these men had done.

He had every confidence Tate would track the former administrators of the prison down and kill each one. He and Hiram Stone had agreed a trial would not lead to justice being served. History is written by the winner. And, their side did not win.

The remaining three fugitives were riding harder and longer into the night. They were distancing Tate.

Tate lost the trail due to the loss of the horse with the distinctive print from the missing shoe and more tracks on the trail.

He came to an intersection of trails where the one he was on continued across the Cherokee Strip and a perpendicular trail turned north into Kansas. Tate's gut told him Bloody Kansas was where the fugitives would go. It was their home ground. So, he turned north and headed for the first town of any substance. It was Wichita. First a trading post on the Chisolm Trail, the town had been incorporated in 1870.

Tate learned Wichita was also the county seat of

Sedgwick County, Kansas. He stopped at the county sheriff's office and the town marshal's office to introduce himself and inquire if anyone knew whether McGillivray, Langston and one other unidentified fugitives may be in town. Neither office had any knowledge of the three, so he rented a hotel room and determined to cruise the saloons and look for himself.

He stopped at the marshal's office after eating dinner and offered to escort a deputy on patrol.

Deputy Jack Rains was a likable man about Tate's age. He wore a Smith & Wesson Schofield revolver low on his left side.

They stopped in all the saloons and sporting houses on Wichita's drinking, gambling and whoring row.

At the Western Lady Bar, the sound was almost deafening. A piano player was making more noise than music and the crowd was unruly.

"This kinda crowd up from Texas makes me glad you are with me. This patrol gets lonesome when a bunch of drunk cowboys are in town. Since I live here, I'm automatically a yankee, they assume.

"Do you 'buffalo' them?" Tate asked.

"What's 'buffaloing' mean?" Rains asked.

"It's something they started doing up in Dodge City. I guess Wyatt Earp taught it to Bat Masterson and he taught it to me. You use your sixgun like a truncheon and knock somebody over the head with it. It will hurt like hell, but usually a bullet hurts a lot more," Tate said.

A couple of cow herders were getting more rowdy as the two lawmen talked. Tate saw Rains eyeing them.

Rains walked over and asked them to hold it down. The retort he got was to do something anatomically impossible. The loudest and drunkest of the several cowboys grabbed Rain's vest and jerked him forward. Tate pulled his right hand Colt and slammed it into the cow man's head hard enough to knock him unconscious. He kept the six-gun leveled on the downed man's companions until he considered they were unlikely to do something stupid.

Tate holstered it and he and Rains each took hold of an arm under the shoulder and lifted the unconscious cowboy partially up and dragged him to a chair, heels dragging. They propped him up and walked back to the group of angry Texas cowboys.

One said, "You damn Yankee policemen up here don't hesitate to harm a Texan, do you? What would you two do if six or eight of us drew down on you?"

Tate, said "I got this," to Rains in a low voice.

"Two things. One, I am a former Texas Ranger from Texas. So, stop calling me a damn Yankee before I get real peeved.

Two: I suspect Deputy Rains is fast. I know, from my own standpoint, I would take down at least five of you before falling. Add it up. All of you would be dead. You want to chance it? It would grieve me sorely to kill my fellow Texans. It surely would."

The group visibly relaxed and hands moved away from revolvers and Bowie knives.

"But, while we're whispering sweet nothings, I have a question. I am trailing a former Yankee army prison warden. Him, his former lieutenant and another man, I know nothing about. The warden is hurt from a woman shooting his horse, which fell on his ass.

These men are wanted for a number of murders, including burning Confederate prisoners of war to death at the end of the war. I've had two resist arrest. They are laying on the trail between here and Raton, New Mexico rotting.

Now, here's the big question: have y'all seen these three? I tracked 'em here."

The Texan who had spoken before spoke again.

"We seen them. Oldest fella, maybe forties or fifties, rode funny like he was in pain. They were right in front of us coming into town. Should be about an hour, mebbe two ago. They rode right on through, near as I could tell."

"Thanks. Sure does help me. Now, y'all enjoy yourselves and tell your friend, next time he attacks a lawman, he might get something more lasting than a headache."

Tate doffed his Stetson, turned then he and Rains walked out the swinging door.

"Even two hours ago was dark. They have put up for the night, either here or on the trail. I think I will do the same after we finish rounds. I just want to make sure they didn't get a room and decide to drink some rotgut before turning in," Tate said.

"Tate, you can walk a beat with me anytime," Rains said. Tate nodded appreciatively, but said nothing. What he had said to the Texans constituted a long speech by Tate's standards.

The rest of the patrol in town did not turn up the fugitives. Just a couple more drunks he helped Rains walk back to the jail. Or, drag back, in the case of one of them.

Tate found a hotel for himself and put Cisco in a livery stable for the night.

Dawn the next morning found him riding north out of town. Stone said he thought McGillivray was from Emporia, Kansas. The trail led in the direction of Emporia and Tate followed it.

Later the next day, he rode into Emporia. Tate's first stop was the Western Union telegraph office. He sent a wire to Marshal Hawkins in Raton to see if murder warrants had been sworn for McGillivray, Langston, and Kelly. The reply was yes and particulars were included. Tate took the paper copy with him to the Lyon County sheriff's office.

The sheriff looked like a real lawman, instead of a politician. He appeared to be of Hawkins's ilk.

"Howdy, Sheriff. My name's Morgan Tate. I am a deputy from Raton, New Mexico on the trail of several murderers. Wonder if you might know them? The leader is supposed to be from hereabouts."

"Well, deputy, you are a far bit from New Mexico. Who is the ringleader of these fellas?"

"His name is McGillivray. He was positively identified by someone who knew him during the war. But, the person did not know his first name. He was a Union major who served as warden of an army prison down by the Missouri border," Tate said.

The sheriff thought for a moment. Tate did not detect any sign of him hiding information about a friend or former army associate.

"I know most of the folks in my county, if not personally, certainly by last name. I never heard of a McGillivray here in the six years I've been in the area. You might walk down to the post office. Elon Huxtable has been postmaster since before the war. He'd know if anybody did. Do you have a warrant?"

"It was sworn after I hit the trail. I have this telegram from the marshal in Raton attesting to it," Tate said, handing the paperwork to the sheriff.

"Yep. This would sure suffice to place him under arrest and start extradition. I think the Kansas Attorney General might require a paper warrant to fully extradite. How many are you looking for? This says three. Right?"

"Just them. There were five. Two dropped off along the way," Tate said.

"Just split with the warden?" the sheriff asked.

"Nope. One tried to bushwhack me on the trail behind them. He winged me, but I got him. Another presented a threat. It was the sergeant. The one called Kelly. He didn't make it either."

"Doesn't sound much like you plan on bringing them back for trial," the sheriff commented.

"I do, if they will stop shooting at me long enough," Tate replied. "They know I'm a lawman. They know they have a hangman's noose waiting for them in Raton, New Mexico for murdering the livery stable owner. And, multiple assault charges. Shooting an old man, trying to shoot his niece. Robbing a freighter. Plenty of charges to go around, if need be."

"I don't need murderous trash like those people in my county. Get yourself on down to the post office and see what Huxtable has to say. I'd be curious to know," the sheriff said.

"Why don't you join me? I'll buy lunch on the way back," Tate offered. He figured having far-flung friends in law enforcement would not be a bad investment of a couple dollars here and there.

"Yeah, I could go for some lunch. Let's see the postmaster first."

The two men walked down Sixth Street and into the post office.

"Huxtable, this is Deputy Tate from Raton. He's looking for a murderer. Mebbe you know the man."

Huxtable looked at them over half-spectacles. He was a bald man who looked like a shorter Benjamin Franklin. Most folks did not know Franklin was six feet tall.

"What's his name?"

"He is Major McGillivray, formerly US Army. I don't know his first name. I also am looking for a Lieutenant Langston," Tate said.

"Murder, eh?" the postmaster said and Tate nodded.

"There was a McGillivray, name of Thomas. Lived on a small spread west of town until the war. He come from back East. New York or somewhere. He joined the army and never came back. The place was sold at auction. I figured he got killed or something. He'd come in here before the war every week or so to check for mail. Never got much. Kinda shifty somebody. No wife or kids. I always figured nobody would put up with his temperament."

"Mr. Huxtable, how about a Langston?" Tate asked.

"Nope. No Langston's here as long as I've been postmaster."

"One last question. There were two more. One of them tried to bushwhack me. Lanky fella with shaggy, dirty dark hair. Carried a Colt conversion model and 1866 Winchester. Another similar-looking fella could have been his brother or cousin. Not sure what he carries," Tate said.

"Sounds like the Franz brothers. Worthless trash. Small time thieves. Headed outta here for parts unknown about the time the Sheriff moved here. Shore no loss to the community. Would steal the hide off a pig if they could catch it."

"You remember the name of the one I described?"

"I'm thinking the one with the conversion model might be William. As I remember, Robert didn't carry a handgun. He had a Green River skinning knife he used to flash around and also a percussion squirrel gun. Two damn no accounts. Anybody hire them would be looking for a couple step n' fetch its. They weren't good for much else," the postmaster ended.

Tate noted the names in the notebook he had left from the rangers.

"Thank you, Mr. Huxtable. You've been a big help. Always nice to have a full name of some fellow about to be hung."

"Good luck to you, Deputy. I hope you get these fellas," Huxtable said and the deputy and the sheriff left for the café they had passed on the way to the post office.

"Your help sure keeps me from riding around the area asking strangers questions," Tate told the sheriff.

"I've heard of the Franz brothers. And, nothing good. Huxtable is right. Them leaving made this a better place. You killin' one made the world a better place. Some people ain't worth a damn and don't add anything. They are better off not crowding the earth," the sheriff said.

"I've encountered a fair share of them, as I know you have," Tate agreed as they sat in the window seats of the café.

At the end of their meals, the sheriff asked "What are you going to do now?"

"At this point, I don't have a trail to follow. No signs to cut. So, I think I will ride to the scene of the original crime," Tate said.

"Where about?"

"A place called Baxter Springs. The three army men were stationed there."

"You think they might go back?"

"I don't know what to think. I am fresh out of ideas. But, I read Allan J. Pinkerton's book on detecting. So, going back to the scene of the crime seems logical," Tate thought aloud.

CHAPTER 8

Former Warden and Major Thomas McGillivray, Lt. Langston and tagalong, Robert Franz, were already in Baxter Springs.

They were at the home of a former corporal who used to go by his birth name of Hiram Stone. Before the damn rebel spy trash had almost killed him and had stolen his good name.

"Of course," he explained to his former commanding officer, "I was gonna change my name anyway. I figured the army was going to come after us and charge us for killing those rebel spies. Once Jubal Paine almost killed me, I figured 'let them kill Paine as me.' So, I stayed right here. Nobody knew me outside of the saloon we used to go to. All those folks scattered after the war. So, I became Will Brown and worked and saved and got this place just before we all reconnected five years ago."

"So," McGillivray said, "you hid in plain sight."

"I did. And, it worked, Major."

"What about your family?" Langston asked.

"I was raised in an orphanage in Philadelphia. I don't have anyone to recognize me or look for me."

"Except the fake Hiram Stone," the major cautioned deliberately.

"The fake one don't have no cause to come here."

"There's a lawman following us. He's killed two already. He might show up here, asking around."

"I don't see much chance of him riding in. Who would he ask for? If he got his information from Paine, Paine thinks I'm dead. And, he has no idea what name I picked if he found out I was alive."

"You might want to pick up our task, since you are an unknown person to Paine. You are the best one to ride over and kill him. You can kill his niece or keep her for yourself," McGillivray said.

"What's she look like?" he asked the major.

"She's a looker," McGillivray said.

"Sure you ain't funning me?"

"He's telling the truth. She is fine looking," Langston said.

"Wal, nobody knows me. The bastard almost killed me then dumped me in a pond to drown. Except for the cold water had not causing me to come to, puking and spitting, I would be dead. I guess I owe him a bullet or a knife in the gizzard. And, the knowledge his niece will be my rag doll after he's gone!"

The former prison administrators laughed and encouraged their most cruel and hated guard. A man the United States Army would have dishonorably discharged in a minute if the army had known of his actions as a guard and stretched his neck if they knew about his part in the killing of all the prisoners of war. And, the administrators orchestrated killing the twenty-five prisoners of war themselves. Their necks were in considerable risk of being snapped by a thirteen loop knot, too. "Will Brown" was just a free gun to turn loose on the man who knew their secret. And, turn him loose they did. With a vengeance.

******

Tate rode the hundred miles or so to the former series of army installations. One of them had to have been the prison. He knew it was a barn into which the Confederate prisoners had been locked then it was set afire. He suspected twenty-five sets of bones would have survived as evidence. But, lawman aside, he was there on a more personal crusade. To save his Eve and her uncle. Two down. Three to go. Four, if he only knew.

The town only had one saloon, which certainly simplified Tate's search.

He walked in to the establishment after dark to see if the prison fugitives were there.

As Tate walked into the first one, two of the four men looked up and recognized him. They drew before he saw them and Langston shot first, hitting the lawman in the side. He fell and the barrage of shots from the two hit several revelers, killing one. The fugitives escaped out of the back door. The newest of their members, Will Brown, was totally confused about what was happening. Robert Franz was always confused, but grabbed his squirrel gun and ran out with the others.

The town constable sent to the county seat in nearby Columbus for the county sheriff. Tate's badge was in plain sight. Having a lawman shot was more than the constable felt he should try to handle.

Larger than Columbus, Baxter Springs had more doctors and two were summoned.

Tate, conscious, identified Cisco to the constable who assured him his horse would be cared for during his recovery.

Tate passed out, awoke in great pain an inndeterminate time later. A doctor was removing a bullet from his side without anesthesia. Not even a pull on a bottle of whiskey.

"Ah, you're awake. Bet you wish you weren't, huh? Figured I could dig this little pill out before you came to. Guess I was wrong." The doctor probed as he spoke and each probe felt like a hot poker jammed into Tate.

"Did it hit anything important?" Tate asked, gasping between words.

"Nope. Would have, but was a little piss-ant .38 rim-fire I'm guessing. If it was a real .44 or .45, you might be dead by now. But, it barely went in, having to pass through your coat, vest, and shirt. Aha! Here it is!"

Tate heard a metallic "clink" as the doctor flipped the bullet into a shiny metal tray beside the operating table.

"Yep! Oh, wait. I was wrong. It appears to be a .32, not a .38. You are doubly lucky. Surprised it even made it through your shirt. Let me put some anti-septic in the wound channel — this is going to hurt," he said as Tate involuntarily screamed out.

"I'm going to stitch this up. You can come back in a week and I'll remove the stitches or you can have your wife do it. I will, however, keep you here overnight for observation. Mainly watching against shock setting in. The little bullet missed everything important, but hit in a place which would make it hurt. A lot. But, I guess you already figured it out, huh, deputy?" the doctor asked.

Tate gritted his teeth and nodded.

"Did the shooters get away?" Tate asked.

"I hear they did. They slipped out the door right quick, according to the night constable."

"Did he give chase?" Tate pressed the doctor for information.

"Henry? Hell, no. He'd have had a heart attack chasing a fly across the dinner table. He reported hearing horses leave from out back as soon as the four ran out the door."

"Four? I was only after three. Already killed two," Tate said between clinched teeth.

"Guess they found a friend," the doctor said.

"Where are my guns?"

"Hanging over on the bedposts of the bed we are going to move you to in a minute," a female voice said.

Tate noticed for the first time a plump woman was assisting. Probably the doctor's wife, he guessed.

"And, my pants," he asked.

"Folded up under the same bed," the woman answered.

"When you get settled in the bed, I'm gonna make you drink a few mugs of water to make up for the blood you leaked out. Especially during surgery. Didn't bleed much from the wound itself," the doctor noted.

Half an hour later, Tate was in bed, watered, and almost asleep. Before he fell asleep though, he removed one Colt from its holster and tucked it under his pillow. Now, he could fall asleep comfortably. Or, at least as comfortably as a man who had just been shot and had the bullet dug out without anything to cut the edge off the pain could.

After a fitful night, he woke up and wrote a letter to Eve. He omitted the small fact about being shot twice since he left her, but gave his location and the name "Thomas" for Marshal Hawkins to add to McGillivray for warrant purposes. Without detail, he said the fugitives now only numbered three. He was unaware the real Hiram Stone, now going by Will

Brown, had raised the number back to four. Tate said he was close to the fugitives and hopefully would be back to her soon.

The doctor bound his torso wound tightly. Tate would put the salve he made on it when he changed the bandage, but neglected to mention it to the physician. He was released and immediately headed to the livery to which the constable had taken Cisco to check on his horse. He assured the black gelding his wound was minor and they would be riding out no later than tomorrow. The owner of the stable stood listening to this, nodding in agreement. A man talking to his horse was a perfectly natural thing, he reckoned. He was impressed, though, when Cisco whinnied and shook his head after the report. "Smart damn horse," the man said. Tate already knew it.

Tate asked for his horse to be saddled and got directions for Ft. Baxter, Camp Ben Butler and Camp Hunter. They were the three army installations in the area during the war. He figured one must have been the prison. He wanted to see the site of the burned barn. He was damn sure there would be twenty-five sets of burned bones in the ashes. What would the army do if it was brought to their attention? He couldn't chance it without an investigation finding Eve's uncle had murdered a union soldier and stolen his identity. But Tate had found it helped to stand at a scene of crime and try to visualize. At the fenced off and closed Camp Hunter, he saw some empty buildings and what looked like a burn site. This had to be it. He did not go past the "No Trespassing Government Property" sign to climb the fence. He just stood waiting for enlightenment. It never came and he rode back to town.

Tate paid the man for last night and tonight then, taking his rifle and saddlebags, walked out into the sunlight.

He found a hotel and got a single room. It was clean by Western town standards. Tate went out and posted the letter to Eve. It sure was nice to have somebody to miss.

He went back to the hotel to figure out what he was going to do next. The only thing left would be to interview the patrons at the saloon and see if anyone heard mention of the fugitives' plans, lubricated by John Barleycorn. He would have to wait another ten hours for the crowd to gather. His side hurt a lot and the ride had made him far more tired than usual. He had always laughed at people carrying small caliber guns. Guns which would not kill a man immediately, but might cause him to die of lead poisoning two weeks later. He liked immediate gratification when he shot somebody.

Nonetheless, he had read Wild Bill Hickok was carrying a spur trigger S&W .32 with a six-inch barrel when he was shot in #10 Saloon in Deadwood two years ago. If it was good enough for one of the deadliest men to ever live, it must be okay. Wild Bill could have carried any gun he chose, Tate surmised.

The weather was half decent out, so he went to the hotel's front porch and commandeered a rocker and sat and watched and thought until dinner time.

******

Langston had told McGillivray he was sure he had killed the lawman who had been dogging their trail since the raid on Stone's ranch. Both saw the man go down hard and not rise to draw and return fire.

The town did not have a newspaper, nor did they have any friends. Will Brown may have been local, but he did not have any friends either. Anywhere. So, they went with the assumption Tate was dead and nobody knew who they were. Only the old man and girl in Colorado knew their crime and faces. And, Brown would take care of them.

There were a few colonels and a general, now long out of the union army who were aware of the intelligence coming out of the secret prison. But, no paperwork remained and they were not about to mention their knowledge or participation in the highly illegal activities there. Especially, a fire which killed twenty-five Confederate spies who were bonafide, if not recorded, prisoners of war at the time.

So, assuming Brown would kill the uncle and do whatever he wished with the girl, they were scot-free to resume their lives in Philadelphia in McGillivray's case and Trenton in Langston's.

Towards late afternoon, the three remaining original fugitives rode into town from their camp to pick up travel clothes and luggage before heading back East on the train. They would use money from the sale of their horses to finance the trip.

McGillivray and Langston were smart enough to want to get away from the shootings and let Brown finish the job they set out to do. They already had a plan for Franz. He was a liability due to his lack of mental acuity. He was going to fall off the train somewhere in the wilderness. Maybe on a bridge. A tall bridge.

The general merchandise was across the street from the hotel upon whose porch Tate was sitting.

As the three fugitives tied their horses to the hitching post, Franz screamed out "It's a ghost! A dead man!" and pointed a finger with a long, dirty nail across the street.

Tate snapped to his feet. A sharp pain shot through his torso.

He yelled "You three! I have a warrant for your arrest! Throw up your hands now!"

Franz scrambled for the squirrel rifle slung on his horse while the two former army officers drew.

Before either cleared leather, Tate was shooting both guns.

Tate winged the major who was trying to duck behind his horse for cover. He yelled and stumbled back on the wooden walkway in front of the general mercantile, landing on his butt.

Tate's left shot missed Langston, but his next one from the right-hand gun hit him plumb center. He folded up where he stood and crumpled to the ground.

Tate was already moving. Move and seek cover was the mantra of gunfighters who lived to tell the tale.

Franz unlimbered the squirrel gun and was taking aim. Tate extended his left arm and fired a .44 bullet into his head. It went into his eye and apparently exited. Tate knew this because of the pink spray hitting McGillivray and blinding him for a second.

The second was enough for Tate to fire two fast shots into the former major. He staggered into the street, gun swinging down at his side.

"Drop the gun, McGillivray! Do it now!" Tate ordered.

McGillivray tried to raise it towards Tate. The distance had lessened. They were fifteen feet apart.

"For Eve," Tate thought as he pressed the Colt's trigger and sent the murderous McGillivray to hell.

Tate approached Langston, who was jerking his arms and legs as he lay just off the wooden walkway in the dirt of the street.

His eyes were rolled back in his head. His brain was dead, but his body did not know it yet. He was not worth the cost of another .44-40 cartridge at this point.

Tate picked up the .32 Smith & Wesson Langston

had used on him. A souvenir, perhaps. He tucked it where his two gun belts crossed in back, turned and walked back to the hotel.

His side hurt something fierce. It was too soon to be drawing, shooting two heavy bore guns and ducking and side-stepping. It felt like the day-old bullet hole might be bleeding. He would give it an hour. If it still felt like it was bleeding, he would walk over to the doctor's office. If not, he would put some black walnut salve on it and call it a day.

Tate sat back down on the rocker and sighed. Now, at last, he could go back home to his Eve. Or, at least marry her and figure out where home would be.

He rocked and watched the town people checking bodies. A county deputy had been riding in and saw it all.

Tate knew he would have to answer a few questions later. He would tell the deputy to wire Marshal Hawkins in Raton. All five fugitives were dead from resisting arrest with violence. Maybe, in a small way, the deaths the Confederate prisoners of war had been avenged. He hoped so.

He rocked on.

The deputy was heading his way, grinning. Nice clean case. Three out of state murderers dead by an out of state deputy. All righteous shoots. Justice served.

******

Tate sent his own message to Marshal Hawkins. He told him the warrants had been fulfilled and to tell Eve he was on his way back. He mentioned he would be riding slow due to a wound, but not to tell Eve about it.

He got the doctor to check the wound and the doctor said it had not opened up. The doctor put his own salve on it and it burned like hell. He re-wrapped it and said Tate could start his ride anytime he figured he could stand the pain caused by the hoof beats.

The next morning, Tate got extra corn pones at the café and bought fresh coffee, bacon, beans, jerky and some canned fruit at the mercantile. He filled both canteens.

Cisco was rested and saddled up. Tate bought some feed to take for Cisco in case forage was sparse. He mounted stiffly and painfully. The trip was roughly six hundred miles. It would take him a week and a half, assuming the pain did not slow him unduly.

He pointed the black gelding west and rode on.

******

Eve and her uncle continued with life during Tate's chase of the people trying to kill them. They were careful, but felt their greatest threat was running as fast as possible away from them, with a dogged pursuer on their trail.

Hiram Stone, or Jubal Paine, as he would be known again for the first time in thirteen years, was recovering. Recovery, he knew, was tougher with the passage of age and with each successive wound. He was blessed, he felt, having his niece come into his life. Come into for the first time. He had never met her. Then, one day, she wrote him and asked for help.

He thought how proud he was of her now since she climbed out of the emotional abyss she was in when he picked her up at the train station.

Probably some credit should go to the young lawman. At least, based on discussions they had, his lineage was Southern. He sat on the front porch and spoke with Eve.

"It took a lot of knowledge, stealth and care to be a spy. Spies, unlike most prisoners of war, were guaranteed a firing squad. I lived as a number of different people during the war. Even different nationalities. It was Pinkerton who finally got me. Got me when I was ferrying intelligence between fellow spy Isabella Boyd in Front Royal, Virginia and General Jackson. We were both released in exchanges for union officers. Both of us kept on spying, but were known spies to the union and we both were caught again," he said.

After the war, Jubal, who was then using the name of the Yankee prison guard he killed, said he saw her in a touring play.

"She was an actress named Nina Benjamin. We used a method of signaling we had used during the war and met in an alley behind the theater long enough to chat."

Ever the good spy, Jubal Paine omitted sharing his new name, even with her.

"She would have understood," he told Eve.

"Uncle, tell me about Rose Greenhow," Eve asked.

"I never worked with her, but knew of her. She gave all for the cause and actually slept with generals and Congressmen for secrets. Pinkerton was obsessed with catching her and he did. It was pretty early in the war. I don't remember exactly when. I was in Canada for a while after the two battles in Manassas."

"Were those 'Bull Run?'" she asked.

"According to the Yankees, yes. We could have chased them all the way back into Washington and ended the war then, but the generals would not allow it. Big mistake, Eve. A lot of good men died on both sides during the three years after."

"Uncle, did you have to kill anyone in the war?" Eve asked.

"I did. Several times. Not like in battle. But, other spies who were trailing me. Or, patrols I encountered unexpectedly."

"Yet, now you just have a union musket and no revolver. Why?"

"It's just part of the role I've had to play. After these attacks, I should have gotten new weaponry. I still might, though I have faith Tate will bring a permanent end to our worries," he said, retrospectively.

"If we go with Tate and you homestead a section

and we homestead another adjacent near Manitou Springs, we might need better arms."

"I believe you are right. You know, Eve, it will be good to farm and grow things we can eat again. Too many bullets in me to ever ride and rope again. I already had some you never knew about," he admitted.

"I will go down to Raton tomorrow and get us some supplies. Money being scarce, we can only get staples. Will you be alright here until I get back," Eve asked.

"I will. I will just keep the Springfield .58 handy. Should be all I'd need. Maybe you'll hear some word from or about Tate."

"I hope so. I worry so much about him. I know he's good with a gun, but one man against five…."

"Well, his mentor was Leander McNelly, a former Confederate raider. He learned from the best how to attack a larger group and pick off the enemy one at a time."

"Do you think he'll dry gulch them, Uncle?"

"I would, if I was him. I am pretty sure he will shoot them one or two at a time. It's the only reasonable approach. He has a murder warrant on them. He does not have to explain to any sheriff or judge how he chose to bring them in," he said.

"But, isn't shooting them from a distance just a form of murder?" she asked.

"The way I see it, what they tried to do to you and me was attempted murder. If he picks them off, I'd call it justice."

She nodded. She did not really care how he got them. She just wanted him to bring them to some sort of justice and come home safe to her. She had kind of loved her late husband. But, it was an arranged marriage. He was a serious man, never warm or affectionate. His wife was his farming partner, expected to bring little farm workers into the family. Sometimes, she felt he looked at her like a breed mare and field hand. She was sorry when the arrow took him. But, almost as sorry for herself.

His suffering had lasted a second. Hers for years. Now, she had a chance for happiness and she was going to put everything she could into it.

Eve went in and got a blanket for her uncle to put over his legs and a cup of water. He had bled too much in the past few weeks, so she poured as much liquid into him as she could. Tonight, they would have soup. It was made as stew. But, to get liquid into her uncle and to save precious money, she had watered it down into beef vegetable soup instead of beef stew.

After looking after her uncle, she resumed seeing to dinner. She had neglected to prepare dough for bread or biscuits, so she got out the heavy cast iron pan, smeared some bacon grease in the bottom and made Indian fry bread. It was one of her uncle's favorites anyway.

******

Tate rode painfully all the next day. He hoped his side would loosen up the following day. Cisco had a good gait. He did not clomp along like some horses did. But, a less than two-day old bullet wound did not make for a pleasant ride. He admitted it beat the fatal wound a rifle or large bore revolver would have made — by a long shot!

He was riding across prairie land, trying to steer a straight shot back to Trinidad.

Tate wondered how the new town marshal was doing. And, where his friend Bat was. Still in Trinidad, dealing faro? Or, moved on like the rolling stone he seemed to be?

He wondered, too, how Eve and her uncle were. Was the former spy recovering from his four bullet wounds in a month? Tate suspected at least one of Stone's was from the .32 Langston had packed and which was in his saddlebag. He might give it to Stone. It was a fairly new model and in new condition.

He had confiscated a rifle and revolver in .44 Henry rimfire for Eve. But, he did not have access to a good repeating rifle for Stone. He thought the man was living hand-to-mouth. Maybe he would buy him one as a present. He suspected Stone was a proud man, so Tate had to figure out a way to give him a rifle without insulting him.

He did not realize he was talking out loud until Cisco whinnied.

"Okay, boy. You are right. It's time to stop for the day and set up camp."

There was almost nothing but tall prairie grass in front of them, but off to the left was a small stand of trees. They rode over and Tate's dismount was stiff and painful.

He unsaddled Cisco and put his hobble on. He unrolled his bedroll and tarp. It did not look like rain, so he put the tarp under the bedroll and the saddle at its head to lean against. Rifle beside the blankets and he opened his camping saddlebag with the food, cooking gear and tools.

Using his trowel, he cleared an eight foot ring of grass and scooped out a pit. Picking up a hatchet, he walked over to the patch of trees and dragged back a couple of long branches. Tate cut these into workable lengths and made a fuzz stick for kindling, using his pocket knife.

He was not sure how cold it was going to get so, without much fuel, he held off making the fire and supped on cornpone, jerky and canteen water.

Cisco got a couple handfuls of feed and a hat crown filled with water. Tate knew he would supplement his grain by munching on grass all night.

Tate awoke cold in the middle of the night. He could not read his watch and the exact time did not really matter to him.

He took his fire kit out and struck his fire steel against a piece of flint. It landed in some charcloth he had laid underneath. He put the charcloth under the fuzz stick kindling and soon had a fire crackling.

Tate tied his bandanna around his head and stretched out in the bedroll. He tilted his Stetson over his face and closed his eyes. The sore side and coolness hampered falling asleep quickly.

After a long night, Tate could see dawn beginning to break. He put more wood on the fire and it built up to a blaze quickly. Water and coffee in his small pot began to brew. He made enough for one tin cup. He was not sure where the next replenishment of water was and determined not to waste a drop.

Tate munched some more cornpone and jerky. He reckoned this would be a long day after a relatively sleepless night.

He wound his watch and looked at the ambrotype of beautiful Eve. The time was seven a.m. when he and Cisco started back on the trail.

Around midday, Tate saw some dust from riders off in the distance. He reckoned the riders were several miles away yet. Indians? Cavalry? Outlaws?

This was wild country and it could have been any of the three. Or, just cowmen returning from dropping a herd off at the railhead in Abilene after bringing them up from Texas on the Chisholm Trail.

Tate knew he was in fairly hostile Indian country. He rode with his rifle laid across the horn of his saddle and ready for immediate use. The 1866 he confiscated for Eve was loaded as a backup in in the scabbard on the opposing side from where his newer 1873 Winchester had been.

He looked behind himself. Tate did not see any trail dust blowing from Cisco's trot along the trail. It is possible the riders had not seen him. He could not detect them altering direction or speed. There was a clump of trees off the trail. He dismounted and walked Cisco into it to wait.

With Cisco standing, reins down, Tate sought some downed trees. He found a couple, maybe six inches in diameter. Not much for stopping bullets, but better than nothing. He dragged them over and erected a makeshift barrier. He set both rifles and the Colt conversion and S&W .32 on his kerchief on the ground. He set out his two canteens.

Tate reckoned he was as ready as he would ever be. No matter who these riders were.

He moved Cisco away from him to help keep him from getting hit by any return fire.

The riders came closer. Tate could tell it was an Indian party. He counted eight riders. He did not know whether they were Comanches, Cheyenne, Kiowas or what. He just saw they were young and well-armed, with rifles. No bows and arrows for these braves.

One was a little bit in front. He was the scout, Tate figured.

As he got within one hundred yards of the patch of trees, he stopped.

Something was bothering him. Smell of man or horse? A bit of lingering dust? The trail was worn enough visible tracks were unlikely.

He raised his hand to stop the other seven riders. Then, he pointed to the copse of trees where Tate and Cisco hid.

The braves spread out and began to canter towards him.

This was a fight Tate did not want to start. But, he thought he had to, if he was going to survive.

His first shot knocked the scout off his pony.

Tate levered and shot the farthest brave, hitting him also. The remaining five opened up and bullets were zinging past and hitting trees.

Tate was shooting as fast as he could. His third shot hit a pony, regrettably. The brave rolled clear and came up shooting. Tate hit him in the gut.

A bullet went through his hat, sending it flying.

"Sumbitch!" Tate muttered as he killed the hat killer. He really liked his hat. Stetsons were not cheap, either.

Four down, four left. They were at the edge of the woods and dismounting. Bad news.

He was levering and pressing the trigger as fast as any good man could fire a Winchester. And, he was having effect. Two more dropped, but the remaining two were on him, knives out.

Tate swung the Winchester at the first one hard enough to break the butt stock off. The brave went down, hurt but not dead.

Tate pulled his Bowie as the last brave jumped on

him, skinning knife held high.

His left arm went up fast and his hand clasped the brave's knife hand. They wrestled for a moment and Tate felt a burn in his wounded side. He thrust the ten-inch blade of the Bowie into the brave. It went in up to the quillons and he twisted. Brave and stoic, the man screamed despite himself and died.

With great difficulty, Tate pulled the knife out and looked to the brave whose head had broken the stock of his Winchester '73.

He had a nasty head wound, bleeding profusely. His eyes were open, but just not right. Tate did not know if he was in shock or had a concussion or both.

Tate exercised his only option and ran the Bowie's blade across the man's throat.

Eight to one. But, he had the superior position.

Tate put his hand to his side and it came away red.

He could not worry about bleeding now. He had to make sure all of his attackers were dead.

Tate went around to each. They were. He checked on Cisco. Thankfully, the gelding had not been hit by an errant bullet.

He reloaded his weapons, except for the '73. Tate then gathered the Indians' weapons for inventory.

He realized he had been generally wrong in thinking they were as well-armed as he.

There was one Winchester '73. It was in foul shape, but the butt stock was sound. There was his repair source.

He set aside another 1866 Yellow Boy in .44 Henry rimfire like the one he had confiscated for Eve. This one had brass tacks decorating the stock and a feather tied to the lever for looks. A swing of the Bowie removed the decoration and Tate kept the carbine for Stone.

The rest were junk, in Tate's estimation. Single shot muzzle loaders. No revolvers. The knives were cheap skinners with brass décor added to the grip scales.

Tate added a few more .44 rimfire cartridges from a buckskin pouch to his ammo stock, and cleaned his Bowie and hands. He found the bleeding was a pull in the stitches on his earlier bullet wound. For now, he added the salve he had made a few days ago.

He mounted Cisco, and carrying the good condition '66, he rode off before the vultures arrived. He saw them circling.

At camp tonight, he would put the Indian's butt stock on his '73. He carried two screw drivers in his saddlebag. One was for a Winchester, one for a Colt. Once he got home, he would sand the replacement stock and rub five or six applications of linseed oil into it, lightly re-sanding between each.

All told, a good day. He picked up a carbine for Stone. He fought the good fight.

And, he was not dead.

******

In a couple days, he arrived in Wichita. He looked up a doctor to see if he needed another stitch. The doctor said his wound had resealed and should be okay. After he left and checked into a hotel, Tate paid two bits for a much-needed bath and applied some of his salve before putting the bandages back on.

His shirt and pants were raggedy beyond repair, so he bought a new black lightweight flannel shirt and some dark pants. He replaced the destroyed Stetson with another in black. Tate thought about sending a letter to Eve, but realized he would arrive before it did.

From Wichita, he would stop a night at Dodge City, then head for the corner where New Mexico, Colorado and the tip of the panhandle of Oklahoma Territory touched. From the corner, he was really close to his temporary home and his permanent girl.

CHAPTER 9

As Tate rode, the pain in his side lessened. Perhaps it was his focus on getting back to Eve, perhaps it was just the healing process.

Trinidad finally came into view. He was tired. Cisco was tired. Overall, they had been thirteen hundred miles. But, their mission was accomplished.

He stopped in front of the hotel he used in the past. The clerk said a private room was available, so Tate took it for several days, with the option to extend.

He moved his saddlebags and assortment of weapons, old and new, up to the room and locked it. Cisco was boarded at the livery with instructions for an extra helping of feed, water, a brushing and a horse shoe check.

Tate went to the café where he often ate and got a steak and lots of strong coffee. He knew he would sleep tonight, despite the coffee.. It was too late to ride down to Stone's ranch and see Eve, so he turned in.

The next morning, after breakfast, he bought some linseed oil and a sheet of fairly rough, one medium and several fine grits of sandpaper. He also picked up a box of .32 cartridges and two boxes of .44 Henry rimfires for the two Winchesters and the conversion era Colt. His last stop was the café again, where he bought six ham sandwiches and a whole apple pie.

He retrieved Cisco and loaded the stock finishing materials and new guns onto the black gelding and rode south.

Tate yelled a greeting before riding in. After the last callers, he reckoned they'd be apt to shoot first and ask questions later.

He saw Stone lean the Springfield up against the wall by where he was sitting in the rocker.

Eve came running out of the cabin smiling while tucking the spur trigger Colt under her apron.

She flew into his arms and stayed there a while. He waved at Stone, who grinned and waved back.

Eve picked up on his grimace and asked if he was okay. He mentioned about being shot and she demanded to see the wound to check it. He promised her in a minute, presents first.

Stone was pleased to add the Winchester '66 to complement his Springfield and Eve was happy to get a repeater also. He gave her the conversion Colt in the same caliber. A gunsmith had shortened the long barrel down to a bit over three inches, which made it handy for her to hide away. The lack of a front sight did not bother her. One less thing to hang up as she drew it from beneath her apron, she thought.

The last gun to be presented was the .32 S&W spur trigger with the six-inch barrel. Tate explained its history with the two of them as he gave it to Stone.

Stone was happy as a kid getting candy and a new pair of shoes on Christmas. Tate included Langston's belt and Slim Jim holster with the revolver.

"Alright, my big tough lawman. Into the house and bare your new bullet wound right now!" Eve said with a newfound edge of authority. Tate moved with some alacrity and once inside, took his shirt off.

She did not have any scissors, so borrowed his Bowie to cut the week old bandage off. The wound, black walnut salve applied daily, had not infected. In fact, with the doctor's stitches, it had healed well.

"Did it hurt a lot, honey?" she asked.

"More than I thought a small bullet should. I went down and was out for a second or two. They got away," Tate said. She looked alarmed.

"But, not for long," he hastened to add.

"Will you tell me about it?" she asked.

"How about I tell you and your uncle over lunch. Which, by the way, I brought with me."

She gave him a more gentle hug before he could get his shirt on, though it would have been considered somewhat scandalous in the day. He did not care a whit. It appeared she did not either.

"Do you have some coffee made?" he asked. Eve nodded positively.

He got the lunch bag, worried about how the pie may have survived. It was okay.

Eve called her uncle in and they ate an early lunch and large slices of pie each.

"So, Tate, did you get 'em?" Stone asked.

"I got all five. Unfortunately, Langston shot me with the revolver I gave you first. Slowed me down a bit. But, in the end, I got them on the street where your troubles originally started. I used guerilla tactics McNelly taught us. I took them down to three men. Then, it was a gunfight in the street like happened in Raton."

"Damn, boy! You tracked and killed five men by yourself!" Stone exhorted.

"Wal, it was a bit more than just them, Stone. On the way back, I was attacked by an Indian war party. There were eight of them. Between the Winchester and my Bowie, they ceased to be a threat," Tate said.

"You mean you killed eight Indians?" Stone asked with incredulously.

"It was them or me. They attacked. I don't have anything against Indians, personally." He looked at Eve. "I know you do, honey," he said, savoring the word she had used.

"They killed a husband I was not too happy with. I'm sorry he had to die violently. But, we did constantly lie to the Indians, take their land and kill their buffaloes. I can understand why they hate us. But, if anyone attacks you, you have the right to defend yourself. This is America," she answered. Both men nodded.

"What do the two of you think about taking a trip up to the Manitou Springs area and looking at some sections I found for homesteading?" Tate asked.

"I'm not sure I can ranch anymore," Stone said.

"How 'bout if we perfected claims on sections adjoining and put the two houses together right on the line. Maybe you could do the farming for food and I could raise the horses or cattle?" Tate countered with.

"It could work. How much land would we have combined?" Stone asked.

"Hundred sixty acres for each claim. We'd each have to build a house and farm or ranch it for five years, or build a house in six months and buy it for a buck twenty-five an acre at the end of the six months. It comes to two hundred dollars each section," Tate said.

"I don't have two hundred in cash, so I'd have to go the whole five years," Stone said.

"How about I give you the two hundred for your house and all and help you build them. And, you put Eve and me in your will as beneficiaries when you die?"

"What if y'all had to wait a while? I might live another forty years," Stone asked.

"No problem with me. How 'bout you, Eve?"

"No, I'm good with it," she said.

"Stone, do you own this place free and clear?" Tate asked.

"No. I didn't homestead it. I got a loan, secured by the land."

"Are you even with it, if you don't mind me asking?" Tate asked.

"I was until very recently. Ever since the first shooting, I have not been able to do any of the money making activities. I suspect the bank would accept it back, since it has a house, well, corral and all. I am not opposed to offering it to them. Maybe a trip into town to visit would be worthwhile."

"Could be. It's your call. I would never ask you to walk away from your home," Tate said.

"It was never a home until Eve got here. Now, it seems like a place to get away from, even though the threats are dead. If we can be close neighbors on three hundred twenty acres, it would be a good situation. Plus, it would be a good opportunity for me to go back to being Jubal Paine once again. I've been thinking about going to my real name for a while."

"Do you want me to hitch up the wagon for a ride to Trinidad to the bank first, or go up and look around Manitou Springs first?" Tate asked.

"Let's see how we fare with the banker first. Once we finish eating, we can ride the couple or three miles to town and visit him."

Tate turned to Eve.

"You have anything to add?"

"I do. And, those words are a hint."

"Will you marry me in Trinidad later today?"

"I will."

"Can I kiss the bride?" he asked.

"Sure. Once she's a bride!"

Tate looked at Stone. Both rolled their eyes.

"I only have one dress. I guess it will have to do."

"You think one of the stores in Trinidad might have another dress to fit your wonderful form?" Tate asked.

"I'd lay money on it," she replied.

"You find it and I'll lay down the money, future Mrs. Tate."

They finished eating. Stone put on his suit and Eve freshened up and combed the long auburn hair.

Tate thought she was the most beautiful woman imaginable. He was not too far off. Especially now she was smiling all the time. He remembered the drawn, haggard and scared woman held hostage on the street not so very long ago.

"Make sure the new dress has a revolver pocket, okay?" he asked.

"I sew those in. You know the soft buckskin Indian bag you brought back with the cartridges in it? I think it would make a really good gun pocket for my new dress."

"Think you could squeeze two out of the buckskin bag?" Tate asked.

"Probably, but I will only have my old dress and

my new one."

"Maybe two new ones," Tate suggested prompting a big smile.

Tate hitched up the buckboard and they helped Stone aboard. Eve drove and Tate rode along beside on Cisco.

The trip to town was quick. They stopped at the bank and Stone went in. He came out in twenty minutes and limped over to the clothing store where Eve was trying on dresses.

"What's the news?" Tate asked.

"Better than I had hoped," Stone said, "The banker said he always liked my place and offered to buy it himself for five hundred over the payoff. I asked if he'd cover any tax stamps and he said he would. He said if I would come back in an hour, he would have the paperwork ready. And, a check. I can keep living in it for another two weeks. Think it will be enough, Tate?"

"I believe it might," the lawman said.

Eve walked out from behind a curtain in a plain cotton dress. It buttoned up the front however high she wanted. The green color picked up her eyes and her auburn hair. Tate nodded and it did not take Pinkerton to get the signal.

She handed it through the curtain and he took it to the shop lady.

The next one was gingham in green and blue. It one went onto the counter also. She picked out some underthings and stockings to go with her new purchases. She put the green dress back on and Tate paid the bill. They walked down the street to the first church they found.

The preacher was a tall, sallow man. Tate thought he did would not have the preaching ability of his new friend Bass Reeves. It was a shame Bass was so far away.

Neither Eve nor Tate were members of his denomination so he refused to marry them. Tate walked out of the church cursing the denomination and its representative in Trinidad.

On an idea, they stopped by the courthouse. The circuit judge was not in, but a magistrate with marrying authority was. The best part was he could marry them and walk the paperwork over to the clerk and file it on the spot.

Twenty minutes and two dollars later, they were man and wife. Tate was still cursing about the "damn holy roller," and his uncle-in-law was nodding support until Eve elbowed him in the side. She really did not mean to hit the bullet wound side, but recognized the error when Tate doubled over in pain.

"Oh, my darling husband, I am *so* sorry," she exclaimed, meaning every word.

He straightened up, took her hand in his and they walked Stone back to the bank. The former Confederate spy was grinning like a jackass chewing briers all the way.

They left with none of them owning a piece of property anywhere, but Stone had the five hundred dollar proceeds check in his pocket.

"You ever carried such an amount before, Stone?" Tate asked.

"Actually, I have. I've taken many times this amount to Canada to pay for English rifles to be smuggled to the South through Mr. Lincoln's maritime blockade," he admitted.

"How did it go for you?" Tate asked.

"Quite well. Matthew Maury's electric torpedoes worked for us many a time. It is said he sunk more Yankee ships than the whole Confederate Navy did with cannons. I believe it. I've heard he and his son actually swam out in the James River in Richmond and blew a Union ship up themselves. He might have been commander of the US Naval Observatory in Washington and chief of all maritime defenses for the Confederacy, but he wasn't afraid to get greasy or wet," Stone said.

"A man who led from the front," Tate observed.

"Indeed," the former spy agreed.

"How about we get you a room, Stone, and Eve can stay in mine? We will put Cisco and your rig up with the livery, have a nice wedding supper, instead of riding back to the ranch tonight," Tate suggested.

"Only if the wedding supper is on the newly-flush and proud uncle," Stone said. Nobody objected and they headed for the hotel.

Tate stopped on the way at the town marshal's office. Chief Deputy Hulon Parker was still in and accepted Tate's invitation to dinner. Bat Masterson, no longer marshal, was dealing faro later, but was contacted and accepted too. Tate lamented he could not get Raton Marshal Hawkins up for the event, but the notice would have been too short.

The dinner went on for several hours and Bat bought chilled Champagne, a new innovation for Trinidad. Tate had a glass, Eve two and the gambler, lawman and former spy finished the rest, and the second bottle.

Thanking the revelers, Eve and Tate slipped away. Well before the morning broke, Tate was convinced he was the luckiest man alive. Eve lay beside him, breathing softly, a white shoulder shining in the moonlight peeking through the window. He found her hand under the sheets and held it softly, staring at the ceiling. Smiling as he never had before, but now planned to forever.

*****

They ate early the next morning and bought food to take on the camping trip to Manitou Springs. Once arriving, they spent the first night in a couple hotel rooms so Stone could rest on a feather bed instead of bunking in the bed of the buckboard on a pallet after the long ride north.

Tate took them to the two adjacent hundred sixty acre sections. Both had tall trees and streams. The one

Tate particularly wanted also had a pool with a small waterfall. The one he had in mind for Stone had a wide meadow area of black dirt, suitable for growing vegetables and running a few head of horses and cattle. Seeing this, Stone agreed immediately with Tate plans to handling the ranching while Stone did the farming.

It did not take long for the three to agree on the two sections. They rode into town and filed claims, walking off and marking trees on both sections. Where there were no trees, Tate hammered stakes into the ground marking corners.

Tate had previously found a construction company in Manitou Springs They agreed to come out and begin construction on two cabins suitable for easy expansion. The two men paid the company two hundred dollars each to commence, the remainder on completion.

Stone filed his homestead claim under his real name, Jubal Paine. He said other than seeing his niece getting married to a good man, it was the best feeling he had in years. He even passed some time chatting with the widow who worked waiting tables at the café they picked as a regular eatery. She was forty-five to Paine's fifty and Eve realized her uncle, given a hair-cut and beard trim would be a fine figure of a man. She looked at Tate and winked as Paine and the woman, Darlene White, smiled and chatted.

They lightly teased Stone, now Paine again, about his new flirtatious ways, to which he replied "they aren't new, I just have not had anybody worth flirting with for a while."

Tate bought a larger tarp for a shelter for Eve and him while Paine bought a canvas top for the bed of the buckboard. A wrought iron tripod and some food essentials, an axe, shovel and bucket finished off their immediate needs.

Back at the camp, the two men erected the new canvas while Eve built a fire and started an iron pot of beans with bacon simmering. Paine noted "everything is better with bacon," to which there was uniform agreement. Eve used the Dutch oven to start corn bread baking. Within an hour, the campground looked and smelled like a good temporary home.

Tate familiarized Eve with the .44 Henry caliber Colt and Winchester, but they put off shooting practice until later. Eve had demonstrated prowess sufficient to give Tate both pride and comfort.

Over the next several days, Tate cleared trees for both house locations. Swinging an axe did not help his bullet wound, and he tried his best to hide the pain. Eve picked up on it and requested he let the construction team finish and he relented. They were due the next day. Given the wagon they would bring with logs, boards, pre-hung windows and doors, the two small homes should go up in several days with a full crew supplemented by Tate and Paine.

Less than a week later, both cabins were completed. They hitched up the buckboard and headed in to Manitou Springs for two beds, tables and chairs and a couple of rockers for each porch.

Paine saw Darlene White and asked her to come to dinner for a housewarming celebration the following night. She accepted and he promised to pick her up in the buckboard.

Eve smiled broadly the next day when her newly trimmed and coiffed uncle climbed aboard the buckboard by himself, Winchester beside the seat and headed downhill to Manitou Springs to pick up his dinner companion.

Tate asked Eve about Darlene. "He better be careful telling someone what he did in the war, without knowing their past allegiances," he said.

Eve replied "Not to worry. He says she was born and raised in South Carolina and is as much a rebel as he is."

"What a relief, because I'm thinking there will be another wedding coming up pretty soon," Tate said.

"Leaving him alone in a cabin was worrying me, though he seems really invigorated since the threat is gone and we are up here. And, Darlene, of course," she said.

"I really never knew how important it was to have somebody to come home to until you, Eve," Tate admitted. She smiled and blew him a kiss instead of getting flour all over his new shirt.

"I'm gonna hold off taking the deputy job until the two spreads are up and running, with stables, corrals and a plot for planting for your uncle Jubal. I think we have enough to get by. Might be tight for a while, but we're both used to not having a lot of money."

"We are. You have saved a goodly amount, Morgan," she said, the question not asked but hanging out there.

"Well, I had a revolver and Winchester when I joined the rangers. And, Cisco. They paid for food, ammunition, and lodging in a wall tent with a floor and four other rangers. So, I didn't have any expenses. I saved everything I made for ten years."

The Scottish poet Burns said the "best laid plans of mice and men oft go astray," and such was Tate's plan. As he was talking to his new wife, a telegram arrived in Trinidad at the Town Marshal's Office.

The Chief Deputy, Tate's friend, Hulon Parker, received it. The Texas Attorney General knew Hulon was not only a former Texas Ranger, but was Tate's current or recent former boss. Hulon had no idea how the politician knew.

Parker needed to get the information to Tate. The ride was one hundred twenty miles, so he wired the El Paso County, Colorado sheriff and requested a note be delivered to Tate with all possible haste. He was to contact the Attorney General of Texas about an urgent matter.

The following day, a deputy rode into Tate's ranch.

The former Texas Ranger looked up. He saw the badge glint in the sun and approached the deputy, who he only vaguely knew.

"Get on down and let me get you some cold water," Tate said.

"I will surely accept some water, Mr. Tate. I got a real important message for you in the meantime," the deputy replied.

Hearing the exchange, Eve drew some water from the artesian well and brought two mugs out to the men.

"I'm Deputy Will Hallstrom," the deputy said, extending his hand before taking the mug.

"Morgan Tate, and my wife Eve," Tate replied, shaking the other man's hand. The deputy doffed his hat at Eve.

They each quaffed the water, then the deputy dug a folded piece of paper out of his vest and handed it to Tate.

It was a wire from the Attorney General of Texas asking if former Texas Ranger Morgan Tate would immediately contact him for a short term assignment on the Texas side of the line with Oklahoma and Indian Territory near the panhandle. Comanches were raiding into Texas and returning to safe haven within the Territory. The Attorney General raised a small company of experienced rangers and former rangers to combat the raid. He wanted to know if Tate would accept a three-month warrant as Captain to lead them.

Tate knew he and his wife of several weeks now had some serious talking to do over dinner with her uncle and Darlene White, who both expected to be family shortly.

"It's only an hour or so 'til supper, Will. You are welcome to stay and eat with us."

"Thank you, but I'd like to be back in Colorado Springs by dark, so I better get going now. Maybe another time?" Tate nodded and the deputy turned his sorrel and headed east.

"What was the wire all about, Morgan?" Eve asked.

He handed her the telegram to read.

They both went into the cabin and he helped her move a table outside and they set place settings for four. The dinner was going to be simple, but good.

The menu was venison stew, homemade bread and peach pie from canned peaches accompanied with water and coffee completed the menu. They heard Jubal Paine's buckboard and saw him and Darlene driving up and stopping.

CHAPTER 10

Over dinner, Tate outlined the offer as he knew it. The title Captain sounded good, but no money was mentioned. Tate knew a town marshal or county sheriff could make more than a ranger captain due to receiving a percentage of the fees the former earned from arrests and taxes collected from saloons and sporting houses. In the long term, he had a sheriff's badge as his career goal. But, there were dues to be paid first. Being a captain of Texas Rangers would take him a long way towards any law enforcement job in the land.

They talked it out over good food and Tate got up from the dinner table outside with the support he needed to wire the Attorney General back with a positive response.

The next day Tate rode past Manitou Springs and into the newly re-named Colorado Springs. He went to the Western Union office and sent a telegram to the Attorney General of Texas accepting the authority warrant for three months, commencing with his arrival by train. Before he left town, he received a telegram back specifying his three-month salary, guaranteeing a good horse, and a voucher for transportation to present at any bank. The meeting was set for the morning after he arrived in Austin.

All were items satisfying Tate. He could leave Cisco for Eve to use and and the voucher prevented him from having to dip into his diminishing funds for train tickets. The orders were to report to Austin to discuss his orders and pick up his men and a couple of wagons with shelters and supplies to convoy to the northwestern corner of Texas.

He would be able to live fine off the food, shelter and transportation provided by Texas and save his captain's salary. He suspected the money to fund the whole endeavor was coming from the federal government. Tate was pretty sure the federals had not yet figured out it would be used to contravene its own safe haven policies for the Five Civilized Tribes. Once it became clear, the money would likely be requested back and denied by the State of Texas. This was a game Texas and Washington played frequently.

Tate picked up a suitcase in Colorado Springs and tied it on Cisco's saddle awkwardly.

He would take a duster, his good suit to wear meeting with the Attorney General, both handguns and his

Winchester, both sets of trail clothes, his razor and two union suits and a big bag of bison jerky.

With Eve watching, he gave special care and attention to the black gelding, assuring him he would be back and telling him to look after Eve. As always, the horse whinnied in answer.

Jubal and Eve drove him to Colorado Springs in the buckboard.

He contacted the man who delivered firewood to the town folks for their stoves and fireplaces. Tate paid him to deliver several cords of seasoned wood to the ranch for both Eve and Jubal. They went to the general mercantile and bought dried and canned foods to help hold the two homesteads over until he got back. They loaded four bags of feed onto the bed of the buckboard for Cisco and Jubal's horse.

Lastly, he gave Eve most of his money, knowing her uncle had a good amount left himself from the sale of his ranch outside of Trinidad.

After goodbye's, Tate boarded the Santa Fe train. He did not check his bag. He wanted to expedite his transfer at Dallas for the quick ride down to the capitol in Austin.

Tate had never ridden a train before and was looking forward to it. It would be as fast as he had ever moved, even on the fleet Cisco at his fastest gallop.

He boarded with a sense of excitement and found his seat. The suitcase fit in the overhead shelf, though barely. He put his Winchester, in its scabbard, up there also.

The train started rolling and he heard the steam engine noise growing. The speed picked up to an amazing pace and the hills and trees flew by. This was an exciting experience and one of wonderment.

He sat locked to the window, watching Colorado go past until he heard his belly growl. It was past noon and all he had had today was a cup of Eve's great coffee.

He stood and walked carefully to the dining car and had an amazingly good lunch with rich coffee and a slice of pie. Tate walked back, holding seat backs as he went down the aisle, the landscape flying past at an amazing pace.

He found his seat and watched until the motion made him drowsy and he dozed off. His trip was almost thirty hours, including the wait for the transfer in Dallas. Tate slept well in his seat, sorry the darkness prevented him from seeing the new countryside.

At Austin, he found a hotel and checked in. He walked around town the rest of the day. The next morning, he cleaned up and donned his best suit.

He began the walk to the state capitol building in plenty of time to arrive ten minutes early. His suit was brushed, as was his Stetson. Tate had his boots shined at the hotel for two-bits. His suit jacked draped just right over the Colt Frontier Model, he figured he looked about as presentable for the big-wigs as he could, selling himself 'way short.

Tate found his way to the three story limestone capitol building at the head of Congress Avenue. Inside, he was directed to go up the steps to the third floor for the Attorney General's Office.

He had never been in a big building before. Tate found this one impressive, though detractors called it a "corn crib with a pumpkin on top for a dome."

Texans, he grinned, have never been ones to withhold their opinions.

He saw an office and inquired of a male secretary about the Attorney General.

"You are at the right place. Who may I say is inquiring?" he was asked.

"Morgan Tate. I have an appointment at nine-thirty. From his watch with Eve's picture, Tate knew he was a few minutes early.

"Have a seat. I'll tell the AG you are here."

Tate sat uncomfortably on a chair which felt like it might crumble under his weight.

Then minutes later, he was ushered in. The Attorney General stood and extended his hand.

"Boy. You look like a Texas Ranger Captain," he said looking up to Tate's over six foot height and into cold blue eyes framed with light brown hair and neatly trimmed handlebar mustache. "A little young for the title, but from what I've heard, you have paid the dues for it."

"Thank you sir."

"Sit down here in front of my desk for an off the record palaver," the politician said.

"Sir, first, why me? I was just a ranger, not an officer."

"I admit I never heard your name until I started asking around for good candidates. I couldn't ask McNelly who rode for me during the war. He had passed, dammit. So, I wrote Lee Hall. He was writing permission to promote you to sergeant when you resigned. Said you were heading up towards Colorado. So, I wrote an ex-ranger who is chief deputy up in Trinidad. He recommended you and so did Bat Masterson. They referred me to Hawkins, the marshal in Raton. He told me you had tracked a group of former Yankees who were outlaws six hundred miles and killed the whole gang. All of which was enough for me, young man. I knew your capabilities as a lawman. I had to take it on faith you'd be a good leader. Hell, boy, you learned under Leander McNelly. So, let's get down to business.

You know the problem from my telegram. Comanches mainly — are raiding ranches and villages near the western border with Indian Territory.

Then, they are ducking back into the Territory, where the damn US Government has granted them safe haven. We can't *officially* follow them back over the line," he said winking and stressing the word "officially."

"Your official Rules of Engagement are to abide by the border line and shoot only in self-defense close to it. Well inside Texas, you can do whatever you damn well need to," he said.

"Sir, a couple of clarifications. First, there is no defined line. No signs. No surveyor's markers. I was recently through there. We won't know where it is and the Marshals out of Ft. Smith, Arkansas will also be guessing where to enforce a line. Second, if there is any expectation of raiding Indian villages, I am out right here and now. I know what the damn US Army does. Slaughtering Indian women and children. I will shoot any hostile who needs to be shot. Any damn where. But, I draw the line at innocents."

"You are right on both counts. Do your best on the line. If you need to stretch it, do so. Don't quote me or use those words as official guidance. Just do what you think is just. As to raiding villages, I deplore what the army does. Any Christian should. So, no worries there."

"Thank you, sir," Tate said.

"Now, if you and I are on the same page, and it seems we are, I'd like you to place your left hand on this Bible and raise your right hand."

Tate did so and was immediately sworn in as Captain, Texas Rangers Special Battalion, as was McNelly's.

The Attorney General then surprised him when he handed him a badge struck from a Mexican cinco peso gold coin. It was a circle with a star inside. On the circle rimming the star were the words "Captain" and "Texas Rangers" along the bottom. Tate immediately pinned it onto the left side of his vest where it showed beneath his suit coat.

"I have a ranger waiting outside. He has a horse for you. It's a good one and you can keep him when your tour with us is over. The badge, too. Who knows if I might need you back real quick?" the Attorney General said, grinning, one Texan to another.

"The ranger will lead you to your men. They are gathered down by Barton Springs. There are several wagons and a remuda of extra mounts. I want you to greet your men with optimism and authority and leave forthwith for the best camp you can find south of the western boundary with the Indian Territory panhandle."

Tate's new mount was an American saddle bred. He was sixteen or so hands high and gray, not unlike Lee's Traveller. The general spelled his horse's name in the British fashion.

"What's his name," Tate asked the ranger, a man called Charlie Bock.

"Thunder," Bock replied.

"Hope it's because he looks like a gray sky before a storm and not his personality," Tate observed.

"Naw, he's a good horse. Can run all day and be happy with sweetgrass for dinner. Strong horse for sure and don't mind gunfire coming from his back."

"Well, sounds real good, Charlie. I suspect we'll be testing the gunfire part real soon," Tate said.

"Tell me about the men. Do you know them?" Tate

asked.

"Some. Most are proven rangers from around the state. No kids in this battalion. Fellas in their thirties and even forties. Been around the block, all of them."

"They transferred over from other companies. Why do you think?" Tate asked.

"Lots of reasons, I guess. Bored. Didn't like sergeants or lieutenant or captain. Mebbe politics not allowing them to enforce the law and sending them to mines and such to keep the peace. Probably, the bored part. Wanting a new adventure. Word is this battalion will chase the Indians into the Territory. We will get rid of the problem and be real Texas Rangers again," Bock said.

"And, it's a three-month duty away from their usual."

"We are going to be walking on some thin ice. The Comanches who slip across the Cherokee Strip into Texas are the wilder ones. They will fight and love every minute of it. The boys all have good weapons?" Tate asked.

"They do. Colts and Winchesters. No more of this Sharps single shot stuff like when I joined up. We have replacement guns and Bowies in the wagon as well as camp building stuff. Axes, shovels for privies, cooking ironwork. And, food supplies."

"You are well informed," Tate observed.

"Didn't the Attorney General tell you?" Bock asked.

"Tell me what?"

"Tell you I'm your sergeant."

"No, but I'm damn glad to know it, Charlie," Tate said.

They arrived at a simple encampment at Barton Springs, a site Indians had communed at since time began. According to the count in the book the sergeant carried, he had thirty men. They looked fit and serious to Tate.

"Men, I'm Captain Morgan Tate. I will be leading you for the next several months while we clear up the problems of Comanches and others raiding, then retreating across the line into Oklahoma and Indian Territory where we cannot officially chase them. Well, we'll see about the chasing over the line part." This got a bunch of nods and grunts of approval from many of the men.

"We will be after hostiles only. None of this damn army stuff of raiding villages and murdering innocents. I suspect, under our circumstances, it will be difficult to take prisoners and deliver them to a court. There are no courts anywhere near where we'll be. We will ride hard and shoot fast and try to fix this situation within three months.

If any of you have second thoughts, come see the sergeant and me as soon as I cease talking. You will be paid for services rendered up until today and transferred back to your original company with no questions asked. Everybody understand?" Tate asked. Apparently, they did. No one stepped forward immediately or later.

Sergeant Charlie Bock called for the men to break camp and prepare for the almost five hundred mile trip to where they would be setting up their camp.

Tate asked Bock if there were any experienced scouts in the group. Bock said there were two and Tate summoned them.

Showing a map of the area of operations, he pointed out several villages near the border with Indian Territory. All were around ten to twenty miles due south of the line.

"When we get within a day or two's ride, I will want you men to ride ahead and pick a campground between the two villages. Look for good forage, a place for our tents and a corral and water. We'll see how much progress we make, but I suspect it will be almost two weeks before you ride out to find our HQ. Before then, I will have you scout ahead of us so we won't run into an ambush of any sort." The men agreed with the need for scouting expeditions. Overall, Tate was pleased with what he had seen of the men so far. The proof would be when the bullets started flying, however.

As the group of men on horses and two driving wagons proceeded towards the northwest corner of Texas, Tate got to know his sergeant and his men better. And, his horse. He tried talking to Thunder, but the horse trotted on steadily without answering. Maybe yet….

The nights were getting warmer and there was no rain in sight. The tents stayed in the wagons and the experienced Westerners slept under the stars. Tate learned the two wagon drivers were cooks and wagon drivers rather than sworn rangers, which made sense to him from his prior service. They were in charge of the camp: pitching tents, with help as required; digging privies; making sure there was sufficient water, feed and food for man and horse alike; and cooking meals.

Tate broke the men into three ten-man troops, knowing he might have to switch some folks around eventually.

He set one guard each night until they got into hostile country. Then, there would be more depending on the threat level.

The two cooks kept them in beans, bacon, stews, cornbread and other standard field items on the trail. They promised fresh meat and fish once the permanent camp was made and hunting could commence.

On the thirteenth day, Tate sent the two experienced scouts ahead to check the area for hostiles and find a good permanent camp, close to the approximate border line and as close as equidistant as possible from the several villages and ranches being raided.

They rode back in on the fourteenth day and invited him to join them to look at their recommended site the following day as the procession plodded on, slowed by the wagons. He agreed.

After a breakfast of bacon, biscuits and coffee the next morning, Tate saddled Thunder and rode off with the two scouts. He left Charlie Bock in charge.

They rode about fifteen miles, passing several ranches and villages and missing a couple. They came to what everyone thought was the line between Texas and Indian Territory.

The two scouts reversed direction and led Tate back to a flat top hill with a stand pines, with a few cottonwoods scattered around. It had two large open areas, fit for a living area and a horse pasture. The edge of the living area slanted down and would be good for the privies. Best of all, a stream ran out of the ground in the middle, suggesting a spring. The water was cold and pure.

"Good job, men," Tate said to the two scouts. "Good cover and water and on high ground. High ground is always a tactical advantage in an attack. Let's get the rest up here and commence to building our home for the next three months."

They did not have boards for either tent floors or privies, so they resolved to put up with dirt floors in the tents and latrines instead of privies.

"Nobody sitting on the latrine will have a hostile sneak up and interrupt his musings, like could happen in a Johnny house," Bock noted, adding "It would be some 'em-bare-assing' way to die". This could be a long three months, his captain thought.

By the end of the second day, the rangers had eight four-man wall tents up for themselves and one for Tate. A canvas roof was constructed over the chuck wagon area and a fire pit dug and wrought iron tri-pods set up and grills, pots and pans positioned.

Tate had a table for writing and a lamp and cot in his tent. A locker had been provided for his personal items and a small file cabinet for official paperwork.

Moving in took all of five minutes. He placed the smelly can of whale oil for the lamp outside the tent under a quickly-built shelter to keep rain off it.

Eve had put his socks and union suits in a cotton bag. He rolled shirts and the clean extra union suit up and put them in the bag for a pillow. He missed his new wife. A lot. He also missed Cisco, his partner for seven years. Thunder was okay for the mission, but Tate thought he would probably trade him afterwards on a mule to give to Jubal for the buckboard and a plow.

The next day, he spoke with Charlie to see who he would leave in charge when the two were away.

Without hesitation, he said "Allen Decker." Decker was the oldest of the two scouts and Tate had noted he had the respect of the men, as did Charlie.

The night before, Tate studied the paperwork given him by the Attorney General. It included the ability to name a second sergeant. He decided to name Decker, yet make it clear Charlie Bock was the senior sergeant.

He made the announcement right away and, with the rangers broken into three companies of ten, named "A, B, and C Companies," he and Charlie took half of A Company on an exploratory ride, with the other half on mounted security patrol in a several mile circle around the camp.

The two senior rangers and half of A Company visited each ranch and village in the area within twenty miles of the line with Indian Territory.

At each stop, they asked the same questions and took prodigious notes in their leather bound ranger notebooks.

"How many raids have you had? Do you know what tribes? What was the general age of the raiders? What day of the week? How many? What weapons did they carry? How many casualties did you have? How many casualties did you inflict on the raiders? What seemed to be the reason for the raid: to inflict casualties on you; to steal horses, cattle or sheep? Did they ride in with war cries or sneak up? What time of day?"

Later, in the evening, Tate and his two sergeants compiled what they had learned.

As a generality, groups of young probably Comanches, had attacked on Thursdays or Fridays. The braves were old enough it was not a rites of passage or trial. They were armed with a variety of repeating rifles. They did not evidence any revolvers. Theft seemed to be the main objective, horses preferred. They came up quietly, then attacked at a gallop and with war cries. Neither side had incurred many casualties. And, importantly, most raids happened at the same time, suggesting a pattern it may be one band doing most or all of the attacks. These facts simplified the rangers plans.

"Since the time of the war, union generals like Sheridan and Sherman and Custer have led their cavalry against the Indians. It may have prevented major attacks like the one at the Little Big Horn, but it has done nothing to reduce the number of small raids by groups of eight to ten young braves. They seem to be looking for mounts. The odd cow is probably for food, not to accumulate to set up a ranching operation over in the Territory," Tate said.

"You know, Boss, we could put two companies just behind some likely villages every Thursday and Friday. Even if they were at the wrong ones, they'd hear the shots and could ride down on the attackers right fast," Bock said. Decker nodded in agreement.

"Charlie, I think you have arrived at a logical approach given what we learned today. This old ranger thing of just aimlessly riding looking for hostile Indians, Mexican or Anglo rustlers is going to be too happenstance for here. Kinda like it has been most places," Tate said, admitting what he had always thought was a fallacy in ranger operations.

"Yep, we surprise 'em with a similar number, like ten, of better armed and trained men. We open fire and take some down, then chase the rest high-tailing across the border. Do it a coupla times and we might put a stop to these raids. The tribes have land, so it's not about fighting to preserve anything other than counting some coup and getting some new horseflesh," Decker added. The other two men nodded.

"Alright. We've had a productive day in learning the lay of the land and developing a strategy.

Tomorrow, the three of us will brief the men.

Since tomorrow is Thursday, one of the historical raid days, we can jump right into this. For now, I'm for hitting the hay. How 'bout y'all?" Tate asked. Both men nodded gladly and got up from around the small table and went to their respective tents.

"Tomorrow will be a beginning, whether we make contact or not. The villagers and ranchers will know we are there to support them and even without a running firefight, we will be practicing," Tate thought. He walked outside and poured the last swallow of his cold coffee on the ground, walked in and stripped to his union suit and laid down on the cot. Not much after he had pulled the blankets up, he was sound asleep.

CHAPTER 11

The cooks were up, as usual, at four AM and the smell of bacon and coffee woke everyone else up around dawn. The outriding sentries came in and the men gathered to eat.

As they ate, Tate, Bock and Decker discussed the findings yesterday and their assumptions from them. They laid out the plan for tonight and probably tomorrow night.

The rangers were anxious to start. They were tired of prepping and ready for action.

Other than taking turns as outriding sentries, the rangers spent the day making sure their Winchesters and Colts were clean and oiled and loaded with fresh rounds. Black powder guns, even cartridge ones, required frequent cleaning to prevent not only corrosion, but worse, having cylinders or rifle actions bind during combat. Some sharpened their Bowies, others repaired or waxed their saddles or tackle. They were aching to get back into action. This was why they had left their previous companies for three months temporary duty.

Just after an early dinner, Tate dispatched Companies B and C to positions agreed upon near villages attacked most. He and Decker took two rangers from Company A, which was protecting the encampment, with them to patrol between the two deployed companies. The instructions from the captain were clear: you hear shots, you ride like hell towards the gunfire. He said riding *towards* danger was the difference between a ranger and about anyone else.

Tate based moving all men towards gunfire on the fact the raiding parties had never hit twice in a night nor during daytime. He felt comfortable playing the percentages.

He and his three riding companions walked their horses between the two companies all Thursday night. The only sounds were the wind, cicadas, a few birds, and one lonely coyote.

Just before dawn, the rangers returned to camp, to eat breakfast and sleep.

Tate told Company B to sleep well. They had the duty again tonight. Companies C and A would swop positions. Bock and two rangers from B would ride with him tonight.

He lay across his cot, only boots and gun-belt removed and slept deeply after coffee, biscuits and bacon.

Most of last night's nightriders slept through lunch, awoke for dinner and made their mounts ready just after. The men rode out, feeling sure tonight would be the night.

It was Tate and Bock and their two rangers who first heard suspicious sound of silence in the night.

Suddenly, Tate raised up his arm, to silently stop the men and have them listen with him. The nights sounds had vanished and only the sound of the wind cold be heard.

The birds had stopped chirping. The only sound was the wind.

Indian ponies were not shoed and made virtually no sound on the prairie loam.

Tate, using the old scout tracker trick, blew the air out of his nose. The fresh air coming in brought a faint scent. It was not man, but hinted at horses.

They were about a mile from Cottonwood Grove, where Company C was stationed. Company A was at a ranch a few miles away...maybe three. The night was clear and the sound of rifle shots should carry over to them.

The four rangers removed their Winchesters from their scabbards. They did not lever cartridges into the chamber and give away their position with the metallic "clack, clack" of the lever opening and then closing as the action pushed a cartridge into the chamber.

They knew the sound would carry on the wind.

They saw shadows. It was at least eight riders, walking their horses slowly. They were Indians, not cow herders from a ranch.

Tate knew he should do the right thing, so he called out "Texas Rangers! Halt!"

As he knew, it was greeted by immediate movement as horses whirled and the braves shouldered rifles.

But, the four rangers were already shouldered and four shots, immediately followed by another round sounded before any from the raiding party.

Several braves dropped. Six or seven returned fire with no effect on the rangers who were still levering and pressing the triggers on their .44-40 Winchesters.

The remaining braves spun their horses around and rode hell for leather towards the approximate boundary of Indian Territory.

The rangers rode in hot pursuit, firing and reloading at full gallop.

With the gunfire, Tate could not hear Company C responding, but he felt it. Soon, he could see the ten rangers arcing off to the right to cut the braves off.

By the time Tate, Bock and the two rangers arrived where Company C stopped, all the braves were down. Two were alive, but grievously wounded and would not survive much longer. The .44-40 bullet in a Colt was powerful, but the additional velocity added by the carbine's longer barrel made it more effective. .44-40 or .45 Colt were both almost half an inch diameter of lead and a mean proposition, Tate knew.

Tate sent five rangers back to where the firefight had begun to recover those bodies and horses.

The rangers collected rifles and knives, put the dead and dying on horses and took them to the Indian Territory line. At least as best they could determine it.

They left them there to be found as a hint to future raiders. "Would it work?" Tate wondered. He doubted it. But, it was a statement.

On the way back, Bock asked Tate a question, with much more temerity than he usually expressed.

"Sir, why did you call for them to halt instead of just opening up on them?"

"It just didn't seem right to start killing them in cold blood, Charlie. There's the difference between good men and bad. We have to represent the good. The Texas Rangers prevailed tonight. None of those braves will ever set fire to a barn or kill a family again. I just hope the message has the right effect and does not start a war. Either way, we did what the state sent us here to do tonight. And, we didn't lose a single ranger. It's a helluva lot better than a lot of ranger patrols all of us remember."

"True, sir. Just wondering," Charlie Bock said.

"Keep wondering and asking Charlie. I want you to always to question things, Sergeant."

They followed the same procedure for the next

week and no further attacks occurred.

Tate knew they may have killed a primary group of trouble makers, but there were five major tribes living in the Indian Territory. His greatest fear was a mass retaliation his thirty men could not handle. Or, survive. Little Big Horn a couple years ago proved such a thing could happen.

Not only did the tribes under Crazy Horse overpower Custer and his Seventh Cavalry, in Tate's reckoning, they used a sounder strategy.

Only time would tell. His plan was to keep two companies at the current positions for a while, then taper down to one alternating the positions.

He decided to send out his two scouts tonight. One would go to each position and at nine o'clock, the western rider would fire three shots with his Winchester. The eastern one would fire five shots soon after.

He would listen to see if he heard the shots from the ranger encampment. During the skirmish last night, nobody at the camp heard gunfire. But, they were closer to the state line. The location put them a crucial couple of miles further away.

Tate's concern, voiced with his two sergeants, was if an unexpected attack occurred on a different night of the week than Thursday or Friday or, during daylight hours. Could the rangers hear it and respond in time to make a difference?

"What do you think, Charlie?" Tate asked his senior sergeant.

"I think it's iffy. Depends on which way the wind is blowing whether we hear shots. Maybe Sharps buffalo gun shots. Pistol cartridges shot in a rifle….I just don't know, Cap."

Tate took out his gift watch from Eve. He admired her beautiful likeness before focusing on the time.

The two listened hard at nine o'clock. They heard three faint shots from the western-most rider. They heard even fainter shots a few minutes later from the one further east.

"You are right, Charlie. A little more wind or distance and they would be impossible to hear. So, my idea of keeping the men here and having sentries listen for shots and rally the men to respond won't work. I am afraid we are going to have to send out patrols on Thursdays and Fridays," Tate said.

"I am afraid so. Two or three guys riding are less apt to get themselves killed. You know, moving targets instead of setting up sentry nests and getting their throats slit," Charlie said.

None of the villages near them had telegraph. One had a small store and stage station. The stage dropped off mail, so the store served as an unofficial post office.

During the day, Tate wrote a letter to Eve and told her how to respond. He also put his reports of the status and action into an envelope for Austin. He was not sure how long it would take to get to the capital, but guessed no more than a week.

It was time for a resupply, so he grabbed three other rangers to ride escort with him. They rode two in front, two in back of one of the wagons on the way to the nearest town. In addition to the voucher paid supplies, Tate picked up two large bags of cigarette tobacco and two bags of chewing plugs for the men. He added a couple hundred wrapping papers. Tate thought about whiskey, but decided not to foster its use in camp.

"Henry," Tate said to the cook and wagon driver as they were loading supplies on the wagon, "Offer the men to fill their pouches with tobacco and take papers and plugs of chewing tobacco as they need during lunch, okay?" Henry nodded.

A wagon with four outriders attracted a bit of attention. Tate noticed several low-life's watching them and warned his rangers, all of whom had their badges hidden by their vests or coats, about it.

Tate went back in the store to sign the Texas Treasury voucher and asked the shop keep about the group of men watching so hard.

"Cap, they're new to town. Rode in last night and drank a fair amount. I have a feeling they don't know y'all are rangers. Your supplies would bring several times the money in Indian Territory. And, they don't know what you got. Might be ammunition and whisky, or ranch cash wages. May want to keep your eyes open on the trail."

"We will. Those fellas look stupid enough to try to jump us. Even without badges, we don't look like pushovers. I think you are right. Maybe the best thing is to go over and have a little talk with them," Tate said.

"Too late," the shop keep said, nodding his head towards the dirt path street as the four men mounted up and rode off fast.

"I guess. Well, listen for the sound of shots in the not too distant future. Thanks for the supplies," Tate said as he signed the voucher.

As he mounted Thunder, he said "I suspect you men saw those four no-accounts watching us. They look like folks who would try something stupid without having a clue who the hell they are trying it on! Keep your guns ready to use on a moment's notice. Same two in front, two in back formation back to camp."

The dust from the four was still in the air as they rode on the trail back to the ranger encampment.

Tate, on front right, looked for an ambush point. The only one he saw was about half a mile ahead. It was possibly within hearing of the camp, but all the wind would have to do is change direction for shots to not be heard by the other rangers.

"I'd say let's keep our long guns in their scabbards until they get in range if something goes down. We should be fast enough to take them down before they get into revolver range. I didn't see any rifles on their horses," Tate said.

Sure enough, when the wagon and its outriders approached the small stand of trees, four riders galloped out from behind it, revolvers out and raised.

All four rangers pulled their Winchesters and the driver came up with a short barrel shotgun and cocked two mule ear hammers.

The outlaws began firing and Tate could see the puffs of dust as bullets struck the ground fifty feet in front of them.

The ill-advised outlaws rode towards them at full gallop with two in front and the two behind shooting over the heads of the ones they followed.

The rangers' rifle fire knocked the front two outlaws off their horses and dropped them under the hooves of those following them. Both men were trampled and one horse stumbled over the body and threw its rider. He hit hard, flopped twice and lay still. The fourth rider threw up his hands, his revolver dropping to the earth.

Tate and his rangers checked the downed men. All were dead. He questioned the survivor, who admitted he thought they were just guards who had gold or whisky on the wagon they were protecting. He seemed surprised to learn he had just attacked the Texas Rangers. Tate formally arrested him for attempted murder of a Texas Ranger, a sure hanging offense. They tied the dead outlaws over their horses and the prisoner with a latigo and returned to the town.

The shop owner seemed to be the most responsible person in town. He would likely be the mayor if they ever got around to such things, Tate thought.

"I am confiscating these horses for the State of Texas. Do you think their guns and saddles would bring enough to bury them and get a one-way stage ticket to Lubbock and one two-way?" Tate asked.

"We could get 'em buried for the guns and saddles. Doubt after we use the gun and saddle money to bury them, the remainder would cover stage tickets."

"Well, do it and I'll write out another treasury voucher for the stage tickets. When's it due?" Tate asked.

"In one hour."

They took care of the paperwork, including Tate writing out the charges against the man and signing them.

He assigned one ranger to escort the prisoner to Lubbock and take the stage back. The shopkeeper promised to look after his horse as part of the deal.

The ranger procession got back to the camp in time for dinner. One cook decided to give out the tobacco supplies as the other cook dished out venison stew to the companies.

Tate spent the time after dinner writing up the incident report and accompanying arrest report for Austin. He included a receipt for the treasury vouchers in the envelope. Like most lawmen, he did not like paperwork. He knew he needed to get used to it if he was going to be a county sheriff one day, though. He then cleaned his Winchester after using it to dispatch at least one of the two front outlaws.

He went out as Decker dispatched the Sunday through Thursday patrols. The three patrols consisted of three rangers from each of the companies. One would patrol around the ranger encampment, one between the western ranches and villages, and the last around the eastward ones. They would be close enough to hear gunfire and respond, after sending one rider back to camp for reinforcements.

Tate came back in with a mug of fresh coffee. At least it was fresh by rangers camping in the rough.

Tate was not a man to note "credits" by carving notches on the grips of his Colt or butt stock of his Winchester. Hell, he thought, if he was, he would have to replace his wood. Then, he reminded himself he already had replaced the stock on his Winchester.

Without a wife or Cisco to talk with, he turned in for the night, hoping not to hear gunfire. He did not.

*****

The next two months did not bring anything of interest. The rangers rested, hunted and fished, providing a good vacation from bacon and beans.

They responded to shots fired in the middle of the night on Thursdays and Fridays six times, always in time to prevent horse or cattle theft or barn burnings.

The villagers, or in one case, ranchers exchanged shots with the raiding parties with no casualties on either side.

On a very still and clear Wednesday night, a volley of gunshots filled the air at two in the morning.

Nine rangers were already out on the three patrols. Tate was not able to determine if they fired the shots or someone else. He scrambled two companies and they rode as fast as possible towards the shots, leaving one company to guard the camp. The guard company was down to seven men, plus the two cooks and wagon drivers.

As Tate, Bock and fourteen rangers rode at full gallop, he wondered if it was a set-up.

Within fifteen minutes, they arrived at a small valley where one of the three man patrols was held up in a gulch.

"Cap, we was bushwhacked by a small group of Indians. They moved off quick. It didn't make sense," one of the rangers said.

They immediately heard a lot more shooting coming from the area of the encampment. It *was* a setup!

"Come on, men! Back to the camp, now!" Tate yelled, turning the big horse on a dime and galloping off, a larger group of eighteen following closely, ready to fight.

But, their leader was damning himself for being taken in by a ruse. He spurred the black horse on, the front brim of his Stetson flattened back against the crown.

When they arrived at the ranger encampment, the attack was over. Two rangers were dead and one wounded.

"It was a better prepared attack than what we have heard about," Charlie Bock said, bloodied but not seriously wounded.

He walked Tate over to the one brave who had been killed and left, saying he thought they hit and seriously wounded several who were helped up onto other's horses and ridden off double.

Tate looked down at the brave. He was a handsome man, probably in his late thirties. His torso showed battle scars from cutting instruments and bullets, long healed. He was lean, but well-fed and muscular.

"Charlie, were the others who rode in here like him. You know, experienced fighters. Not kids," Tate asked his sergeant.

"Just like him. I'd swear some were in their forties," Tate responded. "There were ten," he added.

"This is a retaliation and a message. Get the cooks to put together field ration kits for Company A. I will lead and take Decker with me, okay Allen?" Decker nodded. "If we leave now, dark or not, I can cut some sign. We'll catch up with them before they get too deep into the Territory. 'Specially if a couple are ridding double. It will also aid tracking," Decker said.

"Alright men, listen up. I want Company A, less three men to ride patrol, to come with Sergeant Decker and me. Make sure you have extra ammo and at least one canteen of water. The cooks are fixing up food bags for each of us." He looked over at the cooks. One motioned "ten minutes."

"We will leave in ten minutes and will ride hard."

"I want these experienced braves brought to justice. Tonight, if possible. Otherwise, we'll ride until we get them. Everybody got it?"

Tate looked over his men, not only the scrambling Company A. Everyone was ready for war.

"Charlie Hock is in charge until Allen Decker and I get back. Everybody be careful and alert. Charlie, look to the dead after you get the wound wrapped up."

He went to his tent and got his own bedroll. He already had a rifle and plenty of ammunition on Thunder. His canteen was fresh, but he grabbed a second one and slung it from Thunder's horn.

Tate threw a long leg over Thunder's saddle and yelled "Ride Rangers! And, they took off, Tate and scout Decker in the front.

CHAPTER 12

They rode hard at first, then eased off. The last thing Tate wanted to do was ride up on the Indians without meaning to.

Decker stopped after a half hour and gathered some pine branches and broke them. He struck his steel against his knife by the branches and they flared up from the sap. He used the short-term torch to study the horse tracks in front of him. All were unshorn. Several were deeper.. These were the ponies carrying two men.

"There's no trail dust in the tracks and they are as deep as when the ponies ran by. So, we are within minutes behind them. Captain, I'd slow down or we're gonna run up on them unexpectedly. As long as they are pushing it this hard, I don't think they will hear us until we are real close," Decker said.

"You're the scout, Sergeant. We'll follow your lead," came Tate's response.

They followed for another hour before stopping to confer.

"Cap, I figure we are well into Indian Territory now. They have slowed. See how the hoof prints are closer?" Decker said.

"I do. If they don't know we're after them and they are carrying double and maybe wounded on several ponies, they may plan on stopping soon. These ponies are not as big and strong as our mounts. Carrying double is hard on them."

The ranger scout nodded.

"I am thinking a dry camp with three guards posted. Think it's time for camp, Allen?"

"I don't think we have much chance. Both parties are tired. They probably have wounded to tend. Bad conditions for a fight for either of us."

"Alright men, dismount and prepare a quiet and dry camp. Sergeant Decker will assign guard duties. Allen, make sure I get my turn, too?" Tate said.

"But, you're a captain," Decker began. Tate interrupted by holding up his hand.

"I'm a ranger first. And, we are short-handed. Everybody has to pull his weight," Tate responded.

Tate took the saddle off Thunder and set it where he planned to sleep. He walked the horse over to where a ranger had found some graze and hobbled him after giving him a Stetson full of water from his canteen.

Back at the saddle, he unrolled his bedroll. He did

not have to tell these battle-hardened frontier fighters to keep a cold camp. Some coffee would be good. Real good. But, not tonight. They were right up on the men they were chasing and could not take the chance. Like them, these braves were mature, experienced fighters not to be taken lightly.

Decker rode out before dawn to see if he could identify where the braves were camped. Ten minutes later, the rangers heard shots and hoof beats. They took rifle positions, both kneeling and laying behind saddles because no better cover was available.

They held their fire until Tate gave the command to shoot.

Decker was pushing his buckskin gelding as fast as a fast horse could go, turning backwards in the saddle and firing his Colt as he rode.

Six braves rode hard behind him, firing rifles.

Knowing he was near his own camp, Decker turned off sharply at the last minute and Tate gave the command "Fire!"

Five of the six braves fell from their horses at the withering rifle fire. The falling men tripped one pony and the sixth rider hit the ground. He was dazed when several rangers took him into custody.

Tate saw he had a cut on the forehead and a lump above it. He retrieved his black walnut salve and applied it to both as a ranger tied the brave's hands behind him with a latigo. As he came to, Tate gave him some water from his canteen.

Tate looked up and Decker was not only okay, but had finished checking the downed braves. He looked at Tate and gave a thumbs down, indicating all were dead.

The brave was fully awake, looking around with dark eyes. He did not show fear. Mainly anger and perhaps confusion about being given water.

"Start now. No need to wait," he said in flawless English.

"Wait for what?" Tate asked.

"Whatever torture you do. Or hanging or whatever. Just remember, you are on our ground now. You have no authority here."

"We know where we are and where our official authority ended. But, your war party killed some of my Texas Rangers where *I do* have authority. I believe I am authorized to chase you over a state or territory line. You kill a Texas Ranger and rangers will follow you until they catch you. It's always been the policy."

"How are you called?"

"I am called Tate. How are you called?"

"I am Mukwooru."

"Mukwooru, I have a mission. It's to have these cross-border raids end. Maybe you and I can figure out how. But, if we don't the folks in Washington are going to send a lot of blue coats. And, when you kill one, five more will appear. Nobody wins."

"These raids. They were training and practice for

our young braves. Almost nobody got hurt. White eyes lost a few horses. A few cattle. We don't want to make big ranches and raise these animals. We ride or eat the few we take."

"I understand. But, these animals come from poor ranchers or farmers who also need them for their families to ride or eat. It has to stop before more people red and white die needlessly."

"Perhaps, you should talk with our chief."

"Quanah Parker? The army and Indian agent would not like me talking with him."

"The chief talks with whoever he wishes. He does not answer to those people at Ft. Sill. Only they think he does. The rest of us laugh about it," Mukwooru said.

"Does he ever come this far west?"

"No. But, his sub-chief is nearby now. He is another son of Peta Nocona."

"And, Peta Nocona and Cynthia Ann Parker were Chief Quanah Parker's parents?" Tate asked for clarity.

"Yes."

"How is the son of Peta Nocona called?" Tate asked.

"He is just Nocona."

"If he and I met and made an agreement, would it be binding with Chief Quanah Parker?" Tate asked.

"It would. This is a small thing to us. Young men doing what young men do," Mukwooru observed to Tate.

"How would we do this? You and I ride into the Territory to meet with him?" Tate asked.

The brave nodded.

The rangers observing had mixed emotions. They wanted to hang the brave for his participation in killing some of their own. But, they were wise enough to know a meeting between this sub-chief and the captain could prevent other deaths, including their own. It could, of course, cause the captain to meet his own death, unprotected, deep in the Territory. But, such was his chance to take.

"Allen, could you arrange cooking the breakfast we never had and making some coffee? I'd like to ride up into the Territory with a full belly. I bet you and our new pard here would like to eat something too," Tate asked.

A fire was built and biscuits were removed from bags along with honey and bacon. The bacon was frying within half an hour and coffee was ready earlier.

Mukwooru ate with the rangers. This was not an unusual thing for Decker and a couple others who had shared many meals with other scouts when scouting for the army. The scout contingent was frequently a blend of whites and Indians.

"Allen, you take the men back to camp. Make sure nobody discusses where I have gone or what I am doing, with a single living soul! If Mukwooru, Nocona, and I can work out a peaceful solution to these raids, everybody wins. If not, we tried."

"I'll make sure, Cap. Good luck to you fellas. This beats hell out of us killing each other."

Mukwooru's pony was standing by and the two men mounted. Tate handed the brave his rifle, an 1866 Winchester, as well as his pouch with extra cartridges.

The brave's head was bandaged to protect the head wound from the fall. They rode northeast and the rangers broke camp and rode towards the ranger camp.

The two men who were shooting at one another an hour ago rode for another hour into the Territory.

"Will you remember how to bring people back here?" Mukwooru asked.

"No, but I am trying to remember how to get home from here. I don't care about anything else, nor do I plan to come back."

The Comanche seemed content with the answer. Shortly thereafter, Tate heard an unfamiliar bird call.

Mukwooru answered it with a shrill whistle Tate wished he could emulate.

Twenty Indians on foot materialized from the woods like wraiths. They did not attack Tate. He was pretty sure it was because Mukwooru had his rifle and clearly was under no duress.

Soon the group was at a camp. Mukwooru slipped off the pony and Tate dismounted Thunder.

Tate followed Mukwooru over to the fire. Several Comanches sat at it. All were in their fifties or sixties, yet exuded power and strength. The center man was Nocona.

"Nocona, this man is called Tate. He leads the Texas Rangers. He has killed our young men and the men of my party. We have killed some of his rangers in turn. He comes as my guest to sit and speak with us about a truce. Will you hear him?"

"A truce, or a surrender?" the older man asked Tate.

"We are not at war, so a truce. Mukwooru has told me the earlier raids are young men doing what young men will do. I am here to ask for the raids to stop. Nothing more," Tate said.

"Who do you speak for?" Nocona asked.

"I speak only for myself and the thirty men I lead. They are policemen, not soldiers. I have no other authority, and come to you to talk man-to-man. My government would punish me if they knew I was doing this."

"Tate, what is in this for the Comanches?"

"The only thing is if no parties raid, we no longer have to shoot at each other. Nothing more."

"You do not ask much for a white man," Nocona said.

"I do not," Tate replied.

"I will ask my young men to stop coming across and making you shoot at them."

"This is all I ask of you. I ask nothing else."

"Go back to your people and tell them it is so," Nocona said.

Tate stood and gave a slight bow in deference to the other man's position and turned to Mukwooru. He nodded at the man, mounted Thunder and rode south to Texas.

******

Back at the homestead, Eve finished her novel version of the story about the Union prison for Confederate spies and what happened there. With Jubal's advice, she further distanced the story from them by having a former Confederate Texas Ranger ride after the prison warden and his subordinates and administer rough justice. All names were changed.

Jubal, after giving it more thought, urged her to send inquiries only to Atlanta, Richmond, Houston and Dallas publishers due to the continuing sensitivities between the two sides only thirteen years later. She got five letters underway and began working on multiple manuscript copies to send to anyone who showed interest. Eve also chose a masculine pen name for both her personal security and for marketing purposes. Very few women were yet taken seriously as authors in 1878, something she knew would change quickly with suffrage and women starting to run for political office. She was not far off from being right on the second contention, as a woman would be elected as a city mayor in four years.

She accomplished these tasks diligently during the first month Tate was back in Texas. Now, the wait began. Eve had a set of four backup handwritten manuscripts by the time her husband returned to Colorado, yet had not heard from any publisher.

CHAPTER 13

Tate rode back without a sense of accomplishment. He wanted to trust the two men he just met. But, it was all too easy. Tate knew he could lose his job in Texas for negotiating like this, but had to report it. Carefully report it.

He knew the federals would take great exception to an officer of Texas riding into Indian Territory and negotiating with a Comanche chief. Especially with no federal present and no federal even being aware of it.

Could he be arrested for it? He did not know. Woe unto the federal marshal who came to arrest him for trying to make peace.

He made it back to the ranger encampment just before dark. He had a bowl of stew, some cornbread, and a cup of coffee while briefing his two sergeants.

The three and their remaining battalion hoped for the best.

The next morning, Tate wrote a carefully crafted report to Austin detailing he had an unexpected opportunity to meet with some Comanche leadership on relatively neutral ground and they agreed to cease the raids by wild young braves. Tate went on to say he had some faith they might live up to their promises. Only time will tell. He asked if sufficient funds were available to keep half the battalion in place for another three months, with Hock in charge. He said he needed to get back to his new wife and perfect the claim on his homestead when his contract ran out in a week.

During the remaining time, there was no raiding party activity. Tate, one sergeant and several rangers visited each village and ranch and advised their term had run its course and they were uncertain as to whether a contingent would be left until they heard from Austin.

Several days before the final day of his contract the return letter arrived. The Attorney General said no funds were currently available and his temporary duty rangers were to return to their previous companies. He specified which companies were to get the two wagons, remuda of horses and remainder of supplies.

He thanked Tate and the men for a good job. And, there was nothing else.

On the last day, Tate expressed his own gratitude and received a round of applause from the normally taciturn group of hardened men. He shook hands with each, packed his meager gear on Thunder and headed for a railhead.

He took the train to Denver and found a horse trader. The man was enamored of war horses and wanted Thunder for himself. Tate had a lot of respect for the horse and wanted him to go somewhere he would be taken care of and appreciated. He felt the horse trader would do both. He swapped Thunder for a small paint cow pony for Eve and a young, strong mule. He patted the big horse and thanked him for the loyal service, walking away a bit sadly.

He saddled the cow pony and put a lead on the mule and headed south to home. A word he had not used for a long time.

While the smaller mare felt different, she proved to be a good horse, with the toughness and endurance characteristic of a cowboy's working horse. Her disposition was good and she seemed responsive to conversation, something Tate knew his wife would like. He would hold off and let Eve name her.

The mule was young and frisky, but promised good strength. Famous men like the late Wild Bill Hickok and General Crook chose mules to ride daily. He would check the mule for riding later. But, mainly he wanted him for a replacement for buckboard and plow use for Jubal.

Tate even found himself whistling on the ride home. He did not send a letter saying he was on the way, because he knew with the mail service out of where he was had been in Texas, he would get there before a letter could. Expansion of the telegraph lines would help the far-flung areas of the West, he knew. Still, with the homesteads out from Manitou Springs, they had to check in town for mail and telegrams. Delivery would be many years off.

It was a bright spring day, birds were singing and he could smell the new grass and flowers.

Leaving his men gave him a bittersweet feeling. Though they had only ridden together for three months, some of the times had been intense action.

Tate was honored at the gratitude each expressed upon parting. It was clear to him they respected his leadership and knew he had their backs. A captain of rangers could ask for no more. The second benefit was even more significant; being able to come home in one piece at the end of the tour.

It was around lunch and he was feeling hungry as he rode into Manitou Springs. He checked for mail and sent a telegram of appreciation to the Attorney General. He went to the general mercantile and bought a new dress for Eve. Tate knew the size without even thinking about it. He reckoned the color would show well with her auburn hair, and he added a hair clip for those thick, beautiful locks. As an afterthought, he picked out some dress material for Darlene and asked for enough for two average size dresses.

Mounting the cow pony and taking the lead for

the mule in hand, he headed towards Pike's Peak. He would skirt it and reach home soon.

Before he cleared the woods on the path into the shared big yard between the two homesteads, he sang out "Hello, the ranch!" No need having his wife shoot him on homecoming day.

Jubal and Darlene came out of Jubal's cabin, not surprising Tate at all. Then, Eve came out, broke into a smile, hitched her dress up and sprinted towards him. He heard Cisco whistle in the corral.

Home was the hunter, home from the hill.

He slid off the cow pony and picked up Eve and swung her in a great circle before kissing her.

"Have you been riding this beautiful little horse for three months at your height," she asked.

"Nope. Bought her for you the other day! Now, you have to name her."

Jubal came over and hugged his new nephew as did Darlene White.

"Jubal, I picked up this mule for you. I was thinking about giving your horse a rest from pulling the buckboard and maybe using the mule for your pulling tasks. He does not have a name, so like Eve, you gotta name your new steed."

The former Confederate spy looked over the mule with as much excitement as Eve did her cow pony. Tate gave Eve and Darlene each two bags with folded material from the general mercantile and both were delighted with the respective dresses and material.

"Why Tate," Darlene said, "you didn't have to get me anything, but the cloth surely is beautiful."

"I knew Eve's size and figured you were taller and I better not guess, so the lady in the store said it was enough to make two average dresses," he replied, getting another hug from the lovely brunette.

After dinner together, the couples went to their respective cabins for the night.

Tate finally lay in bed with his wife's head on his shoulder, a strong arm holding her to him.

"Maybe your uncle is not so old, the way he looks at Darlene," he said.

"I think the prison aged him prematurely and turned his hair white. All those bullet wounds within such a short time of each other didn't help either. He's barely fifty, Morgan," Eve whispered.

"I believe Darlene has been a good influence on his health. He looked spryer today than I've ever seen him. Think they will marry soon?"

"Yes. I think they were waiting for you to get back," she responded.

"I'm glad. Jubal's cabin will become a real home, like ours."

"Morgan?" Eve asked.

"What, honey?"

"What will you do now?" she asked, seriously.

"Get the place in shape. Help Jubal get in the seeds

we both need for hay and food for us. Corn, beans, and squash for sure. Maybe a fruit or nut tree to produce for us in a few years. I need to lay in plenty of firewood for the two places for the winter. Then, I guess report to the sheriff and pin on a deputy badge," he replied.

"After being a captain of rangers, will you be content being just a deputy?" Eve asked.

"For a while, I guess, honey. I don't know how long Sheriff Hansen plans on staying in office. Hell, I don't even know his political party. But, I'll have some time to learn, I guess."

*****

At the same time several hundred yards away, Jubal and Darlene were having a somewhat similar planning conversation.

"You know, Darlene, we are very close," he said to the woman lying in his arms.

"Ya think?" she said tugging his beard.

"I know. What I was thinking is we swap histories so there's no mystery about who we are or where we came from. What do you think?" Jubal said.

"I don't have any secrets, do you?" she responded.

"Yes, I do."

"Then, you'd better go first," she said.

"Okay. First off, I am now using my birth name. The one under which I graduated from Virginia Military Institute. I was commissioned an officer in the US Army immediately after. I was an engineer and rose to the rank of major. When Virginia seceded, so did I. I took a position as major in the Confederate secret service. I was a spy. I got captured about a year after Gettysburg and was put in a secret prison for spies. The people who were after us, and who Tate killed, were the army officer wardens."

"Let me interrupt, Jubal," Darlene said. "Why would they want to kill you and Eve. The war has been over thirteen years."

"Because the prison was illegal. It violated the Uniform Code of Military Justice. And, because of the fact they burned twenty-five Confederate spy prisoners to death deliberately upon hearing Lee surrendered at Appomattox. I was the only survivor and got away after killing an escaping guard named Hiram Stone and taking his name. I may look seventy-five," Darlene shook her head vigorously to the contrary, "with this white hair and beard from the starvation and torture, but I am really fifty-two. The four bullet wounds I've gotten in the past five months have not helped my image by impairing my movements either."

"Jubal, can't you report this?"

"Eve wrote it up in a book, but I'm making her call it a novel. Who in the Yankee army would believe a Confederate spy with no proof?" he asked.

"I guess..." she said, thinking.

"I had no family left after the war but a sister and a niece. My sister knew some of the story And my niece Eve learned it recently. My sister is dead. I was listed dead. So, I can just pick up and continue my life now. With you, if you'll have a beat up old spy," he said hopefully.

"Not so old. I am forty-seven. We aren't far apart at all. Do you have more?" she asked.

"Nope. That's pretty much it."

"I grew up in South Carolina and married a man ten years older. We had a farm in Georgia and eventually lost it on Sherman's march. My husband was a good man. Neither generous nor romantic, but not a drunk or an abuser. He was just there. He joined the army in Georgia and died in the fighting around Richmond.

I heard of a group putting together a wagon train to Colorado around the surrender and joined it. I had a couple of mules and a wagon left. And, some furniture I hid when the Yankees came through burning. I hid the mules too, because they killed every living thing they saw. Once I got going, I never looked back. In Denver, I sold the wagon and one mule for some cash and rode the other down here. I was one of the lucky ones. I found a job where we met. Some of the women on the wagon train had to become whores. I want you to know I never did such thing ."

"Darlene is a name I never heard before," Jubal said, his statement more of a question.

"It was my mother's family name. It's a version of Darling. English and Scottish mainly. Just like boys get a family name like Morgan Tate did, I got a family name. Darlene McGregor. Then, White."

"So, here we are, lying here like a couple newly-weds," Jubal began. "We ought to find a preacher or justice of the peace and make us a legal couple. What do you think?"

"It's more romantic than 'I need somebody to push the plow,' so I'll say yes. I'd be honored to be the wife of a former Confederate spy." He kissed her and they laid there staring at the ceiling for a while.

The next morning, each couple had their own breakfast, but met in the middle grass later.

"Morgan, I guess Darlene and I have an announcement to make," Jubal said.

"So, when are you getting married?" Tate asked.

"Soon as we can. I don't want people talking about her spending so much time up here."

"I'm betting nobody's worried about it, but you ought to tie the knot. Maybe have real wedding."

"I was there when the scallywag of a preacher denied you and Eve. I was thinking of shooting him."

"Me, too."

"But lead and powder is expensive."

"There was always a knife. I had my Bowie with me."

"Didn't think of the Bowie. Anyway, I will check with the other preacher. If he's as persnickety as the one you talked with, we'll all four go over to the justice of the peace again," Jubal said.

"Let me know when and I'll put my suit on," Tate offered.

"Then, Darlene and I have to get busy and make up a dress out of her new material Morgan bought her," Eve said with the older woman's silent but eager support.

They planned a trip to the El Paso County court on Friday, two days hence. Tate was going to accomplish another thing, assuming the sheriff was in. He was going to say he would be ready to start as a deputy in two weeks.

In the meantime, Tate wanted to get some firewood cut and seasoned for both families. Jubal had a length of logging chain and they adjusted the buckboard harness to enable the mule to pull logs with the chain.

Tate rode Cisco into the woods and selected trees, which he used the axe to blaze with a slash. He made a point of choosing trees on a hillside so he could fell them downhill and the mule could tow them downhill.

Both Tate and Jubal were recovering from bullet wounds, though the older man had more. Tate did not want him to hurt himself further, but Jubal assured him he could hook the chain to trees and lead the mule downhill to the woodlot they designated convenient to both spreads. The easiest thing would be for the mule to drag the chain, instead of carrying it awkwardly, so only one end was hooked to the harness.

They left later in the afternoon to begin the task. A bucksaw would have helped, but they did not have a saw.

Tate felled two good trees, then chopped the branches off one. He started on the second as Jubal chained the first. By the time Jubal was finished, the second was ready for the chain and Tate was working on another tree. The trees were ones with dying branches, but their main logs were fit for burning after a bit of drying.

They found out quickly the mule could only handle one tree at a time. They started home with the first, but had all three in place by the end of the day. Tate's side hurt where the bullet was removed. Jubal did not say anything, but his movements were obviously slow and pained. Darlene had ridden to work earlier and Eve rode with her on the new cow pony, so neither woman was aware of the toll the wood collection had taken until later.

It proceeded the following day, putting six twenty- foot hardwood logs in the wood yard. Tate was determined to pick up a crosscut saw on the Friday visit to Colorado Springs.

On Friday, Jubal hooked the mule, by now named Tecumseh for the jackass who burned down Darlene's farm, to the buckboard. He set his newly given Winchester in the bed and pulled a tarp over it.

The two women dressed in their new dresses climbed in with him and Tate in a dark suit mounted Cisco.

Tate had not realized how pretty Darlene was, with a new dress from the material he bought her, hair fixed and the glow of a soon-to-be bride, she looked lovely and years younger.

They rode past Manitou Springs and onto Colorado Springs. At the courthouse, they arranged for a magistrate to conduct the marriage and went to lunch.

Afterwards, Jubal and the women went to the general mercantile and looked for a saw for the logs. Tate walked down to the sheriff's office and inquired about Sheriff Hansen.

"C'mon in, Tate and tell me about your term as ranger captain," the white-haired sheriff said.

"We had some fighting and worked out a peace agreement with Quanah Parker's half-brother, a sub-chief."

"Think it will keep the raiding parties on their side of the Indian Territory line?" the sheriff asked.

"I hope so. Nocona was pretty logical and straightforward. I believed him. I didn't ask for much, just for the raids to stop and he said okay," Tate said.

"Wal, I expect it took more politicking on your part than you're admitting to, but the important thing is you negotiated peace instead of bringing in a bunch of soldiers and slaughtering everybody."

"On another subject, I am within two weeks of being ready to work for you.... if the job offer is still open?" Tate asked.

"It is. Let's talk about how to structure it."

"Alright."

"I have two thousand one hundred plus square miles. A lot of its uphill. I have ten deputies. I have a couple of towns and more villages. In addition to Colorado Springs and Manitou Springs, I have Fountain Creek, Green Mountain Falls, Palmer Lake and Old Zounds. Four of these places — the biggest ones — have a town marshal and a night marshal as their only law enforcement. Take a minute and help me figure out how to cover all of these towns and land with ten men plus you."

Tate considered the sheriff's dilemma and applied some logic.

"How about if you worked deals with the places with a marshal and a night marshal to deputize them and offer to supervise them. The towns would still cover their salaries. So, you'd have two men at all times in those areas and your ten patrolling them and unincorporated territory. You'd need a chief deputy or undersheriff to ride herd on the new structure and head the occasional posse and the like. I might be the man to help you there," Tate said.

"I surely will. Have to be the right man," Hansen said thoughtfully. "It would take two separate steps to put into place and I think I can sell both. First, I'd have to get the county government to approve a chief deputy. It would be pretty easy, given our growth. Second, you and I would have to visit the village leaders everywhere else and convince them to keep paying their policemen, but let us deputize them and supervise them."

"If they could get past the ego of managing the policemen themselves, what we would be telling them should take a load off their non-lawman shoulders," Tate concluded.

"You sure hit on the right day. The county commission meets in an hour. I am due to give a status of crime and enforcement. I will give it a shot. Will you be in town another couple hours?" the sheriff asked.

"Yes, sir. I can be. My wife's uncle just got married down the way there. I promised to take them out for a marriage celebration dinner."

"Who'd he marry? Somebody from here?" Hansen asked.

"He married Darlene White, who works over in Manitou Springs."

"I know her. Good looking figure of a woman. She'll make him a fine wife. Is the uncle the one who is perfecting the homestead next to yours?"

"Yes, sir. He is. A fine good man."

"I've known Hulon Parker over in Trinidad and Marshal Hawkins in Raton both a while. They've kept me aware of the attempted kidnapping of your wife and the attacks on her uncle's place. The uncle's been shot up something fierce, hasn't he?" the sheriff asked.

"He has, but he's tough as a cob and has about recovered already. Eve returned fire well enough with a musket and a .41 revolver to stop the last attack," Tate said.

"According to Hawkins, as his temporary deputy, you went after the gang and they all died resisting arrest."

"Well, it was six hundred miles of sniping and shooting, so it was not so clear cut. But, you've got the summary pretty good," Tate replied.

"You want to share how many men you had to kill before you got back?"

"I will tell you, but it might not be a good selling point for the commissioners. They won't want some blood thirsty chief deputy killing everybody. Too much killing's what got Wild Bill fired in Abilene," Tate surmised.

"Tell me the story. I will use my knowledge judiciously," the sheriff promised.

"The three leaders were a major, lieutenant and sergeant who ran an illegal Union prison during the war. They burned it just after Lee surrendered and killed twenty-five trapped men, all prisoners of war. One survived. Eve's uncle. They came after them as witnesses to mass murder. The three added two gofers. Over a distance of maybe four hundred miles they killed some people for horses and shot me. I killed them one at a time, then three at a time. Plus, eight Indians attacked me and I had to take care of them."

"So, you took down thirteen men, Tate. Or, did I miscount?"

"No, Sheriff. Your tally is right. I have a couple

scars to show for it." Tate said.

"Okay, let me get my presentation prepared. I think I can do this and if I do, you and I can start talking with the town elders about the plan one by one."

Tate stuck out his hand. "Good hunting, Sheriff. I will be around town in case you get some fast news."

He walked out of the office with guarded optimism and sought out the rest of his party.

******

Tate found everyone looking at saws. He hefted several, knowing it would probably be a one-man operation, given Jubal's injuries. Finding one to his liking, he bought it and put it under the tarp in the bed of the buckboard. They walked around Colorado Springs for an hour or so.

Tate spied Sheriff Hansen walking down the street as if he was searching for someone. Tate waved to him and found he was the someone for whom the sheriff was looking.

"Tate, we are on! The commissioners loved the idea of a young former ranger captain backing me up as number two. I told them about the plan to deputize town marshals and night marshals and they supported it. More manpower at no extra cost to the county. A product which would sell every time! I won't put you on the payroll for the two weeks you asked for, but while you are in town, I'm willing to swear you in and give you a badge….just in case, you know," the sheriff said.

"Sounds good to me. Want us to walk over to the office and do it now? Then, you can be our guest at the wedding celebration dinner."

"Let's do the swearing in, but my wife has guests coming for dinner at our house, so I appreciate you kind offer, but have to turn it down," Hansen said.

They walked over to the office and Eve held the Bible as Tate swore to uphold the Constitution and enforce the laws of Colorado and ordinances of El Paso County. The sheriff pinned on a gold star and the deed was done. For now, Tate covered the badge on his vest with the lapel of his jacket. The early swearing in was just a contingency.

Tate did not give a thought to the fact his wedding and the one between Jubal and Darlene were quick and celebrated solely by dinner at a café.

This was the West. Weddings may have an element of love, but more often they were matters of convenience. Mail order brides were still common, due to the general lack of available and willing women in the West. He considered himself lucky to have a wife who loved him early on and one to whom he reciprocated the feeling. Usually, in his observation, love came later or not at all. It was hard being a man in the West. But, he knew, it was far more difficult to be a woman.

The dinner was enjoyed by all. The Paine's decided to have a one-night honeymoon, so Tate took the buckboard and Tecumseh to the livery. He and Eve rode Cisco back double. Hell, he thought. Maybe they should have a bit of a honeymoon, too.

******

Tate was under a time constraint to get the spread ready for him to devote more time being a chief deputy and less time being a rancher. He began sawing the logs into sections he could split into fireplace wood. Though he had chosen the driest trees he could, the hearts were still too green to saw easily, so the job was laborious at best. By lunch, he had only gone through half of the first log. He was one man with a two-man job. And, he was still healing from a bullet wound.

Eve called him to lunch. It included sweet tea she made by brewing strong tea and cutting it with cold water from the stream. The rest was beef sandwiches. Tate's side was sore from too much exercise with a bullet wound not yet fully healed, but he said nothing. It would just worry Eve. They sat out on a blanket in the grass and ate, as a spring breeze helped dry the perspiration covering the lawman.

Eve looked at him and smiled. The look and smile would have guaranteed her anything within his power to provide.

Over the next four days, he slowed down a bit, but finished sectioning the logs. The following week, he split and stacked them under a quickly constructed wood shed roof. Ever the gunman, he wore leather gloves and particularly protected his right hand. No longer used to manual labor, his hands were aching, but not blistered.

Every muscle in his body was sore when he put on pants, shirt, vest, badge, gun belt and hat on Monday to ride into Colorado Springs and report for duty as chief deputy sheriff of El Paso County, Colorado.

Cisco could feel the excitement and was glad to be trotting again. Feeling the weight of several nights camping gear and rifle scabbard which signaled he was back on the trail. Tate chatted with him the nine miles to Colorado Springs, something both had missed.

CHAPTER 14

Tate tied Cisco at the hitching rail in front of the sheriff's office in Colorado Springs. He walked in, spurs ringing on the oiled wooden floors. He was in dark clothes. Two bright spots were punctuated. The badge and the ivory grips he had installed on his Colt Frontier Model. Tate had learned a lot from his short time with William Barclay Masterson.

One lesson was a lawman's gun was one of the major symbols of office. Bat special ordered each of his guns directly from the Colt factory, specifying grips, barrel, and more. Tate had a lot of faith in his Colt and the action had smoothed to perfection. So, he dressed it up a little bit and had a gunsmith carefully fit the ivory grips the frame and taper them a bit towards the front so the shape was more teardrop than oval when viewed from the bottom of the butt. It was a trick he learned to enable a better grip on his Colt when drawing fast.

As in many Western lawmen's offices, there was a combination administrative deputy and jailer at a front desk. The sheriff, if in, was at another desk. Or, in the case of a larger office, seated in his own separate office. The latter described El Paso County.

"Howdy, I'm Tate reporting for duty. Sheriff in?"

"Howdy, chief. I'm Horace Keefe. He had to ride up to Denver on business. Left you a note," Horace said.

He shifted some papers about on his desk and handed it to Tate.

It advised Tate his desk was the one outside the sheriff's office door, to begin to walk around town and meet people and they would ride the circuit tomorrow and begin negotiating the deputation of town and night marshals.

"Horace, you have any newer wanted posters I can look through?" Tate asked and shortly received about seven to review.

Five were from the area. They were for horse theft, robbery and one aggravated assault. Tate memorized the faces and descriptions. There would be no rewards as chief deputy, but surely did not want to walk past one of these men on a sidewalk without making contact with him. Maybe in a "buffalo" sort of way, with a Colt upside the miscreant's head.

He finished looking over the posters. Tate saw he needed some supplies. The desk was empty. He asked Horace and was told everyone supplied his own. He nodded and did not respond.

"What's the name of the town marshal? Maybe I ought to go introduce myself."

"Go at your own risk. He's thinks he owns this town and is a major ass," Horace warned.

Tate knew prudence would dictate going with Sheriff Hansen. But, Tate was not prepared to step down before any man.

He walked out the door and headed down the wide dirt street. Some businesses had board sidewalks. Others did not.

He saw the marshal's office diagonally across the street, thought for a minute, shrugged and kept walking in the direction he was headed.

He saw a big man sitting in a rocker in front of the marshal's office. He was smoking a cigarette and did not look up. Tate thought not looking up was pretty careless and a good way to get your head blown off.

He walked up to the man, who still did not look up, but snarled, "You are new in my town. Who in hell are you?"

"Howdy, my name is Tate. I am the new chief deputy for the county."

"So?" the man, whose name he knew was Hill.

"So, nothing. And, I'm not going to have a conversation with someone too rude to look up and acknowledge my presence."

The man spat the cigarette out of his mouth and stood quickly. At six foot four, he was taller than Tate and outweighed him by fifty pounds of muscle.

He walked over to Tate and got into his space, almost chest to chest.

"Look, piss ant. This is *my* town. You got it?" Hill said.

"Well, your damn town is in *my* county, so back off. Do it now," Tate said in a low growl.

Hill made a big mistake. He stepped forward and tried to bump Tate over with his chest. Tate saw it coming and stepped aside. He shoved Hill backwards over the raised wooden walk and his rocker. The big man ended up on his butt leaning against the wall behind it.

Hill started to scramble for his gun, a Smith & Wesson Schofield, but felt Tate's Colt stuck in his ear 'way before he had cleared leather.

"You ever touch me or threaten me again, and you will die on the spot. I have half a mind to blow your damn brains out right here in self-defense."

Tate un-cocked the Colt with the barrel still stuck in Hill's ear. The man flinched as he heard the mechanical clicks.

Tate took the S&W and stepped back.

He walked over to the watering trough and dropped the marshal's revolver in with a "plop."

He turned to the man leaning against the wall.

"We are both on the same side here. One day one of us might have to back up the other in a bad situation. What say you recover your gun and wipe it off and I'll buy you a cup of coffee?"

Hill spit words out. "I'll tell you where you can put your coffee!"

Tate shook his head in disgust and walked down the street, watching for Hill to appear with a rifle or scattergun. He did not. This time. Tate knew he made an enemy. He also knew the only way the enemy could harm him was from behind. Tate's gun had been stuck in his ear before Hill even had a chance to get a grip on his own gun. He was a bully. A damn slow bully.

Tate went into the general mercantile and bought a pad and several pencils. He added a bottle of ink and a pen, then continued his patrol walk, the paper sack in his left hand. His gun hand was always free and available.

It took him less than a half hour to cover the town.

"Did ya meet our friendly marshal," Horace asked

"I did. A real sweetheart. Told me I was a piss ant and it was his town."

"What happened then?" Horace asked.

"Not much, he tried to bully me and push me over."

"Then?"

"Then, he tripped and fell down over his chair. Might say he went off his rocker. Right on his ass. He tried to draw, but found a .44 stuck in his ear, so he changed his mind. His Smith & Wesson is in the watering trough out front of his office right now, unless he already retrieved it."

"Damn, Tate. What a show. Guess he is pretty racked off."

"I guess he is. I made an enemy. One who is a bully and a coward. They are dangerous because they come at you at night and from behind. Not face to face like a man. How did this jerk become marshal?"

"Something, we've all been asking ourselves. The sheriff thinks the mayor recognizes his mistake. It's not an elected job, so he might get rid of him," Horace said.

"You have everything covered here. I think I will go ride around and see what's happening in the rest of the county," Tate said. He mounted Cisco and deliberately walked him slowly past the town marshal's office. No way, he wanted to look like he was sneaking out of town unseen.

He didn't plan to meet up with other deputies because he did not know what Sheriff Hansen had told them about him. Nor, did he want to meet other town marshals before he and the sheriff presented their idea to town or village leaders.

So, he just rode through Fountain Creek and Monument, nodding and tipping his Stetson at anyone who looked up. He stopped in Palmer Lake and got lunch before riding back to the office in Colorado Springs at the end of his tour.

He visited with Jubal and his bride once he got back. He could smell cooking from his cabin and once he unsaddled, brushed and fed Cisco, he walked in.

He found a very beautiful Eve, auburn hair down and brushed until it shined in the sunlight coming in the window. She was wearing only a thin shift which the sun rendered transparent and was barefooted.

"I thought I might give you dessert before dinner," she said softly. Tate unbuckled his gun belt and threw the latch on the door. He had no wish to argue about dessert before dinner at all. Tate picked her up in his arms and carried her into the bedroom and laid her gently on the feather bed, its mattress held by ropes crisscrossed below.

They skipped dinner. Tate got up at midnight and checked the cast iron pot of soup over the coals in the fireplace. He stirred the coals. They were warm enough to keep the soup from spoiling. Maybe soup and corn-pone for breakfast. He yawned and padded silently back into bed. Eve did not awaken but knew his presence and nestled up against him, head on his shoulder.

Tate used to love laying in his bedroll on a clear night looking up at a million stars in the sky. Now, it would be a distant second to nights like this. Real damn distant, he thought as he drifted off to sleep feeling a soft breath on his cheek.

******

The next day, the sheriff beat him in by a few minutes. He went into the office and the sheriff briefed him on some statutory changes he had gone over at the capital.

"Sheriff, will you tell me about the history of this town marshal, Hill?" Tate asked.

"Our beloved mayor has made some whopper mistakes. Hill may be the biggest one. Why?"

Tate told him about the interaction yesterday.

"Well, you probably made an enemy. If he doesn't bushwhack you some night, you should be okay. I feel like his day is coming soon. Real soon. I'd rather the idiot mayor take care of his own house, but if it comes to us doing it, we will. Hill's bullying of prisoners goes beyond normal police procedure. I've gotten lots of complaints and passed them along to the mayor. I told the mayor next time, I was going to have to arrest Hill and put him in jail to await trial for police cruelty."

"How does the mayor respond to your information and threat?" Tate asked.

"The mayor is a do-nothing. He'd watch the town burn down for a half hour before he'd ring the damn fire bell. Just try to avoid a confrontation with Hill unless you see him doing something you could arrest him on and get a prison conviction out of it. I don't need to mess with him. I got high blood pressure and God knows what sort of attack he'd provoke if I got riled."

"Sheriff, if you don't mind me being nosey, what's your background?"

"Ha-ha. You'd never guess with me in this black suit! I explored this area 'way before the war and decided this was where I wanted to settle. I was a trapper. Didn't wear anything but buckskins until the war. Was a young 'un at the last rendezvous. It was on the Green River in Wyoming in 1840. I was twenty."

"You were a mountain man, like Bridger and Carson and all?" Tate asked.

"I was. And, Rube Herring, Smith and Sublette. I might carry this pea-shooting Merwin & Hulbert revolver now, but I still have my .54 caliber Hawkin for serious stuff!"

"The Hawkin kind of preceded the Sharps and the Remington Rolling Block as a buffalo gun didn't it?" Tate asked, fascinated.

"You might say it did. It's a fine rifle, though a muzzleloader. There were no cartridge guns in those days. If there were, where'd we get the proper caliber? So, we carried lead and molded our own rifle balls. We could get powder. Sometimes percussion caps, but most of us liked the old flintlocks. Never knew when you could get percussion caps. We could get loose powder and grind some down real fine for the pan below the frizzen. The old flint in the hammer would spark the frizzen and the spark would fire off the pinch of fine grain powder in the pan. Flame would go through the touchhole and bang! Enough powder would explode to kill a buff or a griz, if you aimed steady."

"Were you one of the first to see this area?" Tate asked.

"No, Captain Pike brought a troop of men through here before I was old enough to even pick up a Hawken. I came through later. And, sure did like it," the sheriff said.

"One last thing, sir. You mentioned a Merwin & Hulbert. Can't you change barrels on one yourself?"

"You sure can, Tate. I have the shorter, four incher on most of the time, but I have a long barrel for the trail. I can change it in a minute, depending on whether I need to hide it or have a long sighting plane. It does not have the balance of a Colt. Nothing does. But, mechanically, I believe it's the finest revolver ever made."

"Maybe you can ride up to our little spread for dinner sometime and let me fire a shot or two with it."

"It's a deal. Now, let's mount up and start politicking those town and village leaders to let us take over their marshals. And, let them continue to pay them!" the sheriff said.

His was the appaloosa Tate had admired at the hitching post next to Cisco. Sure enough, Tate spied something looking exactly like the butt of a Hawken in the scabbard.

"We will meet with the mayor of this fine burg around five today. We may be able to visit the other six before the end of the day tomorrow," the sheriff said as they mounted up.

"I'll be looking forward to how he and his blow-hard of a marshal take to this," Tate remarked.

"He'll do what's best for his political career. We are in the same party and I head the committee responsible for candidate contributions. He's up for election this November."

"Will he stand up to his bully marshal?" Tate asked as they rode away from the office.

"He will probably send a letter and let me handle it. I may let you handle it. Seems like you are able to handle him pretty well."

"Well, I'm afraid blood may run this time," Tate said.

"So, be it. Just make sure none of it is yours."

"I promise I'll do my best to keep mine. I leaked it out twice on the trail after the former prison warden and his gang."

They circled around the county and all three village or town leaders they met with liked the idea and agreed for them to deputize their marshal and night marshal and supervise them. The fourth town was Manitou Springs again, a success.

They had Old Zounds, Monument and Colorado Springs left.

The mayor owned a hotel and they walked into his office there just before five.

Sheriff Hansen introduced his new chief deputy and briefly gave his background. Several things raised the politician's thick eyebrows. The sheriff did not slack on his description of Tate having been a ranger captain nor of his ability to use a sixgun while the other man was thinking about it.

They laid out the plan, including something they came up with on the ride.

Each town had a bell used for fires. Sometimes it

was in town hall, sometimes free-standing, or some-times in a church.

The fire alarm was a constant ringing. Most of the villages could hear it and would send men to help.

The new plan was for the two big towns, Colorado Springs and Manitou Springs. In event of a police emergency, the bell was to be rung three times in succession periodically for Colorado Springs and four times for Manitou Springs. Any other town hearing could duplicate the three or four bell alarm. The sheriff, chief deputy, all other deputies and the day or night town marshals would respond to the emergency.

They all agreed codes for the five other communities would be too confusing. They also had no brothels or saloons hence little law enforcement needs other than shoplifting thefts and things not requiring emergency response.

"I'll let Marshal Hill know he has a new boss. Tate, have you met him yet?" the mayor asked.

"Yes, sir. I have."

"What did you think?"

"I should reserve my opinion until I have worked with him a little bit, mayor," Tate said.

The mayor was too self-absorbed to catch the subtlety in Tate's answer and stood up, indicating the meeting was over.

"Probably good decision to not share your feelings on Hill right then," the sheriff observed.

"But, what did you think of the mayor?"

"Pompous ass. Only cares about his reputation and political career."

"You don't know me very well, Tate. But, based on what you do know, think I'd be a good mayor?"

"I checked around a bit before I came to you for a job. Everything I heard about you was top notch, Sheriff. Based on what I heard, the answer is yes. For sure."

"Well, if I enter the mayoral race in November, it may be real good for you."

"I 'spect it would be good for everyone around here."

"I mean, El Paso County would need a new sheriff."

"Nobody knows me yet. But, I'd sure give it my best," Tate responded catching his drift.

"Your reputation as a straight shooter and a fast one seems to have preceded you, Chief Deputy Tate," the sheriff said.

The next day, the sheriff decided to go with Tate to visit Marshal Hill. It went about like they expected. Badly.

Hill was sitting at his desk when they walked in. He ignored them a minute and then looked up and scowled.

"Hill, did the mayor tell you about the new county policing plan?" the sheriff asked.

"He handed me a letter this morning and left before I could read it. Didn't have the *cojones* to tell me face-to-face," Hill said.

"I believe, as does the county commission, it will give us better policing throughout El Paso County,

Hill. It will give you more authority as a county-wide deputy and a professional lawman to look to for supervisory help. Not a professional politician who does not know his ass from a hole in the ground."

"You saying the mayor does not know his ass from a hole in the ground?" Hill asked the sheriff.

"You put whatever spin on my words you want."

"When does this great master plan take effect?" Hill asked.

"The second the mayor handed you the notice," the sheriff said.

"Your piss ant chief deputy lost his voice?" Hill asked.

"Naw, Hill, I still have it. And, you call me a name one more time and I will beat the living hell outa you. You understand?" Tate said.

"You ain't so big without having your fast gun right handy," Hill taunted.

Tate turned to the sheriff. "Boss, you want to referee a little match in the street?" The sheriff nodded, though looking a little worried as he measured Hill's height and weight silently.

Hill stood up and unbuckled his gun belt and laid it on the desk. Tate unbuckled his and did the same, the long Bowie as prominent as the Colt and cartridges.

Tate slipped on his thin black doeskin gloves as he walked out the door. He wanted to protect his gun hand as much as possible.

"Okay," the sheriff began, "the rules are…hell, there

ain't no rules. Have at it!"

Hill snorted like a Spanish bull and rushed in, head down towards Tate's midsection. Tate stepped to the side at the last minute and jabbed Hill in the ear with his left fist. He caught him at the base of the skull with his right as the big man stumbled and caught himself.

The cry "fight!" went up and a crowd quickly assembled. They all knew this was something eventful, the sheriff refereeing a fight between two senior lawmen. One they did not know, the other, they generally disliked.

Tate let Hill shake his head and recover his equilibrium.

Hill adopted a stiff boxing stance, looking for the world like a professional bare knuckle boxer. He got a big grin on his face and looked confident the fight would soon end in his favor.

Tate circled. He took a painful punch to the left shoulder and did the unexpected. He moved in close to Hill and, head against chest, drove an uppercut with every ounce of strength he could summon up into Hill's solar plexus.

Hill went "Oof," and doubled over. Tate hit him with a hammer blow, again at the base of his skull. The bigger man went down. He sat with his face down in the dust of the street moaning. Tate would have normally kicked him in the head and finished him off, but reckoned he had to play for the crowd and stepped back.

The sheriff bent over Hill and prodded him. Hill just groaned again.

Straightening up, the sheriff decreed "I declare this fight to be over by knock out!" A cheer went up. Tate slipped back into the marshal's office and put his gun belt back on and adjusted it to his satisfaction before walking back out of the door.

He found Hill still sitting in the dirt, shaking his head and trying to make the earth stop spinning inside his head.

The sheriff unpinned the marshal's badge from Hill's vest.

"You are done in law enforcement in El Paso County, Hill. I'd advise you pack up and get out."

Hansen and Tate walked over to the hotel and conferred with the Mayor and gave him the badge. Hansen said he had an older deputy who was getting tired of riding all day and who would be an excellent choice for marshal. The mayor, seeing no way out, politically, agreed. Hansen promised to confer with the deputy and if he was interested, send him to the mayor.

Tate rode to Manitou Springs towards the end of the day to check on the shift change between marshal and night marshal and review the bell procedure with both. He stopped at the post office and found a letter for Eve from a Richmond publisher. He hoped it was good news for her.

Tate made it home before dark and immediately

gave the letter to Eve, who ripped it open excitedly.

She scanned it quickly and smiling, handed it to her husband.

Tate began to smile as he read. The publisher was interested from the proposal letter and sample she sent and wanted a full manuscript. He disagreed with her contention a female author would be detrimental to sales and suggested a pen name and using the fictitious name of her uncle as the author "as told to his niece." She prepared one of her manuscript copies and Tate promised to take it to the larger Colorado Springs post office in the morning.

Tate went down to the icy stream and stripped his vest and shirt off. He splashed cold water on his shoulder where Hill hit him. It was already purple, heading to blue black. He held his hands in the cold water to abate some of the soreness from their contact with Hill's gut and back of his head. Gunfighters knew to punch softer areas and chop hard ones like heads and, Tate had followed the prescription with good results. He would not be shocked if Hill suffered a mild concussion from the blows behind the head.

He walked back to the cabin, feeling better. Eve watched him walk up with both love and admiration. Then, she saw the badly bruised shoulder.

"What on earth, Morgan?"

"I had a final set-to with now former town marshal Hill today. Despite appearances, I won pretty handily."

"How did he look?" she asked.

"No different. I hit him in the gut and the back of his hard head. He went down and stayed down. The sheriff took his badge away and kicked him out of town. We'll see if the part about leaving town sticks. Legally, he doesn't have to. And, he's just bullheaded enough to stay and be a troublemaker," Tate said.

"Morgan, do you think you will ever have to deal with him with other than fists?" she asked.

"Honey, I don't know. I think it's possible. I watched him try to draw on me once and he's pretty slow. I'd almost feel bad pulling my Colt on him….for a little while," he grinned.

"Now, don't make jokes about life and death situations. He sounds like the type who might shoot you in the back."

"It's a possibility. If he does, at least I know I have a wife and an uncle by marriage who will kill him afterwards."

"You can bet your last cent on it!" she exclaimed with enough venom it surprised them both.

He hugged her and she pointed to the table and began serving a simple, but flavorful dinner.

Tate realized, for now, Colorado Springs did not have any police coverage, except when the sheriff's office was open.

They ate, then walked hand-in-hand down the path to the trail leading from Manitou Springs, around Pike's Peak and then to their and Jubal's ranches.

"You know, Morgan. There's a store clerk job in town. Darlene said she could get it for me and we could ride in together in the buckboard every day. It doesn't pay a lot, but cash is hard to come by in any quantity. I've been thinking I should take it. I never thought I could get pregnant but what if I did? Then I'd have missed the opportunity to work and contribute for six months or so."

"All of which makes perfect sense to me. As chief deputy and maybe sheriff in four or five months, I will make enough for us to more than get by. But, a little extra is always nice."

"Sheriff?" she asked.

"Just between us, Sheriff Hansen is thinking about running for mayor. If he does, he wants me to run for sheriff on the same ticket. There's some county party money to fund both."

"Which party?" she asked.

"Darn! I never asked him. The one with some money, I guess. Doesn't really matter to me."

"What if he loses and you win?" she asked.

"He said if it comes out as you say, he'll just retire to his ranch at age sixty and be done with work."

"Be done with work. I cannot imagine what it would be like," Eve said.

"Don't spend a lot of time figuring it out. It will be a long time before we will be faced with not working. A long time. But, we'll have a helluva good time along the way!" he promised. She squeezed his hand tighter as they walked.

Tate visited with Jubal on his way to the sheriff's office the next day. Jubal had purchased a plow and broken Tecumseh to it. He had a large field plowed already, glad to be farming instead of ranching.

"What are you putting in?" Tate asked.

"The three sisters. Corn, squash and beans. The couple acres should keep both families in vegetables here on out."

"I will do my best to bring down a deer or two and put meat on our tables. At least until we get some beeves going," Tate said.

"I guess you are pleased with the news about Eve's book about you?" Tate asked.

"I just hope we hid identities well enough. I ran and changed my name. So, I never took the pledge and got officially pardoned. The government might look at me as an escaped prisoner, though I was never tried or found guilty of anything."

"I wasn't aware, Jubal. Should she cancel the book deal, if and when it comes?" Tate asked.

"No. I don't think so. I'd sure like to know what my liability is, however."

"Who could tell us?" Tate asked.

"Justice Department maybe. Judge Advocate General maybe. I just don't know. And I'm hesitant to push the matter too hard."

"My recent boss is the Attorney General of Texas. He was also a Confederate. Think he could shed any light for us?" Tate said.

"Maybe. But, it would not be binding, just legal opinion. It would take a federal man to render a binding opinion. And, I learned the hard way sometimes they stab you in the back," Jubal opined.

"Sounds like your feeling is to drop the matter and let the book stand on its own legs," Tate suggested.

"Probably. I have a wonderful wife, a damn big chunk of land I think is perfect. Not such bad neighbors. I just as soon not give it all up for a noose or a ten by ten cell in Leavenworth. I already spent a couple years in one of those with regular beatings and torture. And, no legal rights or remedies."

"You sound like you know something about the law," Tate said.

"I had some law classes in college, so I know just enough to be dangerous," Jubal Paine said. "And, to be fearful about whether I am officially an escaped prisoner," he added.

Tate rode on, stopping at Manitou Springs, then continued on to Colorado Springs.

"Oh! Tate. Glad you came in here before patrolling the county. The mayor just hired our deputy, Tom Burton, to be the new marshal for Colorado Springs. You'll like him. Fella about fifty, still chipper and pretty good with fists and gun. Doubt he'll need them too much here, but you never know," Sheriff Hansen said.

"Anything on our pard, Hill?" Tate asked.

"Nobody's seen hide nor hair of him since the fight. His gun was the town's but the mayor isn't going to press the matter."

"I'm going to check with Horace to see if we got any new Wanted Posters in, then go over and meet Burton. He's about the only deputy I had not met yet. You going to advertise and hire a replacement for him on the county force?" Tate asked.

"Nope. You are. You are effectively running this office. I am the distinguished soon-to-be mayor."

"And, former buckskinned mountain man," Tate reminded him.

"Mountain man, too," the sheriff acknowledged.

"I'll probably see you sometime today," Tate said.

"Maybe not. I have some politicking to do. You run the place. Contact me if you need me."

Tate walked over to the marshal's office and introduced himself to former deputy Tom Burton. He liked Burton right off. Tate also noticed he wore his gun like a man who knew how to use it. There were so many clues about others — too low and butt tilted out suggested a swagger, too high, too far back or forward and wrong type of holster told Tate the man carried one but did not plan on using it quickly. Burton wore his Colt about like Tate did.

"I appreciate the sheriff engineering this," Burton said.

"My wife was complaining something awful about me being on horseback and gone dawn 'til dusk. Except for the couple time a year posse's, this will get me home to dinner most nights at a decent time."

"I'm glad it works out to your advantage, Tom. This being married is new to me, but so far I like it a lot. Especially the meals!" Tate admitted.

"Any ideas of a candidate for your replacement in the far Western end of the county?" Tate asked.

"There's a cowboy with the RX Ranch out there who might be interested. He's honest, smart and a good gun hand."

"What's his name?"

"Kit Munro. Spelled M, U, N, R, O. The Scottish way, he tells me," Burton said.

"Would it put him in hot water if I asked for him at the ranch?"

"Might, Tate. Let me send word over for him to contact you."

"I'd appreciate it, Tom. Let me know if you need anything here. I really have not checked out the office. My prior visits have been sort of violent."

"So I've heard," Burton laughed. We had some extra .44 cartridges I think, but Hill must have taken them. There's an 1866 Winchester rimfire. Not much in the power department, but probably okay in town. And, a ten-gauge double scattergun. It has a Long Tom thirty-two inch barrel."

"Why don't you take it over to the gunsmith and get him to saw it off to eighteen or twenty inches? And, see if he will trade the '66 for a '73 in .44-40? Try putting it on the town's tab. If the town doesn't work, put it on El Paso County," Tate suggested, adding "and, maybe you ought to get some fresh shells for both."

Tate made his rounds of all the towns and villages. Eve had ridden into Manitou Springs with Darlene and had secured the job working in the café, starting the following Monday. She was stuck in town until Darlene was through work.

Tate rescued her for lunch and she rode behind him on Cisco back to the ranch. It was a nice surprise for both husband and wife. Tate was glad to note she had the shortened barrel Colt conversion hidden under her apron. Manitou was not a violent place, but an auburn-haired beauty could not be too careful, he thought. Especially his auburn-haired beauty.

Eve fixed some sandwiches with cheese from the store and they had cold stream water with it. Not fancy, but they had neither the time nor money for fancy. The six-month payoff on the homestead took care of their reserves. But, they had a hundred-sixty acre ranch bought and paid for. Four and a half years early.

Tate started back to Colorado Springs. As he got near Manitou Springs, he heard the three-tone bell for Colorado Springs ring several sequences, then the closer Manitou Springs bell repeat. He spurred Cisco to a gallop as he headed to the county seat.

As he rode into town, still at a gallop, he saw a Barlow-Sanderson stage in front of the sheriff's office. A man was laying on the street and the doctor appeared to be checking him. Another was laying, unattended. Apparent passengers were standing aghast.

Tate slid off Cisco and wrapped his reins around the hitching post. New town marshal Burton and county office deputy Horace Keefe were both there, talking to passengers one at a time.

"Where's the sheriff," Tate asked. He was told in "Denver at a political meeting."

"Stage robbery?" he asked and received a nod from Burton.

"Where'd it happen, Tom?" Tate asked.

"Somewhere northeast of here on the main road. The driver's the one doc is working on. He's shot through and in and out of consciousness. The shotgun rider is dead. Has been since the robbery."

Horace walked over to the two other lawmen.

"Hey, Horace, what did you find out from the passengers?" Tate asked.

The deputy paused a minute and organized his thoughts.

"Was thirty minutes north on the main road when they were hit. Five men. Four average, one real big. All white. All with revolvers. Didn't see their horses. Blocked the stage and shot the driver and guard. Took their guns and robbed the strongbox with mail and money for the bank. Also, robbed the passengers. Big fella was rude with the lady and gave her a squeeze up top. She's more mad than embarrassed. She wants to pull the lever at his hanging, I think."

"Horace, please run over to the telegraph office and wire the head office of Barlow-Sanderson Stage Lines. They are in Granada, I think. Tell them what happened. Try to send the name of the guard and the deceased and find out how much was in the strongbox," Tate ordered. "Then, wire the sheriffs in Douglas and Elbert Counties north of here and warn them. Also, Teller County to the west."

"Tom, put together whatever we need for the posse I'm getting ready to call. Maybe food, blankets, a couple of tarps."

Tate turned to the crowd.

"Men, I'm raising a posse to go after these robbers! There are five of them. No rifles or shotguns shown, just revolvers. I'm paying a dollar a day. Anybody who wants to ride needs to be able to be gone a couple days or more. Weather's good, so extra coats won't be necessary. If you need blankets or canteens or extra ammo, we'll get it. Marshal Tom Burton and I are going to run this posse and Horace Keefe will be in charge of the county until the sheriff gets back from Denver. Any volunteers?"

The money was about what a cow puncher would

earn. More importantly, it was a commodity. Cash money. Something of which almost nobody had enough.

Tate got five volunteers and made a formal deal about swearing them in as temporary El Paso County deputies there in the street. Four had decent horses, one had a mule, like General Crook and sometimes, Wild Bill. With a quick tally, Burton found out they needed three canteens, four blankets, a box of .38-40's, several boxes of .44-40's and some .45 Colt ammunition. He got those at the general mercantile along with beef jerky, coffee, and tobacco chaws while Tate got a bag filled with biscuits and sliced beef and some bacon.

Half an hour later, they were ready to ride. Unlike when Tate was tracking the Union prison warden gang, nobody in this gang was injured.

They would have to estimate where the tracking part would begin. They had to ride thirty minutes north and start looking for tracks of a stage and footprints in a busy road. The "big man" part worried Tate and he said something to Tom Burton about it.

"You thinking what I am about the big man, Tom?" he asked.

"Like maybe it's a fella from here we have not seen for several days?"

"Exactly. You think he's crooked, as well as a bully?"

"I think he's crooked as a damn snake, Tate. If he comes back over the saddle, it won't be no loss."

"I figure between him and me, it is destined to

come out with him deceased." The older former deputy nodded his agreement.

They rode out of town at a canter. Tate thought about the fact Eve would have no idea where he was, unless Darlene heard about the robbery in Manitou Springs and told her. But, there was not a thing he could do about it now.

The road was fairly well-travelled and the dirt was packed hard. Tate knew it was going to be difficult to find where the robbery occurred and to track the five men. The posse did not meet or overtake anyone before dark, so information was not forthcoming from further witnesses.

He motioned Burton up beside him.

"I'm going to get the men to ride behind us a little further so we can speak unheard."

Tate turned in his saddle.

"Men, drop back about fifty yards. Marshal Burton and I are going to slow and look for tracks without all the dust a posse kicks up."

These men clearly did not know enough about tracking to know the lawman's words were simply a dodge.

"Tom, before each of us take different edges of the road to look for tracks, are you concerned about the quality of our posse?" Tate asked.

"I surely am, Tate. First shot fired and some will turn and run and the rest will start shooting each other or us by mistake."

"We have not seen hide nor hair of anybody on this damn road, Tom. It's gonna be dark in another couple hours. I'm thinking you and I will look for sign until dusk then find a place to camp for the night. What do you think?"

"I am in favor. Also, one of us should talk to the men about what to and not to do. Like not shooting one of us."

"I'll start it off and you jump in whenever you want."

Burton saw an area on the left of the road where the ground was covered with footprints and wagon wheels. Except, in this case, the two lawmen knew they were stage coach wheels. There were dried spots of blood on the ground. They must have come off the seat box on the stage since neither the driver nor the shotgun rider hit the ground after being shot.

The tracks included one smaller set. Those prints would be the woman. Others were shoes instead of boots.

A lock box did not show up after a thorough search. The outlaws must have taken it with them, Burton concluded.

They split and each took a side of the road. At points when the gang rode side-by-side an outer horse went into the less beaten down dirt and left a clear hoof print. At least with those prints, they could age the print somewhat and determine how long ago it was made and how close or far their quarries might be.

At dusk, Tate spotted a clearing ahead. A creek ran behind it and it had a few trees. He motioned the posse over to it.

"Men, we will camp here tonight. Unsaddle and hobble your mounts and we'll have a quick planning session before a cold dinner. I fear the gang is too close to light a fire. Luckily, it's pretty warm and we'll be fine," Tate said.

He took the saddle off Cisco and spoke to the black gelding for a while. Then, he put the hobble on and cleared a place for his bedroll.

Once everyone seemed done, he motioned them in a circle.

"A couple of things about being in a posse. We are here to try to capture some outlaws. We are not executioners or hangmen. If shooting starts when we are riding grouped up, fan out before returning fire. You don't want to shoot your fellow possemen in the back! If anybody's got a bottle of rotgut, save it in case we need it for medicinal use. We want everybody as steady as they can be if it comes to a firefight, all right? Tonight there will be no fires and no cigars or cigarettes. We have plugs of chaw if you want tobacco. Smoke smell carries and the wind is blowing towards where the fellows we are chasing are. We don't want them to smell it and sneak down here while we are sleeping. Which brings me to my last point. We need to set one sentry. He'll stand a two hour watch and another will take over. I will take the first watch and Marshal Burton will take the final one.

Tom, you got anything you want to add?"

"I do, Tate. Don't fall asleep on watch! We got biscuits and jerky. And, like the chief deputy said, we got tobacco plugs. Don't anybody be sparking their steels and trying to light a cigarette. It is 'way too dangerous under our circumstances. Anybody got any questions?"

"How long will this take?" one man asked.

"I'm hoping we will be done in a day or two, but you never know for sure," Tate said. Burton nodded his agreement.

The night was uneventful and went too fast for Tate. These fellows did not know how to have a quiet change of guards, so nobody slept very soundly.

Breakfast was the same as dinner. There were complaints about no coffee, but neither lawman dignified them with an answer.

About an hour into the ride north, Tate motioned Burton over to where he stopped on the left side of the road. There was a clearing in the trees and it appeared a camp had been made there. They had the posse halt and Tate and Burton went over to the camp, tree to tree, rifles ready.

It was a fresh camp. The ashes in the fire were not cold.

"Damn, Tate. These boys were upwind and could have coffee," Burton said.

"Worse yet, it looks like two split off from here. Let's see if we can find the strongbox from the stage," Tate said.

He motioned the men to dismount and hold in place, while he and Burton searched. They found the empty box. Its padlock had been pried off. The outlaws were smart enough to not risk the sound of shooting it off.

Burton motioned the men to approach, leading their horses and the mule. He told them what the signs indicated.

"We have to go after the larger group. We owe it to the stage company, since they have more of the money than the two who left. We don't have enough men to split the posse. It appears they all left pretty recently from the warmth of the ashes. So, we are close and have to be real careful," Tate said.

"How come they had a fire for coffee and we didn't?"

"Think about it. We didn't because the wind would have blown the smoke smell up this way. The same wind blew their smoke the same way. Away from them and us. Now, let's get going and catch these outlaws," Tate said.

They rode for almost an hour with Burton leading the posse and Tate out front trying to cut sign. Presently, he held his arm up for a halt and rode Cisco back to the posse.

"I detect dust up ahead. Not a lot, but three horsemen wouldn't make a lot. It could be a freight wagon, a group of riders or our outlaws. Since we have not seen any other camps, I'm betting these are ours," Tate said.

Burton was looking down the road.

"Tate, I've been through here a couple of times. There's a diagonal road coming up in about a mile. It runs beside this road, but a mile over. Then it veers off in another ten miles or so. I believe if I pushed my horse hard, I could get ahead of them and set a little trap."

"And, we'd keep on at this pace and then ride and shoot a couple times once they get to you and we hear your shot?" Tate asked.

"Exactly!" Burton said.

"Let's do it!" Tate said and Burton rode ahead at a gallop. The posse saw him turn to the left and disappear in the distance. Tate got the posse up to a canter and held them at it.

Tate began to see more dust from their quarries ahead. He slowed the men and reminded them to not shoot with anyone in front of them.

Three shots rang out. Tate reckoned it was from Burton's Winchester Sporting rifle, which had a barrel much longer than his carbine. The shots were followed by more shots, this time "pops" from revolvers.

Tate spurred the posse on and yelled for them to fan out for clear shots.

"When they are in sight, I will fire a couple shots in the air. You do the same. In the air!" he stressed.

They saw three men on horseback turning back towards them about a hundred yards distance.

He fired several shots up and to the right. The others followed suit as they sped up to a full gallop towards the three outlaws.

The outlaws did the smart thing. They were caught in a pincher movement between one superior group and one unknown group. They dropped their revolvers into the dirt and raised their hands.

Within minutes, the three men were tied with latigos and sitting in grass on the side of the road.

Tate moved the dismounted possemen into a wide circle around them in the unlikely event the missing two returned. He and Burton wanted to have some serious talk time with these three before the other two dropped off the edge of the earth.

"You men talk to Marshal Burton and me and we'll testify in your trials you cooperated. I want to know where the other two are," Tate said.

The men looked at each other. Two nodded almost imperceptivity to a third to be the spokesman.

"We are out-of-work ranch hands. We wuz looking for work and them two promised us easy money. All we had to do was help on a couple of robberies of rich companies. So, we robbed a couple stages. It was not our plan to kill nobody. The fella Brown was the ring leader. He killed the last shotgun man and shot the driver. He was going to take the woman passenger and have his way with her. We pointed our guns over his way and he backed off."

"How long ago did Brown and the big man leave?" Burton asked.

"About fifteen minutes ago. They said they had to kill an old guy and his niece, but were gonna lay low out of state first," the spokesman said.

"What was Brown's first name," asked Tate, writing all of this verbatim in his notebook.

"Will."

"And, the other one?"

"We only knew him as Hill."

"Describe Hill in detail," Tate said.

The man described the former town marshal exactly.

"Do you know which way they were going from here?" the marshal asked.

"Not really. They left going north like to Denver, but I don't think they were going so far. I think they was gonna turn northeast pretty quick."

"We have recovered four hundred dollars from each of you. Did they each take a similar amount when they left?" Burton asked.

"We split even-Steven for us hands," the outlaw replied, "except for Brown. As the leader, he took an extra thousand bucks and Hill got eight hundred total. Hell, what Hill got by hisself was more than any of us make in a year, punching beeves."

"We told you men we would speak for you in court and we will. Now, the marshal and I have to discuss something," Tate said. He and Burton walked off out of earshot.

"So, Brown got a thousand four hundred, Hill got

eight hundred. We don't know where they are going, except for out of state. These prisoners think the two are going to head northeast. The destination could be the corner of Kansas, but more likely Nebraska. What worries me the most is a group of men have tried twice to kill my wife's uncle and her. I'm afraid they are who they are coming back for." Tate said.

"I heard about the attack at the homestead. Wasn't there another one, too. Down south?"

"Yep. They were three hired gun thugs. The one at the homestead was the original ones setting out to kill Jubal Paine. Those five won't kill anybody else."

"Why, Tate?"

"Because I tracked them down and killed every damn one of them. There must be one I don't know about. I have to talk to Jubal about it. But, my best chance at getting to them is breaking off and pushing Cisco hard. Will you take the prisoners and our posse men back home?" Tate asked.

"Glad to. You sure you want to go after two, one being a murderer, alone?"

"I took down five before. These two don't worry me much. I saw how slow Hill is on the draw. I would have time to shoot Brown before Hill got his Schofield in action. I won't give this more than a day. I got responsibilities to the county beyond these two."

"Be safe, my friend. And, you are right, you are a hero if you come back with them dead or not, all in a day. If you are gone four days, people will start second guessing you. And, people are voters. One reason I stayed a deputy and then took this non-elective job in town."

"Just tell people I'm cutting sign and will be back shortly. These two might be anywhere. It'll be like a needle in a haystack," Tate said, nodding and receiving a nod in return.

He got on Cisco, told the posse he was going to look for a trail on the remaining two and would see them back in town.

Rifle over his saddle horn, Tate rode north carefully, scanning both sides of the road for where the fugitives might have turned. He knew the right would lead them north but could not trust they had told the rest of the gang the truth.

He spent the rest of the day and found no signs at all of the Brown's and Hill's tracks or direction.

Frustrated, he turned Cisco south and headed home. He called out as he rode up the lane to the two adjoining homesteads. It was late and he did not want to frighten anyone. Or, get shot.

Jubal came out in his night shirt, Winchester '66 at the ready.

"Jubal, we can talk more in the morning. But, the man who headed this gang got away with the oversized former marshal Hill. Hill is now a fugitive for at least one stage robbery resulting in one shooting and one death. But, in questioning the ones we caught today, they said Brown was coming back to the area. He said he had an older man and his niece he had to kill before leaving the area permanently.

I killed the warden, lieutenant, sergeant and the two jacklegs with them. Do you have any idea who the new man could be? You and Eve have to be his targets," Tate asked.

"The prison was small, not much more than a bigger jail. The men you killed ran it. The only one else was the one I killed escaping. He was the Hiram Stone I strangled and weighted down in a deep pool of water. I know he was dead. He had to be."

"How long did you wait where you killed him?"

"Not long. I was in a hurry to get far away from the scene of what the Yankees would have considered a hanging court martial."

"Could he have been revived by the water and made it to the surface?" Tate asked.

"Tate, I don't see how. But, I have to admit, I was in a bit of a hurry. I figured the fire would bring re-inforcements to fight it. And, I did not want to bump into them wearing prison clothes."

"I will talk to Eve and you to Darlene. We need to keep a sharp watch out. Carry your guns everywhere. I'm thinking we both need a dog. Maybe we can find a pair of canine brothers who get along. And, guinea hens set up a racket when somebody comes around," Tate thought aloud.

"So does Tecumseh!" Paine said and Tate agreed.

"Alright, my friend. I am trail weary tonight and have a big day tomorrow. Sorry this news probably ruined the rest of your night. But, you had to know sooner than later."

They bade goodnight and Tate walked Cisco over to the cabin. Eve in a shift, waved from the door. He was glad to see she had her carbine in hand.

He put water and feed out for the black gelding and brushed him. They conversed for a while and Tate carried his saddlebags and scabbard to the cabin.

Eve waited for him with a cup of hot coffee. She had lost the shift. What seemed like a bad evening had taken a turn for the better.

******

The next day, both Tate and Burton met with the prosecutor and decided on minimal robbery charges for the three in custody. They had given valuable information and both lawmen insisted they be allowed to testify about it. Armed robbery, however, was a serious crime and all three were probably looking at five years in the Colorado State Penitentiary in Cañon City. A magistrate found the charges sufficient for trial and one was set a month off.

Tate wired sheriff's and the US Marshal in Nebraska with descriptions on Brown, wanted for aggravated assault and murder and Hill for stage robbery. Now the waiting game began.

Eve was also waiting. She had sent her manuscript to a Richmond publisher who was interested and they were looking at it. The editor told her it would probably be months before they got back to her. She still had several duplicate copies already prepared for other publishers if needed.

On the rare daylight times they shared, mostly Sundays, Tate and Eve rode all over the quarter section homestead. They found and used picnic spots on bubbling streams and Tate sought deer sign for the approaching fall.

Despite the domestic tranquility seeming to pervade his life, he practiced drawing and firing his Colt on empty brass virtually every day. To not use the empties could well break the firing pin on the hammer and render his Colt inoperable. He always protected his gun hand with a glove when doing manual work like preparing wood for the fire. Every week or two he and Jubal, and often the women, would engage in target practice in the woods.

It was deadly serious for all, especially the lawman and the former spy, who had not picked up a revolver in almost fourteen years, yet showed amazing proficiency with one. The man who had led a secret life continued to amaze Tate.

Tate fell into a comfortable gait with the sheriff job. The county was relatively low crime and the alarm system and the cross-deputizing of the town police were working well. The reappearance of the mysterious Will Brown and the damnable Hill was always in the back of his consciousness. He was sure it was to Jubal Paine also and was glad he had slipped back to his old secret agent persona and well-armed.

Jubal was close-mouthed by nature and training. He admitted he had been friends with someone like McNelly at the University of Virginia before going on to Virginia Military Institute. It was a small, frail man who was constantly badgered by bullies and finally shot one through the throat with a pepperbox pistol. The man was kicked out of the university founded by Thomas Jefferson and studied law in prison until pardoned. The war had interrupted the man's law practice, but they reconnected as friends and operatives when he began to deliver secret messages to his friend, John Singleton Mosby. Known as the Gray Ghost, the northern part of Virginia was begrudgingly known as "Mosby's Confederacy" by the Union officers who Lincoln thought controlled it. Paine got caught in plain clothes trying to deliver a dispatch to Mosby and was quickly moved to the secret spy prison. Before he could rescue Paine, Mosby's Rangers were moved out of Northern Virginia to the area around the Rappahannock River near Bowling Green for some reason Paine never knew. He had heard of a plan for Booth to kidnap Lincoln, but did not know if it was just a rumor.

Every now and then, Jubal Paine would mention some famous Confederate to Tate in passing. Too young to serve, Tate lost his brother and father in the war and like many, was bitter about the way most of the South was treated after the war. He listened closely to understand better.

Paine shocked Tate one day when he stated the death of Abraham Lincoln had been the worst thing possible to happen to the Confederacy. Tate wanted to learn why, but time and chores delayed any further discussion.

The trial had come and gone for the three stage robbers. Tate and a deputy had taken them to the Colorado State Penitentiary in Cañon City. These were not bad men, he thought and hoped they would be released on parole in three years. He wished them the best as he turned them over to the assistant warden and turned Cisco back towards Colorado Springs.

Eve, who was sure her badly performed abortion prevented her from ever becoming pregnant, began to throw up in the morning. Over the next several months, her belly began to swell. She prayed it was a baby and not something wrong inside her. The doctor in town did not perform examinations like she needed. She was left with a midwife. A good person to deliver healthy babies, but Eve feared she needed much more. Eve put off talking with Tate about it. She knew he would want to take her to New York or San Francisco to a specialist. She did not want such a trip. She just wanted to be well.

Tate knew Eve did not feel well today and had not accompanied Darlene into town where they both had jobs.

He had to check on some things with a deputy in the county's north district, which gave him time to go by and check on Eve and have lunch with her.

He rode straight to Green Mountain Falls and met with deputy George Fuller about a possible horse rustling gang operating in the area.

He turned Cisco towards the homestead west of Manitou Springs. It was a beautiful day. Still warm enough to not need a coat, the smell of fall was in the air. This was why he relocated to Colorado. Soon the trees would turn a myriad of reds, oranges and yellows, the evergreens adding a clean scent to the proliferation of colors.

Tate had told Eve he might be late enough for lunch they could call it dinner and he would not go back to the Sheriff's Office.

He was pleased over the swelling in Eve's belly. He did not know of her worries, only of the past conviction she could not bear him children. He was convinced this was proof to the contrary.

CHAPTER 15

Brown, Hill and three other ruffians Brown hired rode into the homestead fast. There were two cabins a hundred yards apart. One belonged to the target, the other to the prize.

"Hiram Stone or Jubal Paine. Whatever you are calling yourself. Come out!" Brown, the real Hiram Stone, called out. Receiving no answer, he sent the three thugs into the cabin. They came back shaking their heads. "He ain't here, boss!"

They remounted and the five rode over to Tate's homestead cabin.

A very sick, very scared Eve Tate was hiding behind the door, her lever action Winchester cocked and ready.

"Get away!" she screamed. "My husband is the sheriff and he will be here any time."

"Step out girlie and lets us take a look at you!" Brown yelled.

Eve made the tactical mistake of doing just what he suggested, carbine at her shoulder.

They all drew and she fired at Brown, missing him.

The five men fired. Three hit her in the torso and she crumpled to the ground.

She laid there cursing Tate for not being here once again. Then, a great darkness came over her and she was no more.

Brown dismounted and squatted down by her.

"Yep! This is the niece. I don't know anything about her sheriff husband. But, he ain't but one man. He comes riding up here now, and they are gonna have to call a new election. 'Cause he's gonna be dead!"

He nudged her roughly a couple times with his boot and got back on his horse.

"She's dead. Let's ride boys! He's in," he stopped for help from Hill, "Manitou Springs."

They took off, leaving Evelyn Hudson Tate dead in the dirt near her front door, bleeding from three fatal bullet wounds.

Tate found her a half hour later. Tears streaming, he picked her up and put her on the bed. He pulled the blanket up over her face and kneeled at her side and sobbed.

Then, anger took over heartbreak. He arose, leaned over and kissed her one last time.

He knew what destiny had decided for him. It wasn't his choice. Not at all.

He loaded food and .44-40 ammunitions in his saddlebags and filled two canteens. He put the rest of his travel gear behind the cantle of Cisco's saddle. He put all their cash money in a leather bag and included it with his trail kit.

Tate saw Jubal's buckboard was gone, but walked over and looked inside the cabin to make sure the man he had grown to think of as an older brother was not lying dead inside. The man who, in Tate's mind, was the replacement for the older brother the war took, was not there.

"C'mon, boy. We've got to deliver a lot of hellfire today. Let's get on with it." He knew Cisco understood and the big black gelding took off at a full gallop without the single touch of a spur.

They followed five sets of tracks into Manitou Springs, rifle out of the scabbard and ready.

"I'm looking for five horsemen. One is a big fellow. Former marshal in Colorado Springs gone bad. Seen them?"

The man, a freighter unloading grain sacks at the general mercantile, immediately responded.

"I seen 'em. Not long ago. Came riding in here like the devil hisself was chasing them. Looked all around town. Real careful. Then, one said to the big man, "He ain't here. We gotta go to Colorado Springs. He'll be there! And, they spurred and rode off in a cloud of dust. I wouldn't want to be the one they was looking for, Sheriff."

"No, mister. You wouldn't want to be *them*!" Tate said as the spun Cisco and galloped off.

The freighter watched him. He had never seen a look of such death and violence like in the sheriff's eyes.

"Yep, Sheriff. I sure as hell wouldn't" he said aloud and lifted a bag onto his shoulders.

Cisco showed his blood and breeding on the way between the two Springs.

Tate slowed as he approached town, but then heard shots.

******

Jubal Paine had awoken early, as he was wont to do. While Darlene dressed for work, he fixed them breakfast. Looking out the door, he could tell Tate had already left. The young man put a lot of miles behind him and his black horse, he thought. He really was not cut out to be a rancher. He was cut out to be a lawman. A damn good one. Just as Jubal knew he had been cut out to be a secret agent. He just could not pursue excellence in his career because his side lost. It was not like he could have reported for duty to Allan J. Pinkerton and said, "I ruined your day so many times, you should hire me now this mess is over."

He went out to hook up the buckboard for them to take into town to work. Usually, Eve was up and ready to go. No sign of her.

Jubal walked over to the cabin to check on his niece.

He found her sitting on the bed, still in a night gown crying softly and holding her stomach.

"What's wrong girl? You are usually ready to go to go 'way before now. You okay?"

"Uncle, I have not told Morgan, but I think something's real wrong in here. I don't know if this swelling is a baby or something else," she said.

"Something else? Like a growth? A tumor?" he asked.

"My fear is a growth. But, I don't think the doc in town is who I should see. Neither is the midwife, particularly if it's not a baby. Or, the baby's not right."

"Honey, you need to talk to Tate. Then, you need to go see a real specialist. Maybe the Medical College in Richmond, or one in Philadelphia or some large city," he said.

"Those are far away and take time and money."

"So what? Tate does well as county sheriff. He can take the time. God knows he works all the time as is. Talk to him. And, don't wait."

"You're probably right. Tell Darlene I'm not feeling well today and see if she will tell my boss I won't be in, will you?"

"Of course. Are you sure you won't ride in with us and at least speak with the doctor?"

"Not today. Maybe tomorrow."

Jubal leaned over and kissed his niece on the top of her head and walked out the door.

He saddled the old horse for Darlene, having need for the mule and buckboard himself to pick up some tools and materials he ordered in Colorado Springs.

Husband and wife left together and rode all the way in side by side. Each considered the other a late life's blessing.

******

Folks did not usually wear revolvers in town. Jubal Paine kept his carbine in the back of the buckboard, covered with a tarp. Most people kept a rifle or shot-gun that way, if they had one.

Jubal had an ominous feeling today. Maybe it was Eve. Maybe it was what Tate told them about this fellow Will Brown. Was he really Hiram Stone, the nasty and mean prison guard from his past?

He slipped Lieutenant Langston's .32 in his boot just in case. The fit was tight enough to hold it and loose enough to draw. And, it was unseen.

Jubal, ever orderly and disciplined, decided to go to the places with the least weight to carry first.

He stopped in the doctor's office and had to wait for ten minutes. He told the doctor about Eve's problems and fears. The doctor recommended a specialist much closer than Richmond or Philadelphia. He said he knew of a good one in Denver. It was a relative rarity. A female physician. Her practice, he said, was exclusively women and pregnancies. He gave Jubal a piece of paper with her contact information on it. Not having pockets, he shoved it in the boot without a revolver already in it.

Jubal went on to the general mercantile and picked up a small sack of necessities and a treat for the two women in his life.

While he was in the doctor's office, Will Brown, Hill and the three hired guns arrived in town, walking their horses slowly. Hill knew his replacement would be on duty and told Brown he was someone representing a threat to them. He also knew Horace Keefe would be at the damn sheriff's office, also a threat.

Stupidly, they walked in a group searching for the former Confederate spy.

Brown spotted Jubal coming out of the general mercantile and without thinking, pulled his gun. Seeing this, Hill and the others not only pulled, they started shooting at Jubal.

Jubal turned towards the gunfire and looked eye to eye, from fifty feet, at a man he thought he had killed almost fourteen years ago.

The former spy whipped the revolver out of this boot and shot the spectral figure in the chest twice before ducking back into the store. His spy talents had come back with a vengeance.

"Everybody down!" Jubal yelled.

Will Brown, holding his chest, staggered towards the general mercantile. The others spread out and began moving towards it.

The scene seemed to move at a snail's pace.

Sheriff Morgan Tate rode fast into Colorado Springs, sheathing his Winchester

At the first shot he heard, he slid a cartridge into the empty chamber on which he kept the hammer down for safety. He did this with Cisco at a full gallop and now had six rounds in his Colt before going to his rifle.

He slid off Cisco, not wanting him to be in direct danger from the gunfire.

Running fast from one protective barrier to another, Tate got to within revolver range of the spread out shooters.

He fired at the largest target first and Hill went down, holding his crotch and screaming like a little girl. Tate shot him again, killing him.

One of the three gun-hands fired at Tate and Tate brought him down for good.

Jubal continued to shoot at Brown, or Hiram Stone, until his revolver was dry. He ran to the gun counter and grabbed another box of cartridges and reloaded on the run back to the door.

There were still two shooters representing a threat and Brown who had not decided whether to just die and be done with it.

Tate squatted behind a full water barrel and shot at one of the gun thugs. He winged him, but the man still shot back. So, Tate shot him again from an estimated forty feet. The slug caught him in the center of the forehead and he went down permanently.

One more. Tate could see Tom Burton easing down the street, with a double barreled shotgun at the ready. Tate stood and waved. Burton nodded he saw and recognized the sheriff.

The last man was spinning around in the middle of the street, looking for help and for a target. There was no help. But three targets. One badge toter on each side approaching him and one man with a long barrel, popgun in the store in front of him.

Tate reloaded and holstered his Colt.

The man looked at him in disbelief. Tate could not see his two friends in this gunfight, but so did they.

He walked towards the man with the gun.

"Who killed my wife?" he asked in a soft voice.

The man, his Remington revolver still pointed at Tate, said "Brown did," and nodded towards the man still staggering around aimlessly some distance over.

Tate, in the same soft voice heard only by the man with the gun, said "Thank you."

Then, he drew and fired faster than any onlooker could have imagined and hit the man in the Adam's apple. He went down and stayed down.

Tate walked over to where Brown was staggering in shock from the small bullets Jubal had put into him.

"You killed my wife," he said, not really expecting an answer.

Brown looked and tried to focus on him. He could not. He tried to raise his revolver.

At the first movement of the gun, Tate shot him in the mouth. He crumpled into the dust like a worn ragdoll.

Tate stood over him and cocked the Colt Frontier Model aimed at the dead man's head. Somebody, probably Tom Burton, distantly said, "Tate, don't!"

The deadly lawman who had just killed five men in the space of two minutes looked up at Burton as his friend approached. Jubal walked out of the store, his revolver still in hand.

Tate eased the hammer down on the Colt and holstered it.

He reached in his large vest pocket for the bag with all the money he had in the world.

He handed Jubal a fistful of gold coins.

"Would you bury her? Real nice? In the town cemetery." The uncle nodded, having heard the conversation about his niece being murdered.

"Jubal, my homestead and everything on it are yours. Tom, you are the witness to what I just said."

Tate unpinned the gold star from his chest and dropped it on Brown's body.

His tan face tearstained, Tate turned and walked back to where Cisco stood, reins on the street.

Former sheriff, former Texas Ranger, Morgan Wood Tate. Dressed in dusty black. He reloaded his Frontier Model and then swung a long leg over the saddle.

He turned the horse north on the street and rode out of the life he had loved, never looking back.

CHAPTER 16

Several days later, Eve Tate's funeral was held. The crowd was small. The Paine's, Burton's, several deputies, the Hansen's and the folks she worked with came on a bright fall day.

Jubal used the money Tate gave him for a nice monument, which was put in place a month later. As Tate requested, Jubal buried her in the town cemetery.

Marshal Burton and several other witnesses testified before the circuit judge about Tate giving his property to Jubal. The judge decreed it be filed and the deed amended. Jubal now had three hundred twenty prime Colorado acres. He planned to hold it for Tate and drew up a will leaving the whole thing to him after he and Darlene passed. He hoped Tate might be drawn back to the only home he had ever cared about. But, he truly did not know.

Getting the cabin, stable and corral part of his land

ready took what little was left of the growing season. He and Darlene had a small garden behind the cabin and it provided corn, beans and squash for their table needs during the summer and into the early fall. Darlene put some by for winter consumption in a root cellar Jubal had dug and closed in. He and Tecumseh plowed land for the larger vegetable garden next spring.

Husband and wife missed both Eve and Tate and wondered what Tate was doing. Had he become a drifter, a drunk or a gun for hire in his misery and melancholy?

Over his loud remonstrations, Tom Burton accepted the governor's appointment as sheriff to serve out the almost four remaining years of Tate's term. Burton had two deputies to replace, the position he vacated and the one vacated by the deputy who took his place as town marshal of Colorado Springs.

******

Molly Winthrop was a handsome woman in her sixties. She was wealthy. But, in land rather than cash. A widow, she ran a seven hundred acre ranch ten miles outside of Hastings, Nebraska. She made enough money to pay a minimal number of wranglers and to keep food on the table, but hardly more.

This late fall day had started off well. She was coming back from Hastings with a small box wagon pulled by two mules. She was given everything she needed on credit at the store in Hastings. Molly had enough food and supplies for her and her wranglers for the next month.

Then, she hit a rut in the road and the left rear wheel started vibrating. She was sure she broke something, but decided to keep on going.

Several hundred yards later, the rig became uncontrollable and she yelled "Whoa!" and pulled the brake lever.

Molly climbed down and uttered a curse word, since the mules wouldn't tell. Her left rear wheel was off and flat on the side of the road. The loaded wagon, bigger than a buckboard, was leaning and unsteady. She knew there was little danger of dumping over. She also knew it would not move safely from its current location until fixed. She acknowledged readily to herself she did not have the knowledge or strength to do move it.

She had a couple of options. Unhitch one mule and ride him bareback the six miles back to the ranch and get a couple of her riders to come out and fix it. There were several negatives associated with riding home. First, she had not ridden anything bareback for forty years. Second, she stood a good chance of losing supplies for which she had not even paid yet by leaving them unattended on the side of the road.

Molly's only other alternative was to sit and wait for help. She had her shotgun in the bed of the wagon. If someone came by who could not assist, but could take a message to her wranglers, she could guard her cargo. Without it, she would be in big trouble.

Molly decided to try waiting before trying bareback mule riding. So, there she sat.

After about an hour, she saw a rider coming towards her, and Hastings.

As he got closer, she could see he was dressed in all black and on a black horse. The only thing she could see differing from the black was an ivory grip on the low-riding Colt he wore like a gunfighter. She did not need to make an overt move for the shotgun. It was within easy grasp.

The man appeared to be tall. He had a short beard and was dark as a Lakota. His eyes were as light blue as today's Nebraska sky.

"If you have some tools, I think I can get you on the road again," he said in a deep voice.

"I'd appreciate it if you could, stranger," she said.

He dismounted the beautiful black and left the reins hanging straight down. The horse walked over to the side of the road and began munching some grass.

He searched around the wheel and looked up at her.

"Ma'am, do you know when the wheel nut came off?"

"I'm not sure. I hit a rut real hard, back there," and she pointed to a clump of trees several hundred yards behind them.

"The wheel nut does not seem to be here, so I'll walk down the road and see if I see it. Do you have wheel repair tools and grease?" he asked, knowing it was standard to carry repair items in every wagon or buckboard.

"There's a tool box in the rear of the bed. I have not looked at it, but I think its wheel repair items."

"Guess I better search for the nut first. Even if you have an extra, there's no use wasting money by leaving a perfectly good one behind."

He turned and walked down the road, scanning the side for about six feet out from the track. At the trees, he found the greasy square nut covered with dirt and walked back trying unsuccessfully to blow the dirt off.

"Have you found the right one?" she asked.

"Should be. Want to slide the tool box over to the tailgate?"

She did and he found a spare smaller nut for a front spindle. Wagons such as this usually had forty-four inch wheels on the front and taller forty-eights on the rear. There was a greasy rag and can of axle grease in the box. What was not in the bed was a wagon jack. He walked around the side of the road. Nothing. A trip into nearby woods provided a seven foot log about four inches in diameter. He found a wooden box of nails and staples in the rear he could put under the wagon and use as the fulcrum of a jack.

The next step was to grease the spindle. Once the grease work was done, he sat the box on end to give some height and put the log over it.

"Ma'am, I'm going to need your help. You can either hold the jack handle — the log here — after I prop up the wagon bed, or you can start the square

bolt on. I'll finish it with the wrench. Your choice."
She picked the nut.

He set the wheel up against the wagon and pushed down on the end of the small log. The wagon lifted and Molly placed the wheel on.

"It's a reverse thread, so screw it backwards or to the left," he said.

She did. She got it as far as she could with her hands and he lowered the wheel onto the ground. Moving the box and log out of the way, he took the square wrench and finished tightening the nut.

He set the box back in the bed and threw the log off into the grass, away from the road. He then wiped his hands on the grass.

"Thank you stranger. Can I pay you a bit?"

"No thanks, Ma'am. But, do you need a ranch hand for a short period?"

"Stranger, I need about eight. But, I cannot afford one more."

"How about for a week for room and board only?" he asked.

"You a wanted man?"

"I'm afraid nobody wants me now."

"Were you wanted before?" she asked.

"By the law? No. I enforced the law. I didn't break it. But, it's okay. I better be moving on."

"No, wait. Room and board for a week. Wrangle my remuda?" she asked.

"I could handle it."

"I'm Molly Winthrop. I own the Lazy W Ranch. It's six miles or so from here. Just follow me back and we'll get you settled."

"Thank you, Ma'am," he responded, failing to identify himself.

The ranch house was long and low with unpainted boards and a shake roof. There was a big corral, a fairly large stable and barn and a bunkhouse. There was an unused bunk back in the far corner and he chose it. He saw to his black horse and washed up, finishing just before Molly Winthrop rang the dinner gong.

He heard the other employees ride in and head for the trough to wash for dinner.

"I guess I better find out your name before I try to introduce you to the other riders," Molly said.

"Just call me Tate, Mrs. Winthrop," he said.

"Alright, Tate it is."

As they gathered around a large, wind worn wooden table in the yard, Molly began to bring large pots of beans and green out. The riders sat and waited. Tate got up and helped her. The roasted beef smelled good, but it wasn't the brisket he grew up eating in Texas.

"Boys, this is Tate. He's going to be with us helping with the horses for a week or so. You make him welcome, ya hear?"

Each looked up and nodded and dug into dinner with the vengeance of a working man who had worked through lunch.

The food was good, especially compared to the trail food Tate had lived on for several months, drifting through the West.

Per custom, riders refrained from speaking much during meals, especially dinner. This meal was characterized more by Nebraska wind, hardwood smoke from the stove, the aroma of the food and the ever present smell of the prairie. It was a good smell. A homey smell. Tate was reminded of Eve and the home they had begun to make together. And, baby Tate. The son or daughter he would never hold or teach to talk or ride. He lowered his head and ate, glad there was no need to talk. He would check the barn loft after dinner. He saw several cats roaming around the barn. Given the cats, it was unlikely there were rats or snakes in the top of the barn. But, he had to know for sure before moving out of the bunkhouse and spreading his blanket on straw to avoid talk and questions. He did not need people now. They were just irritating noise.

Five riders were in for dinner. Tate reckoned there must be two or three others left out to watch the herd of cattle.

Dinner finished, the men sat around drinking strong black coffee and chatting.

The peace of the almost dusk was penetrated by a high velocity rifle shot, followed by two revolver shots.

"Regulators!" one of the men yelled.

The men jumped up as Molly ran into the house to grab a couple Winchesters. A couple of the riders had no guns at all. Molly handed them the Winchesters. The other three pulled different revolvers from their saddlebags.

Tate had already saddled Cisco and was riding off.

He had memorized the direction from which the shots sounded. This was flat prairie land. No mountains or hills for the sounds to reverberate off. He rode, a string of five riders behind him, but not catching up.

Tate saw the two riders, one on his feet and one on his back.

He swung off Cisco as the standing cow man aimed his gun at him.

"I'm with Mrs. Winthrop. Point your damn gun in another direction and tell me what happened!"

"Two riders rode up. One shot Melvin with a rifle. He's dead. Has to be regulators hired by the big ranchers. One or two have been trying to buy this place. They figure killing us off will put her out of business."

"Which way did they go?" Tate asked.

The man pointed northwest.

Tate he could see a trail from the shooters retreating across the prairie.

"Tell the boys to get this man's body back to the ranch and to protect Mrs. Winthrop, all right?"

Tate could see the buffalo grass pushed down where the two riders rode through. He followed the path they left. They had a ten minute head start, but did not expect pursuit and were riding at a brisk pace, but not like men running from sure death.

He rode close enough to see the men. The grass and dirt below did not amplify the noise of the horses. Tate did not see them look back during the chase. They slowed from a canter to a trot. Cisco automatically did the same as Tate was not urging him on. He figured this late in the day, the men would stop and make a camp instead of riding to some ranch. Regulators were generally guns for hire and on their own. The odd thing to Tate was two men instead of one.

He had mixed feelings about what to do with them when he caught them. Most big ranchers were tied in with the sheriffs and judges. A trial would likely be a travesty of justice. The work of capturing them unscathed and transporting them to Hastings for trial was sure to be a waste of time. As far as Tate was concerned, these were cold-blooded murderers.

He based his planned actions on logical justice, not morals or the law.

The two slowed even more, suggesting to Tate they were looking for a place to stop for the night.

Sure enough, they stopped just before darkness. If there was any wood for a fire in this part of Nebraska, its presence eluded Tate. The earlier prairie fuel standby, bison dung, was long gone. It did not really matter to him, his duster was already tied behind the cantle of his saddle. He had sufficient ammunition, and food and water with him each time he put the saddle on Cisco. In this cool, but not cold weather, he could camp comfortably without a fire.

The grass was getting higher. Tate thought switch-grass, maybe.

Tate unsaddled Cisco and spoke with him quietly. The wind was against his back, so there was a chance his words or a whinny or snort could carry on it to the regulators. He gave Cisco a crown full of canteen water in his hat.

He spread the waxed canvas duster on the tall grass and laid on it. The grass was an imperfect mattress, but better than the ground alone. Tate munched on a piece of jerky and had a sip from one of his two canteens.

He developed a plan as he dozed off for a couple hours.

About three in the morning, Tate awoke and took Cisco off his hobble. He told him to stay and hiked to where the two regulators were camped.

As with the tracking by horse, the grass and soft loam in many places made for silent stalking on foot.

Tate made it to the regulator's camp sooner than he expected. He knew this would be quick and close, no matter how it went down. He left his Winchester with his saddle at his own camp and would depend on the dependable Colt Frontier Model.

He stood there quietly watching the sleeping pair.

After a while, one man stirred and got up and wandered half asleep, about ten feet off. He fumbled for a while and finally began to urinate.

His senses were not very good he did not feel Tate directly behind him. He may have felt the blow from the ivory butt of the Colt against his head, but Tate doubted it.

The man's gunbelt must have been where he slept, because it was not around his ankles like everything else.

Tate holstered and dragged the man back into camp. The slight noise awakened the other man who reached for a long barreled rifle, maybe an 1876 Winchester.

Tate dropped the urinator's shoulders and drew before the other man could heft the big rifle. Tate fired two fast shots from seven feet away, killing the murderer of Molly Winthrop's rider. The urinator regained consciousness and wrapped his arms around Tate's legs. He went down hard.

The man was on top of him fast, swinging a flurry of blows with both fists. Tate grabbed him by the shoulders and rolled him off, but he came up swinging again. Tate blocked a round house and jabbed his bare fist into the man's throat. Damn! He hated to fight with his gun hand unprotected. But, the throat was a relatively soft target.

The man went cross-eyed and started gagging. Figuring he was dying and had nothing to lose, he pulled a Barlow knife out of his vest and started to open the blade. So, Tate shot him.

Tate did not have a shovel to bury them. There were no rocks to gather for a cairn within a three-day ride.

He thought a minute and decided to build a crime scene where two partners had falling out and shot each other.

Tate looked through their vests and their saddle bags. In one saddle bag, he found a small bottle of what he suspected was really bad whiskey. He took it out and dumped half on one man and half on the other, being sure to get some in their mouths. He dropped it on the ground between them.

He arranged the bodies in a position which suggested a shootout.

He strapped the gun belt on the one who had been the sniper.

Removing each revolver, he checked the loads. Both were carrying properly with five rounds and the hammer on an empty chamber to prevent accidental discharges if the hammer was struck by something or the gun was dropped.

He took the sniper's revolver and shot it once in the air. Tate then put it in his hand.

Since he had shot the sniper twice, he took the urinator's revolver and shot twice in the air. To avoid the implications of a pants-down gunfight, he hitched up the urinator's pants and buttoned them before putting his gun belt on. He dropped the conversion Remington Navy on the ground where the wounded man might have dropped it before dying.

He relieved both men of their cash, except for a couple dollars each. The sniper had fifty dollars in a separate leather wallet. Apparently fifty bucks was the fee for killing Mrs. Winthrop's rider.

He would take the horses, saddles and all. While it would be logical to have saddles laying around, but the horses would have run off after the gunfight, Tate had a use for both. He doubted Allan J. Pinkerton himself would be examining the crime scene.

Tate checked the rifles. One was a Winchester Model 1876 in .45-75 caliber. He knew the action of the Centennial year Winchester would not handle the length of the government .45-70, so Winchester made a cartridge for the rifle.

He might want to keep this one piece of equipment he was confiscating. The other was a Spencer of war fame. Good gun, but not a '76 Winchester. Not by a mile. But, still fit with his intentions.

Tate led the saddled horses back to Cisco. The sniper had a lariat on his saddle, probably to hang some poor small rancher for effect. When he got back to the black gelding, he cut the lariat in half with his Bowie knife and knotted both cut ends so they would not fray. He attached each to the bridle of the commandeered horses and headed back to the Lazy W Ranch, horses led behind Cisco.

It was early morning and still dark when he left.

Tate arrived back at the ranch not long after breakfast. Most of the riders were getting ready to ride out to the herd, but did not when they saw the man in black on the black horse leading two horses with empty saddles.

Tate rode up to the porch where Molly Winthrop was waiting for an explanation. Tate dismounted and took the two rifle scabbards off the led horses.

"Perhaps we can step inside and I will let you know what's going on, Mrs. Winthrop.

She turned and he followed her in. She motioned for him to sit. He did after leaning the two rifles against the corner wall.

"We feared you were dead when you didn't come back last night, Tate."

"I followed the two regulators until well after dark. Maybe I should say one regulator and one regulator in training. I knew I was close, so I made a cold camp. Well before daylight, I walked to their camp with full intention of capturing them both. One awakened, and I introduced his head to the butt of my Colt. I dragged him back to the camp, waking the other one up. The second man is the one who killed your rider. He reached for the long Winchester," Tate nodded towards the longer gun propped in the corner, "and, I had to shoot him. The other one attacked me and we fought for a while. He pulled a knife and I had to shoot him, too. Ma'am, I suspect the big ranchers who hired these two are in cahoots with the judges around here. Even if I had brought them in, they would have been back out in a day or two. It's better this way."

"Where are their bodies?" she asked.

"They were shot justifiably, but I arranged the crime scene. Are you sure you want to know?" he asked.

"I do, Mr. Tate. Pray continue."

"I shot the sniper who killed your man twice and the other once. So, I rearranged them like in a gunfight, poured their whiskey on them and fired the appropriate number of rounds out of the appropriate guns. Two trailhands got drunk and killed each other. Their horses ran off. End of story."

"How did you learn how to stage a crime scene?" she asked.

"I was a lawman until recently, Ma'am."

"Will you tell me your story? I have a legitimate reason to know. I'll tell you why after you tell me."

"I will share the short version. I was a Texas Ranger who left to homestead in Colorado. I got married. The rangers called me back to be a captain for three months. I did it and returned and became sheriff. Five men killed my wife, who was expecting. I rode in right behind them. I trailed them into Colorado Springs, where my office was. We had a shootout. I killed them. I dropped my badge in the street, handed my wife's uncle enough money to bury my Eve and rode away. It was a few months ago now."

The woman was rightly struck by the story.

"I thought, though you seemed a good man, you were trying to get away from somebody," She said.

"I 'spect I am, Mrs. Winthrop."

"May I ask who?"

"Myself."

The two sat silently for a few minutes before she spoke.

"I guess I can understand what you are saying. I was being nosey to find out if I should ask you to stay on as foreman. You clearly are a step up from being a horse wrangler or cow hand. I don't have any money, so it would have to be on shares."

"It's real kind of you Mrs. Winthrop. But, I just walked away from a quarter section of rolling hills and green trees and, too many memories. I need to keep riding. Before those memories catch up with me again."

"I'm sorry about your loss, Tate. Real sorry. You always have a roof and a bunk if you need it here. God knows I need the help. But, I cannot hire it. I need help cooking and with the house in addition to outside. What I could have really used was a daughter or two, but it wasn't to be," she said.

"Thank you, Ma'am. I have a small bit for you, actually. Those two fellas who killed each other with a little help contributed two good horses and saddles and a couple of rifles. One good and one okay. And, this."

He handed her the leather wallet with a total of seventy-three dollars cash and gold coins in it.

"It's not much. If the dead rider had family, it could go to them. Otherwise, put it in the account for your ranch. It might buy a little something."

"Hank didn't have any family we know about. I didn't think he did, so I asked the boys. They verified it. Two horses, saddles and cash will always help here," she said.

"If it's okay, I'd like to keep the Winchester. It might be helpful in my travels," Tate suggested.

"Of course. You've been generous enough. Will you stay a few more days?" she asked.

"I'll wrangle the horses for the rest of the seven days I agreed to. But, then I have to get going."

"Where to now?" she asked.

"Winter's coming. Maybe south to Santa Fe or somewhere warmer. I don't know. Somewhere. Doesn't really matter where as long as I'm able to outrun my memories."

"How's outrunning your memories working out for you?" she asked.

"Not well. Not well at all," Tate responded.

"Will you ever go back to your land in Colorado?"

"I doubt it. I gave it to my wife's uncle. He's a good man. He said he'd hold it for me, but I don't think I could ever live there again."

Tate rose and picked up the Winchester.

"I better see to Cisco. He could use some feed after eating grass for two days. I'll get on the horses in the

corral and make sure they have everything they need."
He smiled a small smile and walked out the door.

"What a waste of a good man," she thought sadly
as he left.

He fed, watered and turned Cisco loose in the corral. Then, he checked on the remuda already there. A
couple needed shoes, which he found in the barn and
nailed on outside. He brushed the ones who needed
it and talked to them. Tate thought about the difference. He calmly talked to these horses. He talked with
Cisco, but his pard talked back.

He did his job conscientiously, but without joy for
the rest of the week, then thanked Molly Winthrop.

Tate pointed Cisco in a southwesterly direction
and rode off, not looking back. The woman at the
ranch silently prayed for him.

CHAPTER 17

Fifteen or twenty miles from the Lazy W, Tate saw a small ranch ahead. He and Cisco could both use a drink of water, so he headed over.

As he approached, he heard yelling, a woman screaming in agony and the sounds of fists hitting flesh. Hitting hard. Tate pulled on his gloves. He could not abide by what he was hearing. Retribution was called for. And, it had just arrived.

He slipped off Cisco and bounded to the door. He kicked it open, not caring a damn whether it was locked or ajar.

He saw a man wearing just a shirt beating a woman. He was older. It was hard to tell her age with blood running down her nose and her hair awry. Maybe twenties. Tate quickly took in marks on her naked body. Red recent ones, purple bruises and older black bruises. This woman had been subject to hard beatings for a while.

"Well," Tate thought to himself, "the beatings will stop here. Forever."

The man turned as the door slammed open against the wall. His face was a mixture of anger and surprise. The two men rushed each other and Tate's right fist landed soundly on the man's forehead. The man staggered backwards as the tingling pain went all the way up Tate's arm into his shoulder.

As the man staggered back from Tate's blow, Tate struck again. He brought his right boot up into the man's bare crotch as hard as he could. He thought the man's eyes were going to pop right out of his head as he went "whoof…" with an expulsion of air before doubling over. Tate drew the Colt to apply it to the back the man's skull, but the woman had already jumped the man from behind. She reached around and dug her fingers into both of his eyes.

The noise the man, made was more a whimper than a scream. She slid her hand down his face to his neck and began to squeeze, her bare legs wrapped around his waist.

She was average size. By now there was not much personal about her Tate did not already know. But, she must have been pretty strong, since the man's damaged face turned blue very quickly.

Tate let her enjoy her murderous catharsis until almost the end. He gently took her hands off the man's neck. She collapsed into Tate sobbing.

He did not have another choice, so he let her cry it out. Tate pulled the blanket off the foot of the bed and wrapped it around the shoulders of the woman pressed into his chest. The man on the floor was making raspy breathing noises, but he sure was not going anywhere.

While the woman cried into his vest, Tate kicked the man in the side of the head. The raspy breathing stopped.

Ten minutes later, the crying stopped also.

"You might want to wash the blood and eyeball goo off your fingers before it dries permanently," he said to the woman. "You can put something on, if you've a mind to, also," he said as he arranged the blanket around her now she was not tight against him.

"I don't care. This is the way he made me stay all the time anyway," she responded in a voice sounding more like a thirty-year old than the younger woman he thought.

"Other than all the bruises are you injured, Ma'am?" Tate asked.

"No, just sore like I am all the time."

"How about down there?" he asked, pointing below her navel.

"What? Didn't you see him before you kicked the living hell out of him? He's not man enough to hurt anybody with what he's got. I figure it's why he beat on me, because try as he would, day after day, he was worthless in the bed department."

Tate reached down and touched where the man's pulse should have been. It was there, but very weak. He guessed his boot must have done it. If ever a man deserved getting his head kicked in, this one seemed a top candidate. He may die as he was. Or, he may need some help.

"I'm taking it from your attack on him, you don't care if he lives or dies?" Tate asked.

"I hope he dies and burns in hell forever," she said. He thought for a minute.

"Could he write?" Tate asked.

"He could write a little and do some ciphers."

"How about this place? Is there a mortgage on it?"

"No, he was a squatter. Nobody ever came up and tried to claim it. Leastwise, since we've been here."

"How long have you been here?" he asked.

"Maybe six months. Six months of hell. I was in a wagon train. When my new husband died, I couldn't keep up. Luke," she said pointing to the man on the floor, "didn't have a wagon. He was just walking with a blanket and some stuff on his back. Fool didn't even have a rifle. He helped me bury my husband on the prairie. The wagons moved on, mine included. It was taken by some no-accounts. Luke spotted this place and we walked over. Then, I found out a man who had not said twenty words to anybody in two hundred miles was a demon from hell. He was crazy. I hope he dies right now."

"He will. One way or the other," Tate promised.

"Ma'am, what's your name?"

"It's Lila James. No kin to Jesse, by the way."

Tate smiled at this. A little bit of sass was coming back. He held up a finger for her to wait, cut a piece of sheet with his Bowie knife and walked outside to the well. He dampened the cloth and went back in.

Tate gently washed the smeared, dried blood off Lila's face from the nose bleed.

"What's your name, stranger?" Lila asked.

"Tate."

"Just 'Tate?'" she asked.

"Why don't you get something on. I need to take this piece of dung out into the barn. We have some unfinished business," he said, ignoring her question.

He dragged the almost-dead man as he went out the door and around the corner of the shack to the ramshackle barn.

He found a length of rope and made a slip knot. To hell with a hangman's note. He put the noose around the man's neck and tossed the free end over a rafter. Dealing with effectively dead weight, Tate strained to pull the man to his feet. Then, with a last burst of strength, Tate pulled the rope until the man's feet were five feet off the ground. He then took a barrel, emptied it out and placed it on its side as if the man had stood on it, fastened his noose, then stepped off to hang himself.

Tate went out to Cisco, still standing patiently with his reins straight down. He took a nub of a pencil out of his saddlebag and reentered the barn.

He took the pencil and wrote on the wall. His note said "I hurt her bad. She left. I kaint live," in crude letters. Satisfied. He replaced the pencil on Cisco and went to the door of the shack and tapped.

"You decent?" he asked and got a laugh in return.

"As if it really matters now!"

"I'm from Texas. I have to ask. It's the way my mama taught me."

"Yes, come on in Mr. Tate."

"No 'mister' necessary," he said. She was wearing a worn but clean dress and her hair was brushed. With the blood cleaned off her face and the body full of bruises hidden, she was quite pretty. At closer look, Tate thought his last guess of late twenties or early thirties was probably close.

"Lila, where can I help you go? Do you have any family you'd like to go to?" Tate asked.

"My folks are dead. No brothers or sisters. Tate, I don't have anywhere to go or anyone to go to. I envy men. You have choices. You can get on your big black horse and ride off without any idea of where you're going to end up. If I did it, people would think I was a soiled dove going to another town or just a crazy woman."

"I have some very personal experience with how hard it is to be a woman."

"You want to talk about it?" she asked.

"No, Lila. It's something I have not figured out how to deal with myself yet."

"Sometimes, it helps to talk with a caring stranger. I owe you, Tate. You probably saved my life. If not today, then some other day. But, you seem to be a decent man. I'd help you anyway."

"Let's get you taken care of first," he said.

"I helped out an older lady with a ranch a couple hours northwest. She needs help with her house and cooking for her riders. She doesn't have any money to pay, but I bet she'd love to have you there for room and board. Then, when the ranch gets back in the money, she's pay you."

"Do you just ride around and help ladies in trouble, Tate?"

"I missed helping the one meaning the most to me by a few minutes. If I can make up for it even a little, it would be worth it."

"So, the thing you don't want to talk about is related to her? The one you missed helping?"

Tate did not say anything. He did not have to.

"How 'bout we get me a six gun and I just ride with you?" she asked. Tate thought about it. He grinned. This one does have some sass to her. He wondered if it was possible. A female, gun-packing pard. Well, maybe. Just not based on knowing her twenty minutes though.

"Can you even shoot a six gun?" he asked.

"Not really, but I'm a real fast learner!"

"What's wrong with moving in with Mrs. Winthrop and helping her?" he asked.

"Oh, probably nothing. Maybe I'd just like to ride with you."

"Yep. All you need is a sad, guilt-ridden pard."

"Tate, I can promise you I have had worse. You just killed one. The one back on the wagon trail did not beat me, but he was awful disappointed I could not fill a farmhouse with little workers in his exact image. And, whether I can or cannot is kinda up in the air, given the two men I've had," she said.

"You just speak it right out, don't you. Don't hold back at all."

"Life's too short to mince words, Tate"

"You're pretty smart, Lila," he observed.

"Why don't you see what you need to take? Keep it light, because Cisco is not used to carrying double."

"I already packed. I am wearing it," she said.

"I hung your friend. Then, I knocked over a barrel to make it look like he used it to drop from and break his neck. Finally, I wrote a crude and badly spoken suicide note on the wall."

"Sure looks like you have done this before. What were you besides a lady helper. Did you assist in suicides for a fee?"

"Don't worry, I was on the right side of a badge. I've seen a lot of murder scenes," Tate said.

"Well ain't you the jaybird!" she said, barely able to contain her smile.

"I thought about just burning the damned old barn

down with him lying in it, but I was afraid of starting a prairie fire and roasting us, too," Tate admitted.

He looked at his pocket watch. Lila caught a quick look at the pretty woman's picture in the lid. Certainly fodder for a conversation later. She was going to have to pump information out of this tall Texan in black like drawing water.

"It's already eleven in the morning, Miss Lila. It's going to be cold on the trail tonight. Do you have a coat and heavier shoes," he said, noticing the thin ones she was wearing.

"I have the horrible looking brogans I wore across the prairie in the wagon, then walking here after we got left," she responded. "And, I have a wool long coat, a scarf I can wrap around like a hat."

"Better get them. You got any food in there? Biscuits for the trail, or something?"

"While I'm getting a blanket and my warmer clothes, why don't you gather up the food. I made Indian fry bread. We have a little coffee, dried beans, salt, and flour."

"Good! I'll get it put together and in a bag. We have to be careful about weight, since we are riding double. Cisco isn't used to it."

He gathered the food and cut another square off the sheet, put the food in and tied it at the top with a latigo. Lila came out, her blonde curls sneaking out of the scarf wrapped around her head and tied around her neck.

Doing something scarily familiar, he took the small

.41 Colt spur trigger pocket revolver out of its usual hiding place and presented it to Lila after showing her how to cock and fire it.

"So, does the mean we *are* going to ride the trails together?" she asked.

"Uh…well, at least to outside Hastings to the Lazy W Ranch. I'm a little worried about the sky. Does it look like snow to you?"

She looked up and thought for a long time.

"I think it is going to snow. And, a lot. How long, riding double to get to the ranch?" she asked.

"It was a good half day with Cisco just carrying me and at a canter. We'll be at a walk, so I figure unless we hit a big blow, it will be rest of today, camp, and get in around dinner time. Probably ready for a hot meal of beef and beans and maybe even pie!" he said.

"Don't try to get on my good side with food. It might work," she responded.

They mounted Cisco. The horse looked back at Tate with a distinct look of disapproval.

"Cisco, this is what we have to do. You need to just accept it," Tate said in a conversational tone.

The horse snorted derisively.

"Do you and your horse have these chats often?" Lila asked.

"Yes. He understands English pretty well, so be careful what you say. He has a pretty sensitive temperament for such a big, tough horse."

"I'll keep it in mind," Lila responded, only half buying Tate's statement.

As she shifted, trying to get a more comfortable position, she asked "why do you have two rifles?"

"I have a big one for big things and a smaller one for smaller things."

"Well, sure makes perfect sense. Does your horse agree?" she asked.

The answer was so obvious to Tate, he did not dignify her question with a response. He changed the subject.

"You know what's missing out here?" he asked.

"No, what?"

"Buffalo manure."

"And, it's important to us why?"

"Well, it's obvious trees are missing, so I was hoping we'd have buffalo scat for fuel. It's gonna be really cold tonight and, like we talked about, probably snowing," he said.

"I guess I took it for granted we'd have it. Buffalo manure was a lot of our fuel on the wagon train. We came through this part of Nebraska, but long after turning off from some real wild country. It still had buffalo. And, as we found out, some pretty angry Indians."

"They got plenty to be angry about."

"I don't doubt it. But, it's hard to remember when you hear war cries and arrows and bullets going past your head."

"I know the feeling really well." Tate admitted.

"Tate?"

"What, Miss Lila?"

"It's getting really cold out."

"You need a wool blanket to wrap over your coat?"

"Yes. Like you wrapped me up in the cabin. You were kind and a gentleman. Most men would have just stared at me in my state of undress."

"It *was* a rare moment," he said, leaving her to puzzle his response, as he dismounted and got his heavy blanket out of the bedroll and wrapped it around her shoulders. He checked the time, Lila craning to see the picture, and mounted Cisco.

"It would normally be 'way too early to stop and make camp. But, we have to gather a big bunch of the largest sage brush sticks we can for tonight. A lot more than it would look like we need, because they will burn fast."

He looked for a spot to stop off the trail, but everything looked about the same. Tate spied an area with taller sagebrush. Maybe a different variety. He stopped there.

Tate took a small trowel out of his saddlebag.

"Would you scoop out a fire pit while I chop a lot of sage brush? I stopped here because they look taller, which might mean thicker stems."

He removed the wicked looking, but highly effective Bowie knife he had carried since a young ranger. Soon, he had a pile of sagebrush taller than his six foot plus height.

Lila instinctively dug a perfect fire pit. It was two feet in diameter and a foot deep. She saw which bag had the camping gear and removed a grill and coffee pot. She found the next bag had coffee, salt and beans and, lots of ammunition. She placed the coffee by the pit while Tate chopped the thicker stems and branches into foot-long fuel. He watched the woman as he worked. Normally, he would have not liked someone searching in his saddlebags. But, her actions seemed unobtrusive and perfectly natural. Early to tell, but she seemed like a pretty good pard.

The wind picked up and snow began to blow hard.

Tate got out his flint and steel box and made a fire. He brewed strong coffee while Lila set out the fry bread.

Since the wind was working havoc on the fire they needed for warmth, Tate took the small tarp he usually put over his blankets and made a low lean-to over the fire. He pulled the two bedrolls, such as they were, in close to the fire, putting a rifle on each side. He left the rifles in their scabbards to protect them.

Using precious water from one of his two canteens, he shared it with Cisco, who he hobbled close by. Tate used the saddle to further help block the fire pit from the wind. He also put Cisco's saddle blanket under Lila's bedroll to keep the cold ground from affecting her as much. She noticed and turned away so he would not see her wide smile.

They drank the hot coffee quickly as it was not holding the heat well in the wintry conditions.

The two adjourned to their bedrolls to munch fry bread for lunch. Or, dinner. Or, whatever the poor excuse for a meal was.

The sky was so dark it was not possible for Tate to determine whether it was day or night. He did not want to stir cold air by checking his watch. He decided it did not make a damn bit of difference anyway. It was snowing, cold and dark. And, it was going to continue for a while. He did not even want to hazard a guess how long a while would be.

Tate could see some of Lila's face despite the wool scarf wrapped around her head and throat and the blanket pulled up as high as she could get it without exposing her feet to the penetrating cold. What he saw was pretty. All of what he had seen of her was pretty. He felt guilty thinking of her in such a manner. It had only been several months since Eve had been murdered. He hoped the retribution he had wrought would bring her some peace and forgiveness.

Tate gave the matter a lot of thought as he lay there cold. He could not be everywhere he needed to be as a lawman. He got to Eve too late, but only by minutes. He had no way of knowing one of her uncle's nemeses would have gone there. Gone there right then. Gone there just ahead of him. Well, he sure wouldn't go anywhere else now. Outside of hell!

His soul searching was interrupted by a tiny voice. "Tate?"

"Yes, Miss Lila. I thought you were asleep," he responded.

"I was. But, the cold woke me up. It's really cold! Could I get in with you?"

"Sure. Get up with your blanket around you to keep a little of the warm air around your body. I'll rearrange the bedrolls."

He dragged the saddle blanket over to where she would lay next to him. He motioned for her to lay down on it while he checked on Cisco. The horse, tough as nails, was making out fine.

Tate lay down beside her. He put his blanket over top of hers and slid underneath both.

Lila moved over against him and put her head on his shoulder. She was shivering.

Tate put his arm around her and hugged her in close. The prairie wind and the snow blew.

She slept some and thought when she was not asleep. Her smile was hidden because her face was pushed into his shoulder. She felt cold, happy, safe and optimistic all at the same time. Lila wondered how Tate felt. She had found Western men, perhaps men in general, were not very forthcoming about what they thought or felt.

Not a shrinking violet, she determined to ask Tate how he felt about a number of things and why a nice man was so sad. She knew it had to do with the woman whose ambrotype picture was in the case of his watch.

She was tolerably warm now and snuggled in closer to Tate's shoulder. Lila liked the strong arm around her. It was warm. More importantly, it was comforting. She felt safer than she ever had. She dozed off, the snow and prairie wind howling.

CHAPTER 18

The night went slowly, but the two people were warm enough to survive, except when Tate had to get up to push more wood into the fire pit.

Lila felt dawn coming. It always seemed to get colder just before and just after the sun came up.

She opened hazel eyes. She and Tate were covered with a couple inches of snow. The insulation may have helped them make it through the night. She looked up at Tate. He opened his eyes with the instincts of a panther. She gave him a dazzling smile, which he returned.

"Hello, my dear," she tried out.

"Did you sleep well?" he asked.

"Once I got on your shoulder. If I had some money, I'd try to rent some space there for every night, Tate."

"It was pretty nice. I let the fire go out. You stay in here and be warm. I'm going to put snow in the coffee pot and melt it for Cisco. One of the bags you saw yesterday is feed. He's going to need all the strength in his great heart to get us to the Lazy W before dinner time."

The black horse heard his name and whinnied.

"I'm coming, boy. Just hold on for ten minutes."

Tate filled the coffee pot and set it down by the cold fire pit. Sufficient sage brush stems were left for what he had in mind.

He lit a fire and put the pot full of snow on it. As it melted down, he added more. Soon, the pot was full of clean water for the horse. Tate stuck his finger in it. The top was barely warm, but it seemed hotter further down. He poured a crown full in his hat and laid it on the ground for Cisco to drink. The rest boiled with the coffee he put in. By the time Tate took his hat over to Cisco, the water was the right temperature to hydrate the horse, but not be over hot or cold. When the horse had drunk his fill, Tate cleared a place and put the whole small bag of feed under Cisco's nose. He felt the horse's excitement at something other than cold prairie grass.

"All things being equal, boy, tonight you'll have feed, water and a brushing. Then, you can sleep in a warm stall at the Lazy W. I hope, anyway."

He walked over to the coffee and poured some in their only tin coffee cup. He took it to Lila, still covered with snowy wool.

"Here you are M'lady," he said handing it to her.

She sipped some and handed it back to him for a sip. They traded back and forth until the cup was empty.

Tate poured the remainder in and they continued the ritual until the last bit of coffee was consumed.

"For less than a full day acquaintance, we've developed some routines. It's pretty interesting, huh?" she asked as she put the cooking gear back into the saddlebag and handed Tate one of the two last pieces of Indian fry bread.

He stopped, thought about it and nodded. She keenly watched his expression to see if she had pushed too hard too soon. But, it seemed like he considered her words, decided he was fine with them and nodded agreement.

If Lila James was to have her plan come into fruition, she needed to push as hard as she could without scaring this brave man off. They expected to get to the ranch where he was going to drop her tomorrow afternoon. While she doubted he would drop her and leave soon, it was possible. And, she may not see him again.

The snow was over a foot deep and still snowing lightly. But, it was cold enough each flake stuck. Tate feared they would end their trip in two feet of snow.

They rode double for several hours. Then, Tate dismounted and lifted her over the cantle into the seat of the saddle.

"Time we lessen Cisco's load by a hundred seventy or so pounds," he said as he lifted her over.

Taking the reins, he led the black horse down the road.

"At this rate, do you think we will make it tonight?" Lila asked.

"I reckoned on this speed when I said late afternoon, so I hope so. We don't have anything but some coffee for lunch or dinner. We sure won't die. But, we'll go to bed with our bellies growling if we don't make it, Lila."

She noted this was one of the first times, if not the very first, he called her without the "Miss" in front of her name. She was getting there, but time was running out with every mile they trudged through the snow.

After almost four hours, she offered to walk and let Tate ride. He had a better idea. They both would walk in the snow for a while and let Cisco rest by walking without a load.

They made it to within a mile of the ranch house when they heard shots. A lot of shots.

Both mounted and rode another three quarters of a mile and dismounted with the ranch house a bit over a hundred fifty yards distant.

There were a dozen or so riders dismounted and shooting at the house. Tate could see several of Molly Winthrop's wranglers returning fire from any barricade they could find in the yard. Periodic shots came from the house. Tate reckoned those would be fired by Mrs. Winthrop herself.

"Guess I should have asked you this earlier. Have you ever fired a rifle?"

"A bit when I was growing up. My husband didn't think it proper for a woman to shoot." Tate frowned at this. "What an idiot," he thought, but did not say it.

"A little reminder," as he handed her the carbine.

"Lever it to put a round in the chamber. Line the dot on the front sight up in the U in the rear. Put the dot on the target. Press the trigger back while holding your sight picture. But, from this distance with a revolver caliber carbine, you should hold a foot over your intended target. The bullet is gonna be like a rainbow. So arc it over."

"Got it!" They moved away from Cisco to protect him from being shot.

Laying on their stomachs on a little rise in the land, both took aim. One dead on with a .45-75, the other a foot over with a .44-40.

"Give 'em hell, Lila!" and the two opened up.

A couple of the shooters looked around in surprise. Several more just fell down, dead or wounded.

"I got mine!" Lila yelled.

"Good job! Now, slow down and make every shot count," Tate said as the big rifle cracked and another man spun around and dropped. She kept shooting, pacing herself.

With fully half their partners laying on the field, the other half jumped on their horses and rode off. They had no respect for their friends, because no effort was made to help or take anyone, dead or alive.

As the last man mounted and started to spur his horse, Tate picked him off from two hundred yards. The horse kept going, the rider hit the snow and stayed there. Tate was pleased with the big Winchester.

After the last five riders got far enough away to be dots on the prairie's gray horizon, Tate and Lila arose and carried their rifles and extra ammunition over to Cisco. Placing both in his tackle, they walked to the ranch, leading him. Ranch hands were already on the grounds checking the dead and wounded. The latter proved to be dead by the time the hands walked to them, carefully, guns forward. After collecting guns, they rounded up the casualty's mounts.

They greeted Tate with appreciative waves and Lila with confused stares.

Molly Winthrop walked out of the house with a Sharps carbine in her hand and a bandolier of thumb-sized cartridges slung around her neck and shoulder.

"Well, Tate! Welcome back. Looks like every time I need a guardian angel, you appear. And, I sure am glad."

"Howdy, Mrs. Winthrop. Say hi to Miss Lila James. As you can see, she shoots like Jesse, but I don't think she's kin."

"Oh, my goodness young lady! You have fallen into some pretty good company with this fellow. Thanks for your help. Come in and get warmed up. Tate, are you here for a while?"

"Depends on you, Mrs. Winthrop. If you need help with these regulators and big ranchers, I'm your man. Room and board would be welcomed and nothing more."

"The boys seem to be doing a good job cleaning up

the mess in the yard, so let's us go in and warm up," the rancher said.

She prepared a bucket of hot water and some soap. Tate took it out to the men. Several had gotten bloody gathering the dead. Lila came out in a minute and set a big black pot of coffee on the outside table where everyone ate in warmer weather. Molly Winthrop followed with a tray of mugs.

As the three walked back in the house, Tate asked "What about the bodies? The ground is too hard to plant them. Want to deliver them to whatever rancher sent them?"

"I know exactly who sent them!" she said. Lila listened and took it all in without speaking.

"Bernard Mays was behind the two regulators you tracked down and killed," she said. Lila's eyebrows raised on this new information.

"Where is he Ma'am?"

"He's got a thousand acre spread five miles south. But, he is never there. He owns the Jolly Time Saloon in Hastings. He stays there most of the time. He's got a ranch manager who runs his spread. He wants my land so bad he can taste it!"

"What bigwigs is he in cahoots with?" Tate asked.

"Just a couple, but they are big ones. The judge and the sheriff. Mays is a heavy-drinking blowhard. He thinks he's a fast gun and a ladies man."

"I wonder how much the judge and sheriff would

back him if push came to shove?" Tate asked.

"I have wondered the same thing. Both are elected officials. Neither is very popular. The three hang out at his saloon most of the time."

"Sounds like the place to deliver the bodies then," Tate said. "Are you doing anything in the morning?"

"Riding to Hastings I suspect. Now, young lady. I'm thinking Tate brought you here for some reason. What's your story?"

Lila told a short, but succinct version of her life and how a knight on a black horse came riding in and saved her.

"Well, Lila, if Tate likes you, I'm sure I will too. I've been watching Tate while you've been talking, and I'm pretty sure he likes you a lot. Even if he hasn't figured it out himself yet," she smiled.

"You do know I'm sitting right here?" he asked.

"Indeed I do, Mr. Mystery Man Tate. This might be a good time for you to tell Lila the story of why such a good man is riding alone. Or, I can do it if you wish."

"Ma'am, I hate talking about myself. The worst thing about being sheriff of El Paso County, Colorado was politicking!" Lila looked at Tate with surprise. She knew where the county was. It was a big deal to be sheriff there.

"How about I go check on the boys and tell them the plan for tomorrow. How many can you spare to go into Hastings with us?"

"Four, I should think. Now you do your checking and we will have some girl talk."

He left and Molly Winthrop told about him being a Texas Ranger, a deputy under Bat Masterson, and a bad man to draw a gun on. Even if you brought some friends. She also told her about a dead wife and a homestead left behind. And, the dead bodies of the men who killed his wife.

"He killed the man who was keeping me. And, a bunch of the men here today. I made noise, but he made business for the undertaker," Lila said.

"How long have you known Tate?" Molly asked.

"Since yesterday morning. But, I knew he was special right away. I'd follow him anywhere and know I would be protected and treated like a lady."

"I expect you are right, Lila. I've known him a week longer than you. He's already saved me three times. I wish I was your age. I'd compete with you for him. But, instead, I might back your play. I was pretty good at figuring him out and I think I have a good read on your character, too."

"It's sweet of you, Mrs. Winthrop. But, look at me. A raggedy old dress, a coat a stray dog wouldn't sleep on. And, not a copper penny to my name."

"Lila, those are easily fixed things. Assuming we don't shoot up the whole town tomorrow, maybe we'll do some shopping in Hastings. It's been a boomtown since the railroad came through. I have some credit at a store in town carrying ladies wear," Molly offered.

"If you help me get presentable, I'll work it off many times over. I promise."

"We have a deal, then. The only possible fly on the pie is whether Tate shoots the whole town up. Now, why don't you go up to the third room on the right upstairs and I'll heat you up some water. You've been on the trail and I'm sure at least a sponge bath will make you feel better. Then, come down and help me make some dinner for these starving cow punchers and horse wranglers."

"A bath, even out of a pitcher and bowl sounds like heaven, Mrs. Winthrop. Thank you so much!"

"Let's make it Molly, alright?"

Lila went to the room, her room apparently, and stripped to her shift. It was as holey as a revival church. Molly came in shortly with some towels, soap and a bucket of hot water. Lila noted with relief it was a different bucket than the one the wranglers used to wash the blood off.

She raised her arm to wash, sniffed, and wondered how Tate had been able to stand sleeping with her. Then, she thought, he had been on the trail, too, and they both probably smelled pretty much alike. Shortly, she was dressing with the same clothes, but with a sweeter body. She wished Tate could get a whiff of her now, but figured the trail clothes would mask Molly's fancy soap. Well, maybe soon. Hair brushed, she went downstairs to help Molly.

At dinner, Lila was strangely quiet around the wranglers. Maybe because they all looked at her with unabashed appreciation. To shoot like she did and look like she does made one perfect package in the minds of these Westerners. It was pretty much the conclusion of the Westerner who had brought her here, too. There were a lot more men than women on the frontier. Tate knew ones like this were at a real premium. Even after only less than two days, he knew he should not risk one of these young cowboys catching her eye. Little did he realize, her interest was just on one man. She was filled with interest down to the tips of her toes.

After dinner and after Molly and Lila cleared away the dishes, the men adjourned to the bunkhouse for cards and stories. Some would saddle up and ride out in the snow to spell the two already there.

Molly offered red wine to Tate and Lila. Tate opted for coffee and Lila joined Molly with a stem of wine.

"I want to speak candidly with you both if I may. Tate, I offered you the job as ranch manager for shares for a reason I will divulge shortly. I was impressed enough to wire a few people and made some inquiries about you. You are what you claimed…. and, so much more. In addition to bravery and capability, you are a leader of men.

I loved my late husband. We worked heart and soul to build this ranch. While we are currently cash-poor, but part of the reason for it is seasonal and part is the harassment by Mays and some of his associates.

I own the Lazy W Ranch free and clear. I want my husband's, William, and my work to continue after us. We had no children. Nor, are there nephews, nieces or even cousins. So, Tate, when I said work for "shares," you didn't know it, but I meant *significant* shares.

I have not been feeling well. The doctor in Hastings sent me to Chicago to see a specialist. He said I have something terminal. I can feel it getting worse, though it doesn't show from the outside. But, I am getting weaker. Day by day. I don't want this life work to be sold at auction, Tate and Lila.

Sign on and it will be yours sooner than later. And, yes, Tate. I heard your need for trees. But, might not an established big cattle and horse ranch trump trees?"

The room was silent for a few moments, as Molly's words sunk in. Tate could see tears forming in Lila's eyes.

"Tate, this part is kind of none of my business. But, as an older woman with one foot in the grave, I'm gonna speak my piece on it. Grab 'hold of this beautiful thing sitting across from you and marry her before someone else does. I have not known her long, but I can see into her heart. I see a good person who loves you immensely. Lots of us have lost people before their time. It's life. You are not the first one and you will not be the last. Get over it and live!"

At this, Lila began to sob softly. Tate arose and took her in his arms and stroked her hair. She squeezed him tightly as she pushed every inch of her as close to him as possible. Molly smiled. She knew he had been pushed him to action just like she hoped.

Tate lifted Lila's wet chin and kissed her lips.

The two sat back down. It was time for more commitment and planning.

"Ladies, before I can commit to managing the ranch to one and propose to the other, we have to get through tomorrow. It's going to be dangerous and people will die. Molly, if I may call you by your first name in view of our discussion, does Mays have a group of gunhands hanging around him in addition to the sheriff?"

"Of course, I cannot go into the saloon. But, I send my hands in to check on him. He usually has about three and, the sheriff. Nobody knows how fast on the draw or how many men any of them have shot. It's all talk for now. So, my answer isn't much help. My boys — your boys now — say the men around him vary from tough-looking gunmen to just thugs."

"Which are the most dependable, best gunmen for the four we will take with us tomorrow?" Tate asked.

She told him who she would chose, admitting none were experienced gun hands, just honorable men.

Tate lay in his new bedroom upstairs. Lila was next door. He heard her bed squeak as she got in or out of it. He was not sure which until his door cracked and he heard a whispered "It's me." Luckily, Molly slept downstairs, which avoided a look of impropriety.

"What do you need?" Tate whispered.

"To be held. Nothing more. Tomorrow scares me."

She slipped into bed and onto his shoulder in her ragged shift. He put his arm around her. She smelled sweet and clean. She nestled her head in and was asleep almost immediately. He continued to stare at the ceiling, figuring different ways he might handle the situation with Mays and the probably crooked sheriff.

The only dishonorable lawman in his more than ten-year's experience was Hill. He was not so naïve as to think there were not crooked ones in high positions, he just flat out did not like it.

Tate then shifted his thoughts to the more immediate. The pretty, saucy woman in his arms. If he married her, would he lose this one too? He knew it was a stupid presumption. Life was too short to forego happiness because of an illogical worry. People lived and people died. He reached over and kissed her top of her head. She stirred. He did not see the wide smile since her head was buried in his shoulder. The kiss sealed his decision to move forward with her. She already knew he would, but she was glad he finally figured it out for himself. "Men..." she thought.

******

The hands had the bodies laid on straw in the same box wagon Tate fixed the day he met Molly. Molly selected the four and Tate armed them where needed from the attackers' guns and ammunition.

Thinking about having given his backup gun to Lila, Tate went retrieved his second gun and its left-hand holster. He made sure any rider who wanted a second revolver, along with a rifle, had it.

Before passing out the extra guns, Tate found a double action .41 Colt Thunderer in the collection and gave it to Lila. It was powerful and had a short, concealable barrel. He did not want her to go, but learned stubbornness came with the sass. The Colt fired .41 Long Colt, a more powerful center fire than the .41 rimfire in the revolver he gave her.

They mounted up and rode to the sheriff's office in Hastings. There was one deputy on duty.

Tate suggested politely, but strongly, for him to get the sheriff and be quick about it. He did, and the aggravated senior lawman left his breakfast at May's and stomped over.

"What in hell is this all about?" he growled, then seeing the two women and the look on the face of a tall, two-gun man in black, calmed his rhetoric.

"Sheriff, these men, and an equal number who rode away leaving them dead, attacked my ranch yesterday," Molly said.

"I want you to take the bodies and to ride out to the ranch. There are a passel of red spots in the snow where they fell, so you will be able to see they were trespassing. There are also casings by the red spots from the ones who reloaded. These men are from your friend Mays ranch. I want him held to account today!" she demanded.

"Well, Mrs. Winthrop, it's not up to you to tell me how to do my job. How will I really know you didn't kill these men elsewhere and invent this story?" he asked haughtily.

The next voice was deep and spoken quietly.

"She just told you how to determine the crime from the scene. If you knew your ass from a hole in the ground, you'd understand rules of evidence," Tate said.

"Who are you, and why do I care about your opinion?"

"He's the former sheriff of El Paso County, Colorado and former captain of the Texas Rangers. I should think he's forgotten more about being a lawman than you'll ever know," Molly said.

"I don't need to take this kind of talk from you people, old lady included," the sheriff said as his hand strayed near his Colt.

It was a bad move on his part, especially with the growing crowd of spectators.

As soon as the sheriff's hand got within inches of the handle of his revolver, Tate drew faster than anyone there had ever seen.

Tate did not fire. He held the cocked .44 several inches from the sheriff's ear.

"I have enough witnesses to blow your damn brains across the street and claim rightful self- defense. Or, big man, were you gonna draw on the lady?"

There were many disapproving comments in the crowd.

"You can't draw on a lawman!"

"It looks like I just did. Why don't I just finish it and shoot you?" Tate asked in the same voice.

"There's no call for all this bickering! Let's go over to May's place and work it out," the sheriff said.

"Sure, where I'll have to kill him and four or five of his outlaw friends, instead of just you?"

"No, no. I'll keep things calm."

"Start by handing Mrs. Winthrop your revolver. Lift it out of the holster with two fingers."

Once he complied, Tate un-cocked the big Colt and slipped it back in his holster.

"Lead the way, Sheriff. You can have your gun back once the negotiations are complete. I can't say as I trust you very much," Tate advised.

The sheriff, Tate, Molly, Lila, four Lazy W hands loaded to the teeth and a crowd of twenty walked to May's bar and went in the door.

"What's all this? Hey! We don't allow no women in here!" he said in a somewhat high, irritating voice upon seeing the two women.

"You do today, Mays!" Tate said loudly to the pot-bellied man in a flashy suit and wearing two guns, like Tate. Tate thought he looked more like a circus clown than a big-time gunman and rancher. But, he had been fooled by appearances before and was alive only because his speed and resolve were good enough to overcome the mistakes.

Mays looked at the sheriff, and noticed his empty holster.

"You people took the sheriff hostage! I'm a special deputy and am gonna place the whole bunch of you under arrest."

"Not in your lifetime, Mays. Which is getting shorter by the minute. We came to talk. You listen to reasonable demands and you get to live at least through lunch."

Molly spoke up next to the shocked man.

"You already know about twenty of your hands attacked my ranch yesterday. They were specifically shooting at me. You figured if I die with no heir and you could get the ranch for a song. Shooting at a little old lady! You ought to be ashamed of yourself, Mays!" Molly said followed by a chorus of agreement from the crowd and even the men in the saloon restaurant.

Mays turned red and got madder and madder.

"You are lying, old woman!" Mays screamed.

"Watch how you speak to a lady!" Tate ordered.

Blowing spit he was so mad, Mays grabbed for his Colt.

Tate shot him between the eyes before he cleared leather. The group of men behind and beside Mays pulled leather. Tate started shooting both revolvers as fast as a great gunman could cock and press the trigger. His ranch hands, who had fanned out beside him, were firing too. One of Tate's men dropped, as did four of May's men. The unarmed sheriff did the only smart thing so far. He dove for the floor. Unfortunately, one of May's men accidentally shot him in the top of the head, killing him instantly.

The place was filled with acrid black powder smoke. Everyone's ears were ringing with the sound of large revolvers fired inside.

One of May's better gunmen was on the floor with a stomach wound which would likely cause a painful, lingering death. As Tate scanned the room for any remaining threats, he raised his gun and shot Tate.

Tate, close to the bar, staggered and fell against it before sinking to the floor.

Lila, screamed "You son of a bitch!" and ran towards the man firing her .41 Long Colt until it went dry. Then, she stood over the man and emptied the smaller Colt. Everyone in the crowd was sure he was dead. Probably by the first or second of twelve shots.

Lila pocketed her guns under her apron and ran to Tate.

"Don't you dare die on me, Tate! I just found you and I will not give you up!"

Tate looked up and said "Honey, would you fold my bandanna into a square and push it real hard on the hole in my shoulder. More the back of the hole. I think it went all the way through."

The Lazy W riders were kicking guns away from bodies on the floor, especially after they saw a downed man shoot Tate.

While Lila tended for Tate, Molly spied the man she needed to talk to in the crowd.

"Judge, you saw everything. One of May's men killed the sheriff. It may have been an accident, but he did it anyway. Mays, then his men, drew on us first. We have a whole crowd who will testify it was self-defense on our part. Think carefully about the upcoming election. These men and their friends will pick a new sheriff. Make the wrong decision here and I'm sure they would pick a new judge, too," Molly said.

"Are you threatening me, Mrs. Winthrop?" he asked.

"No, just stating the obvious."

"Yes, I guess you are. Doesn't really seem anything illegal was done by the survivors, does it?"

"No, sir. It does not. If you will excuse me, I better see to my ranch manager."

"Who is he?" the judge asked.

"Texas Ranger captain, county sheriff, and about the worst man in this part of the world to draw on. Maybe anywhere, Judge."

She turned and walked over to Tate, her stomach aching badly. She saw Lila holding a compress on the shoulder wound in back, where the exit wound was bleeding slightly. Molly Winthrop knew, for the first time since her husband died, the Lazy W would go on and grow. She felt she could die in peace and be with her husband for eternity. But, she still had to make sure her successor was fully ready to take over.

EPILOGUE

Spring at the Lazy W Ranch saw some changes. Molly Winthrop was resting beside her husband in the small graveyard near the house. It was on a rise, looking over the wide expanse of prairie.

After the shootout, the county commissioners came to Tate about being named sheriff, then running in the upcoming election a month later.

Tate turned them down. He had other commitments now. His creed was to always fulfill his commitments.

Lila's name changed to Mrs. Morgan Wood Tate. She was putting in a vegetable garden and enjoying a new filly her husband had given her for her birthday.

Tate, who always hated the prairie he spent so much of his life on, grew to tolerate it. He spent, he thought, too much time on the books, but still had enough time to ride Cisco out, talk with him and check the cattle and horses. They would put in timothy and alfalfa for a hybrid hay this year.

Once a week, he and Lila went out in the prairie. She fixed a picnic. He took saved peaches cans.

He practiced his draw and fire. Though she had seen it in real life, she still watched him in wonderment.

In many ways, she thought she was his gun-packing pard on the trail like she talked about their first day. She even started talking to Gracie, her cow pony. Gracie had not answered back yet, but Lila knew she would.

Today, after lunch, Tate looked at his pretty wife with love and pride.

He stared out into the vastness of the prairie.

Then, he looked at the tin can on the ground thirty feet away. He drew in a flash and the can jumped. He hit it again in mid-air and, again.

He fired several cylinders full of cartridges. Then, Lila fired. She was getting really good. It was important to him.

He would always stay close to his wife. He pledged to himself to never lose another one.

And, he would always practice with his Colt Frontier Model.

He never knew when the skill would be called upon with no notice.

And, he was so right. So very right.

A LOOK AT: ARIZONA GUNMAN

A WESTERN STORY OF GOOD OVER EVIL, LAW OVER CRIMINALITY.

County Sheriff James Duncan is fast and honorable. An Arizona lawman who rides rough country, often going up against dangerous men and gangs alone. Dealing with bank robbers, kidnappers and rustlers with his fast gun. Much of his tracking ability comes from his Scottish father, who served as an Indian scout. Valuable experience as a Rough Rider with Teddy Roosevelt, then as an Arizona Ranger.

Outlaws and corrupt government tend to stand in Duncan's way, but he manages to overcome all obstacles with integrity and really fast guns.

AVAILABLE NOW

ABOUT THE AUTHOR

G. Wayne Tilman is a full-time author. He retired from the Federal Bureau of Investigation several years ago. Prior to the FBI, he was a Marine, bank security director, deputy sheriff, investigator, and security contractor.

He holds baccalaureate and master's degrees from the University of Richmond and has been an adjunct faculty member there, as well as the University of Phoenix, St. Petersburg College and Florida Metropolitan University.

Some of his law enforcement subject matter expertise includes threat assessment, continuity of operations, security and executive protection, counter intelligence, international terrorism, and small arms. He has been an instructor in those subjects in a number of training academies, conferences and seminars. Mr. Tilman holds the internationally-recognized Certified Protection Professional board certification, generally accepted as the highest in the security profession. He also earned a US Coast Guard 50 Ton Inspected Vessel Master Captain's license.

G. Wayne Tilman's primary interests are family and writing. His avocations are bushcraft (survival/primitive camping), hiking, boating, kayaking, shooting sports, and travel.

He wrote his first novel over thirty years ago and has now written thirteen novels. Genres include espionage thrillers, mysteries, and Westerns.

G. Wayne Tilman's impetus to write in those genres comes from both personal experience and heritage.

A direct ancestor was a sheriff in Virginia Colony in 1680. Another ancestor was the lawman who brought in outlaw Bill Doolin singlehandedly and helped to decimate the infamous Doolin-Dalton outlaw gang, sometimes known as the Oklahombres. Bill Doolin was the Desperado of song fame. Closer to home, his mother was a counterintelligence agent for what is now the Defense Intelligence Agency or DIA.

www.ingramcontent.com/pod-product-compliance
Lightning Source LLC
Chambersburg PA
CBHW030639020726
47493CB00006B/1781